The Karma Con

by Rad Johnson

One Global Vision.
One Divine App.
One Non-Believer.

∞ **www.RadAuthors.com**

The Karma Con

Published 2024 by RAD Authors
www.radauthors.com
Text Copyright © Rad Johnson 2024
www.radjohnson.com
Paperback ISBN 978-1-7385426-0-4
First Edition 2024

Edited by Greer Glover www.greerglover.co.uk

Additional editorial services by Kim Kimber www.kimkimber.co.uk

Cover design concept by Rad Johnson
www.radjohnson.com
Cover design artwork by Hutchins Creative Limited
www.hutchinscreative.co.uk

Rad Johnson

ACKNOWLEDGEMENTS

Some heartfelt words of thanks. Firstly, to my loving,
supportive and tolerant family,
S, T & S xxx – I love you beyond measure.

Secondly, thanks to Ali and my early draft 'guinea-pig'
readers, Sharon, Michèle, Les, Mike, Steven, and Ian, whose
valuable feedback helped progress this novel.

Thanks also goes out to Clif High and all the free-thinkers for
their dissemination of critical thinking processes, alternate
truths and woo-woo concepts.

Lastly, my special thanks to everyone actively and selflessly
working towards lifting humanity, and all that it entails, in a
world where disunity, distraction and dread are made easy
paths for the unthinking. Question everything.

Maybe it is incumbent upon us to begin the process of awakening in this life, afore we fully awaken in death.

– Rad Johnson

For Humanity

1

Helmand Province, Afghanistan
9th November 2012

Sam Angel watched himself lying lifeless below.

No feeling of sorrow, no pain.

Just rapidly increasing exaltation.

Bliss. Serenity. Silence. Peace. Love.

Pure love, indescribable, fulfilling love.

The only breath was one of a sense of growing, infinite awareness.

Then… a heartbeat.

Instantaneously, Sam wore the familiar weight of life again.

He lay stretched out in the glorious autumn sunshine. Its radiance tingled his cheeks, but this agreeable feeling contrasted with the acrid smell of burning which was becoming increasingly apparent. A sliver of blurred light penetrated his half-opened eyes.

Is that mist or smoke?

As he attempted to move, Sam became aware of his considerable discomfort and then rising agony; sharp stones and rocks were digging into his back and he was cognisant of ringing in his ears. Overlaying all this, a muffled, unintelligible, yet panicked voice could be heard nearby. He laboured to sit up. Reality was beginning to clearly emerge, but he was still struggling to fully comprehend the situation.

A caustic smell emanated from the burning, twisted army Land Rover which lay just metres away. That, coupled with the essence of detonated explosives, there was only one conclusion. 'IED,' he mumbled.

The panicked voice grasped his attention again, only this time it was clearer, urgent. 'Angel... Angel! Help me, man! Help me!' Wincing in abject pain, he turned and looked left. Corporal 'Tinks' Taylor sat propped up against a boulder at the foot of an embankment. 'Fuckin' help me, man, I can't stem it... fuck, fuck!'

Finally understanding the situation, Sam scrambled in considerable discomfort towards Tinks and automatically jammed his thumbs hard into the right side of the Corporal's groin. The blood spurting from his leg subsided. 'What the fuck, Tinks! Where's my medi-pack?' Sam said loudly, still auditorily affected, frantically looking around for the life-saving equipment.

'I dunno, Angel, I don't want to die, I don't want to fuckin' die! Fuck... the pain.' Taylor's contorted face pointed skywards; every sinew straining in his neck as he tried not to look at his own severely damaged leg.

Scanning everywhere, Sam spotted the medi-pack. 'Tinks! Tinks! Stay with me, Tinks. Look at me, look at me!'

Taylor did as he was told, but Sam could see his respiration rate increasing and his pallor worsening. Tinks' eyes widened and he stared at Sam unblinking.

'OK, I've got to get my pack. You're gonna have to hold

your femoral artery like I'm doing, so I can get a tourniquet. Are your arms OK? No breaks?'

Tinks impatiently signalled no with the smallest shake of his head and then spat, 'Don't leave me. Don't you fucking leave me!'

'Remember your training. You can do this. You've got to do this! We're like brothers, yeah? Brothers do what brothers need to do! Now, get your thumbs just up your leg from mine.' Sam scanned the desolate locale, looking for any further lurking danger. He looked back down and saw Tinks' arms had failed to move. Clenching his jaws due to the continuous exertion to arrest the haemorrhaging, he shouted, 'Fucking now, Tinks. Now! Do it, now!' Slowly, Tinks' arms moved and he positioned his thumbs above Angel's thumbs.

'On the count of three, you're gonna press down, hard as fuck, OK? It's gonna be alright, alright?' Tinks gave just the slightest of acknowledgements, but that was enough for Sam.

'One, two, three.' The thumb swap was complete. But more blood began streaming from the large gash on Tinks' inner thigh. Within milliseconds, Sam had this covered and manipulated Tinks' thumb positions slightly, pushing them down harder to stem the flow. 'Well done, mate, but you need to hold and maintain this much pressure.'

As Sam slowly retracted his thumbs off Tinks', the bleeding seemed to reduce significantly. 'I'll be back,' Sam said in a poor Austrian accent, a vain attempt at humour, just one of the catchphrases he and the boys liked to use from his unit's limited choice of seven DVDs, *The Terminator* having been watched the most.

The embankment was steep, a mass of friable rocks and rubble that formed the only useable track for miles around. Sam scrambled his tall, athletic frame up the incline, weaving his way through debris and apparel, parts of their vehicle and its contents. Pain jolted through his lower back, probably only a superficial injury but there was no time to corroborate that assertion. As he moved, his thoughts arranged themselves. He'd need to radio in for help, but stabilising Tinks was the priority. And, as he had been taught and heard many a time, there was often still enemy danger after an IED attack.

The medi-pack sat at the edge of the embankment top, on the fringe of the roadside. Although now scorched and squashed on one side, the backpack-sized bag still clearly displayed its red cross emblem, a symbol of reassurance for Sam in his seven-year service as a combat medic. In his career, he had known nothing other than active service, serving in Iraq for the first four years and the remainder in Afghanistan.

As he reached out from behind a series of large boulders at the brow of the hillock to grab the pack, the all too familiar sound of an AK-47 assault rifle rang out from his left, seemingly from a small, square dirt building, positioned on the far side of the embankment. Instinctively, he hit the embankment, aware of plumes of bullet-graze dust thrown up in his vicinity from the weapon. Sam grabbed his radio. 'Foxtrot-Charlie to Lima-Golf, we've been IEDeed and in contact with the enemy, one click north of Karwangah on the main route to Bastion. Over,' referring to his home base, the British military base of Camp Bastion. Seconds later, though aeons to Sam, static crackle was followed by 'Lima-Golf to Foxtrot-Charlie. Understood. Standby. Over.'

Another spray of shots rang out. Sam was just below the level of the road and only a couple of metres from his medi-pack. Glancing down, he saw Tinks still pressing on his leg but throwing his head back and giving out continued grunts of effort and cries of pain. Tinks' strength would soon give out.

Irregular boulders of varying sizes marked a rudimentary guide to prevent inadvertent driving over the embankment edge. Sam's priority instinctively changed again as he was forced to engage the enemy.

A stab of doubt entered his head as he readied his standard army issue SA80 to single shot; this was the first time in all his service that he had had to fire at the enemy.

Sam slithered up to the nearest boulder between himself and the sniper. He raised his head slowly and as low as possible to get good sight of the enemy, relieved he was not facing the sun.

Sam estimated the outpost building was less than fifty metres away, the doorway open to the roadside with an unglazed window opening to the side. The apparently lone shooter was right-handed and pointing his rifle out of the portal on the right-hand side, thus managing to hide most of his head. Sam noticed the barrel of the AK-47 was unsteady, as if the shooter was anxious or perhaps not well-trained.

Without allowing himself time to dwell on the fact that he must kill this sniper, Sam repositioned himself with the gun, but this time with his SA80 pointing at the outpost window.

As the Taliban's shooter's head appeared over the base of the window opening, Sam composed himself and fired. The unfamiliar mechanical 'clack' was not the expected result. *Jammed? Fuck, no!* He turned back to reclaim the full shelter afforded by his rock-shield. As he lay the weapon down, he checked it over as his training had taught him – there was damage to the aluminium magazine; the rifle was useless. Unclipping and readying his Browning pistol, he resumed the shooting position and aimed at the enemy again, revealing the least possible hint of his presence, but aware of the reduction in accuracy of his handgun over his rifle.

Sam flinched as a static crackle came through his earpiece. 'Lima-Golf to Foxtrot-Charlie. Assistance on its way, six clicks and closing. Report intel on enemy positions and provide casualty report. Over.' Ignoring the interruption and recomposing, Sam focussed on the shooter. He held his breath. Using both hands to increase his accuracy, he squeezed the trigger.

'Crack!'

Within a second, the enemy shooter's AK-47 dropped to the ground, landing below the window.

'Oh fuck, forgive me,' Sam said, exhaling. The adrenaline pumping through his body and the rising level of nausea to his first career hit had to be ignored. There was no time to dwell.

'Lima-Golf to Foxtrot-Charlie, please copy. Over,' spat the radio link. Grabbing the medi-pack, Sam again ignored the message and slid down the shale incline.

Drenched in sweat and now panting and shaking violently, Tinks was just holding on, as more blood seeped from his weakening arterial hold. Sam grabbed a tourniquet and succinctly applied it. 'OK, Tinks, you can let go now.' Tinks relaxed and let his arms go limp while Sam rigged up a saline drip.

'Lima-Golf to Foxtrot-Charlie, please copy. Over.'

'Foxtrot-Charlie to Lima-Golf, enemy neutralised, casualty stabilised. Over.'

'Lima-Golf to Foxtrot-Charlie. Understood. Cavalry one click away. Over.'

'That's the fifth IED in this sector in the past eight days,' Sergeant Lucas proclaimed in his privileged accent, but it was really more of a thinking-out-loud statement, something he was well-known for. He was all too well aware that the increased threat from improvised exploding devices had fuelled another layer of mental anguish for his men. As he surveyed the carnage at the scene, and tuning out the background hubbub his squad created, he played with his moustache and began to mull over the security brief he had just sent up the chain of command recommending further operational measures to mitigate just such an attack, which included yet another seemingly futile plea for improved armoured vehicles. His train of thought was abruptly interrupted.

'Sarge?' Lucas locked eyes with Corporal Robins, giving him silent permission to continue. 'Perimeter secured and is all-clear, Sarge.'

'Well done,' Lucas replied automatically, whilst watching Robins then make a good fuss of Tex, the squad's explosives sniffer dog, a full-of-beans black and white spaniel. *If only the military hardware was as reliable and effective as Tex*, Lucas thought bitterly.

As Tinks received further medical attention and was stretchered off to the waiting Bell 212 helicopter, shamefully deployed by army logistics in jungle camouflage due to its hasty redeployment from Brunei, making it an easier target for the enemy, Lucas made his way over to Angel.

'I'm fucking impressed, Angel – taking out an enemy combatant and saving Tinks. Fucking hero in my book!'

'Er, thanks, Sarge,' Sam replied, still sitting and assessing his own aches and pains and his comprehension of the incident. A light breeze blew noxious smoke from the smouldering Land Rover towards them. His first attempt to stand to move away from the fumes failed and Lucas grabbed his arm on the second to make it successful.

Sam struggled back up the shaley embankment, back to the road, using the shorter and stockier Lucas as a prop to assist his passage.

'You sure you're OK, Angel?'

'I'll be fine, Sarge.' he said unconvincingly. 'I took someone's life, I took someone's life,' he muttered inaudibly to himself. His eyes had started to dart around, his breathing rate was rapidly increasing and Lucas saw strength was evaporating from his legs. When they reached the top of the embankment, Lucas helped Angel reach down to sit on a slab of rock.

He gently spoke in Angel's ear. 'Take some time for yourself here, it's a lot to take in.' He walked over to ever-straight-talking Corporal Steve Sage, who was taking a long draw on his roll-up. 'Keep an eye on him here, Sage,' he said, nodding in Angel's direction, 'he's in a bit of shock.'

A hissing and muted phut from the charred and twisted wreckage at the bottom of the embankment gained Lucas's attention, leading him to thank the gods that his boys had got away with their lives from the explosion and crash. 'How are we supposed carry out our duties in these flimsy pieces of tin,' he muttered, but not quietly enough.

'And those MP fuckers back in Parliament keep cringing every time the news shows more coffins being flown home. I'd love to see the Prime Minister come out here and go out in a Landy; then I could enjoy watching him shit himself,' Sage said, as he spat out a string of tobacco that was caught in his lips.

Lucas looked over to the outpost, awaiting a report from the reccy of it. Once received, he planned to get the squad back to base for a late lunch and look to formulate another request for better hardware, but being careful that it was not taken as a complaint. *God forbid that we would have the nerve to complain!* he thought sarcastically.

Corporals Patel and Nicholls were returning from checking out the mud hut and were about halfway between the outpost building and Lucas. Affectionately known as Goon One and Goon Two by the squad due to their constant juvenile antics, such as playing football with anything small and not bolted down and their incessant, immature banter. Lucas had given the goons slack, reasoning their asinine behaviour was a coping mechanism, and he didn't want to pull away their crutch to everyone's detriment. But now Lucas was taken aback by the contrast presented to him; he could visibly see them both doused in solemnity. No cheeky grins, no innate banter, just walking like they had aged drastically in the past few minutes. He started to walk towards them to find out what was going on.

Sam had composed himself somewhat, by closing his eyes and forcing his mind to imagine he was on a tropical beach whilst consciously controlling his breathing, pushing out any thoughts not related to this fanciful ideal.

'Angel, yous back with us?' Sage enquired light-heartedly, with his Geordie accent dialled back somewhat.

'I think so, Onion,' Sam said, attempting to act normal.

Sage rolled his eyes at hearing his nickname, rueing the day he had unwittingly asked the mess cook for more sage and onion stuffing last Christmas. 'We'll have to get you a nickname that's not your real name. I'm sure your halo'll slip one of these days, Angel.'

Sam looked at Sage and had a sudden urge. 'Any chance of a ciggie?'

'Didn't think yous smoked. Is that your halo slipping already?' Sage chuckled at his own quip and handed Angel his half-finished smoke.

As Sam took it, he had a momentary but lucid flashback where he looked down on himself just after being hit by the IED. A long draw on the butt, he started to ponder on this as he turned his head to look towards the outpost. This contemplation was quickly cut short as he coughed heartily from the alien nature of the smoke. His stare re-locked on the hut, the epicentre of his confusion, and he watched as the goons turned round, taking the Sarge back with them towards the outpost.

Sam offered back what was left of the cigarette – starting to smoke now was not for him. 'What's Sarge going over there for, Onion?' he said.

'No idea. The goons seemed oddly sheepish for once,' Sage said.

Ignoring the call for attention from his severely bruised lower back and possible broken ribs, Sam started to wonder why a report from the goons wasn't enough for Lucas and why the goons were not gooning, and all three of them were returning to the hut. Unsure if he was being paranoid as an after-effect of the attack, Sam was suddenly struck with a dark foreboding. It may have been the smoking or it was this new notion making him feel queasy. Sam laboured to an upright stance and started to journey to the mud hut himself.

'Oi! Angel, I've got orders to keep an eye on yous here.' Sage caught up with Angel, took a last drag on his roll-up before flicking it away. 'This won't be of benefit, mate,' he pleaded. 'Let's get you in the Landy for a bit of rest.'

'I've shot someone in the head; they're probably dead!' Sam snapped, quickening his pace up a notch. 'I've taken a man's life, maybe a husband, a father but certainly a son to his family,' he continued, feeling his emotions rising.

'We're soldiers and when at war, we're trained to kill if needed. You needed to kill this bastard else he'd have killed both you and Tinks. This little shit waited for you to drive by the IED and detonated it. And just in case yous two survived, he waited to pick you both off with his AK-47!'

Grimacing through the pain, Angel walked as fast as he could to reach the hut and try to shake off Sage's unwanted sermon. His mind raced with thoughts and images of the guy he had shot, his life, his dreams, his soon-to-be grieving family.

'I enlisted to become a medic, Sage, and fucking save lives. I never wanted to kill anyone! It's not me! It's not what I'm about!'

Sage responded in a more compassionate tone. 'You're not thinking straight, mate. You're still in shock, we all are after the first. If it wasn't for your actions, we'd be picking up your body and Tinks' too. You made the right choice.' Sam felt Sage grab his wrist to stop him, but Sam snatched back his arm and pressed on to the hut's window.

With his heart pounding and the sick feeling in the pit of his stomach refusing to ease off, he heard the voices of Sergeant Lucas and the two goons in the hut, having arrived a minute earlier.

'What the fuck are you doing here, Angel?' barked Lucas. 'I told you to rest up back there. Go back!'

Sam didn't take any words on board. He peered into the dim hut, craning his head right inside. He needed to know. But he had to wait for his eyes to adjust to the darkness. Slowly, he made out a figure on the floor, the goons and Lucas standing silently beside it.

His eyes adjusted scarcely a little more, but just enough to reveal the truth before him. Through tears of incredulity, he stared at the Afghani body with a bullet wound in the right side of his forehead.

'No-no! He's just a kid! I've gone and killed a fucking kid!' he blurted. He collapsed to his knees, his world imploding, and he howled, wept and retched in equal measure.

'Sage! Get him away from here – back to the Land Rover,' commanded Lucas.

Reverting to his usual goon-like form, Corporal Patel shook his head unsympathetically. 'Bad karma, Angel,' he said. 'Bad karma.'

2

Colorado, USA
13th June 2018

Laura Lafayette purposefully strode past the first of two twenty-five-ton blast doors, sentinels defending the North Portal of the Cheyenne Mountain Complex from a thirty-megaton nuclear strike. Her insistence on wearing sneakers whenever possible gave her confidence that she could use her fitness and agility at any time needed, but she felt a little conspicuous wearing them as they boldly squeaked on the polished concrete flooring. She was accompanied on this trip from CIA Headquarters in Langley, Virgina, near Washington D.C., by Intelligence Collection Agent Adam Stables, an equally youthful and fit CIA worker but subordinate to Lafayette's position of Special Agent by some stretch. Being his first visit to NORAD/USNORTHCOM, the military organisation providing aerospace defence to the continental United States of America and Canada, Stable's eyes were darting everywhere to take in all he could of this fabled installation. His nerdish characteristics were projected by his wearing of sixties-inspired, black-framed glasses and one of his trademark V-necked, knitted sweaters.

Laura had enjoyed her previous trip to this facility in Colorado as it afforded her fresher air and mountainous terrain which was missing from Washington DC, which she now called home. It was also an environment which had been absent from her childhood in muggy Mississippi, some fifteen years before.

'Better hope this isn't a wasted trip as we're getting close to a solution to our little Iranian situation,' Lafayette quietly declared to Stables, breaking a long stretch of silence more than anything else, whilst she adjusted her heavily starched, white blouse collar to stand upright to attention. It was a signature of hers to convey power, attention to detail and more than a hint of intimidation, mainly to her male counterparts.

Stables felt compelled to respond as he liked to take every opportunity to sell to her his worth. 'Yes, Ma'am, but confidence was rated at over ninety-six per cent that this thing's going to happen – whatever that is – which in a CIA analyst's vocab is as good as certain.'

Laura wondered again why she had been sent on this trip, which was shrouded in secrecy and at a time when her Iranian project needed her the most, in her estimation anyway. It was most unusual.

After speed-walking through several identical looking tunnels, they arrived at the five-acre main chambers area. This housed fifteen three-storey buildings, all of which were isolated via spring-damper systems to minimise movement from explosions or earthquakes to a mere twenty-five millimetres. Laura noticed Stables couldn't get enough of these statistics and the enormity of the project needed to carve out this command bunker from a mountain of granite.

Another two minutes' walk saw the agents at their destination, the entrance of 'Building 3A, Command Centre', clearly marked in three-foot high, white military font. After another round of security checks, including retinal and facial scans, they were escorted through the airlock system and on to the desk of US Air Force Staff Sergeant Mike Collins.

Again, Stables' head was turning like an owl at the array of screens and technology adorning the desks and on all the walls of this high-ceilinged centre, his mouth unconsciously dropped open like the proverbial kid's in a candy store. It would have been an information overload for most CIA operatives, but Laura could see it was received by Stables as a feast for his nerdy eyes.

'Special Agent Lafayette,' Laura said confidently, holding out a firm hand, 'and Intelligence Collection Agent Adam Stables reporting on the demand of CIA Head of Special Operations, Jacob Rozen.' Mike Collins jumped out of his seat and fired a sharp salute before shaking both their hands and introducing himself.

Collins pulled up two wheeled office chairs and invited his guests to sit. He hand-groomed his full, ginger moustache into place.

'So, Staff Sergeant, thank you for your time at such short notice. What can you tell me, er, us,' she quickly corrected, 'about this object of interest?' Laura always valued rapidly getting to the crux of a meeting; it gave her male peers very little time to allow their minds to wander when processing her attractive appearance. She was also mindful that there was no time for chit-chat; there was a world to save and it needed saving now.

Laura regarded her good looks a disadvantage in a world fixated on glamour. They belied her outstanding grasp of mathematics, information technology and statistical analytics, woven with an acute understanding of psychology, which caught the eye of the CIA when she was a freshman at the Massachusetts Institute of Technology back in 2002.

Collins started his debrief in his relaxed but attentive Texan patter. 'OK, ma'am, sir, our object of interest is a decommissioned experimental satellite called *ConchaSat*, covertly launched on March 6, 1965 from Cape Kennedy – now Cape Canaveral – upon a specially modified Gemini 3 test rocket.'

'Now, we have been monitoring it and re-calculating its orbital demise for years; that's one of the main objectives of our sub-project here, tracking all man-made orbital satellites. We expected it to burn up in the atmosphere in a few years' time, but due to the unexpected increases in the sun's electromagnetic activity recently, which had been steadily reducing cycle after cycle over the past decades, it created a subsequent thickening of our atmosphere which has led to the satellite's orbital degradation to drastically speed up. Also, *ConchaSat's* re-entry angle of attack has gone from a long-predicted steep angle, guaranteeing a burn up, to a gentle angle, leading to a greater possibility of survival, i.e. debris reaching earth's surface. Instead of a 1.8 per cent chance of re-entry survival of the satellite, the probability has now swung to a 92.7 per cent chance of surviving re-entry and increasing.'

'Jesus, it's not often that statistical math is turned upside down to such a degree,' Stables chipped in.

'You're darn right, sir,' Collins said. 'But statistical math for space projects has never seen the likes of the changes in sun-cycle activity that we've witnessed in recent years. It's creating a whole new field of work for us to understand, to then be able to utilise and input into projects such as ours.'

Fingering her collar again, Laura enquired, 'Say the satellite keeps slowing down, enters the atmosphere and say it survives re-entry; it'll most likely splash into the sea somewhere or what's left of it will smash into pieces if it hits land. Either way, it doesn't sound like the satellite could fall into the wrong hands in a useful way. Can you brief us as to the purpose of the satellite?'

'To counter your first point, usually, your assertion would be spot on, Ma'am. However, we have the conjoining of three unfortunate facts. The first is that we calculate the satellite will most likely return to land. Secondly, that land is predicted to be potentially unfriendly, somewhere in Western Asia, maybe China, perhaps the Tibetan Plateau. And thirdly, we do not have access to full records of this satellite project as many details were shredded in Operation Sweep in the 1970s under President Carter to clean up top-secret paper trails. But we do know that the rocket's cargo was packaged with heat shields and a landing parachute system.'

'That system is over fifty years old, what's the probability of its successful deployment?' Stables asked.

Collins referred to his calculation notes. 'It might be old tech but it was simple and made from the best materials of the time, so there's around an eighty-seven per cent chance of successful deployment, sir.'

'Let's see if I've got this right,' Laura said. 'We have a 1965 military satellite about to return to earth with a high probability of landing intact in China!' Her eyes widened at Collins to get his reaction to her assessment. Collins slowly nodded.

'So, what the hell are the Chinese about to receive and when?' she asked, her voice pointed.

'Ma'am, all we know is that *ConchaSat* was part of the deeply secret Project Arc which specialised in aspects of warfare relating to alternative energy. When I say "deeply secret", it's because effectively it was beyond top secret. It was set up as part of a whole host of projects at the time to try to get ahead in the Cold War against the USSR. Project Arc was the most secretive of projects due to its nature – Arc for Arcane; hidden. It dealt with strange phenomena and the likes. There are scant records left in the archives so if the project was ever internally compromised and failed in its objectives, it would not deal a psychological blow to the US military – hence it was buried deep and hidden from most of the military itself. And you can bet the government of the day knew nothing of this.'

While Collins spoke, Stables furiously jotted down notes on his phone.

Collins took a slug of his coffee. 'Could you imagine, if the Russians found out we were trying to defeat them with "woo-woo"? They would have had a public relations feast and the US, a world superpower, would have been a laughing stock. And...' Collins paused and clicked a few keys on his keyboard. 'The latest estimate for touchdown is 16:44 UTC on 30th June, so in a couple of weeks' time.' He pointed his guests to the largest screen on the wall in front of him which showed a technical orbital map of the world and a simulation of the orbital decay of the *ConchaSat*.

'So, in a couple of weeks, the Chinese will potentially recover some form of US woo-woo material from a mid-60s top, top-secret project but we can't assess if this will have any impact on the US or our allies as we don't know what it is!' Laura surmised indignantly. 'What do the Chinese know about all this?'

'Ma'am, they are aware that a small piece of space junk is due to return soon and may land in a sparsely populated part of Western China but they suspect it'll be nothing but twisted junk once on the ground. Though they are not making too much noise about it at the moment, we expect them to capitalise on its landing on sovereign soil if it is determined as no material use to them. Of course, they'll keep quiet if they can make use of the payload.'

'That's probably what they want us to think. But we can't rely on that notion, we know the sophistication of their intelligence agencies. You got some questions here, Stables?'

'Yep, quite a few. Firstly, any significance of the name

ConchaSat?' Stables asked.

'Well, *Concha* is Latin for a shell, you know, from the sea. Around here there's a thought that it's to do with a shell in terms of a weapon of some sort.' It was the best answer Collins could offer.

As Stables launched into more minutia, Laura wondered why her director had sent her out here to investigate when she had been so busy on the follow-up to the Stuxnet worm attack on the Iranian atomic project. This looked to be nothing other than a shambolic dead end with a possibility of a small diplomatic spat between the USA and China. With the evidence provided thus far, this satellite issue paled into insignificance compared with the regional and global threat, and the ramifications of an Iran with nuclear weapons. Something didn't add up.

'… at about an altitude of eight hundred kilometres on a sun-synchronous orbit so that each successive orbital pass occurs at the same time of day, so good for comparisons,' Collins concluded, responding to Stables, who was lapping up the technical juice.

After another ten minutes of questioning, the meeting wrapped up. Formal goodbyes were exchanged and then Lafayette and Stables left Building 3A.

'Wow, what a buzz that was!' whooped Stables, instantly toning down his demeanour to appear more professional. 'It seems they've got quite a dilemma on their hands.'

'Our hands, Stables, our hands,' Laura quickly corrected, as she tried to access the situation. 'We haven't been whisked over here for a bit of light entertainment.' But without an objective, without knowing what impact the satellite falling into enemy hands could have, and without any orders, she remained perplexed as to their role in it all.

As they exited the North Portal tunnel, they were greeted by a rush of fresh, mile-high thin air and a burst of strong sunshine. Laura inhaled deeply and felt a wave of relaxation, contrasting with their past hour in the heart of a mountain. A line of nondescript black sedans, each with a driver, were parked up on the kerbside, tasked to ferry government officials mainly to and from Peterson Air Force Base, some ten miles away.

Both Laura's and Stables' phones started pinging and beeping as a backlog of messages were served, pursuant to effectively having been cut off from the outside world once inside the mountain. Strolling to the sinister-looking taxi rank, they were each catching up with the latest comms when Laura spotted a text from her boss, Rozen. It read, 'Call me. Right now.'

'Sir, what the hell is…' Laura started but Rozen talked over her.

'Lafayette, I've got to put you on hold, hang on.' The line went silent. She let out a sharp sigh of impatience. Laura and Stables reached the head of the rank just as Rozen reconnected the call.

'Right, stop what you are doing – are you still at Cheyenne?'

'Yeah, just sat in a car to return…' He talked over her again.

'Tell Stables to continue to Peterson and wait for you there. Get out of your car and return to the mountain. There's another meeting you need to have – from hereon in, everything is now between us, just us. Other than this meeting, you are not to discuss anything with anyone except me. Clear?'

'Got it. Who am I to meet?' Only as Laura ended the question did she realise that Rozen had abruptly ended the call.

'Hi. I'm back again,' Laura said to the officer at the first checkpoint inside the North Portal. The officer on duty didn't react; but he did recall her, owing to her only having left ten minutes before. 'I'm here to meet someone but my superior has not let me know who it is I'm to meet. It's more than a little awkward,' she said with a wry smile.

'Ma'am, I gonna need more to go on than that,' the officer replied, now with a hint of a smile. 'We have over three thousand people in here on a good day!'

'I'll take it from here, officer,' boomed a voice sounding like it was coming from behind her. She spun around to find the outstretched hand of an impeccably-dressed General darting its way towards her. 'Ms Lafayette, I'm guessing?'

'Er, yes, sir, er, General, er...' Uncharacteristically flustered, Laura was not sure whether to shake hands or salute and got caught in between the two.

'I'm Chief of Staff of the United States Air Force, General John Q. Hill Please. Come this way,' General Hill directed with the outstretch of his palm. As they walked, he now lowered his volume as he spoke, 'We have much to discuss, but back in my office, not here.'

As they continued in silence through a whole new warren of tunnels and doors, accompanied by the rhythmic squeal of her footwear, Laura found she was quite disorientated by the time they reached General Hill's secluded office.

'Special Agent Ms Lafayette,' General Hill started as they took their seats either side of his large but utilitarian desk, in what must have been the most drab-looking office that any General had been allocated in peacetime, Laura thought.

The insertion of "Ms" in the General's address to her did not go unnoticed as it was an unusual inclusion but she noted how it was delivered in a warm manner. A physically fit, good-looking and confident man, Laura guessed he was in his mid-fifties but other than some noticeable forehead and laughter lines, his skin's appearance could pass for that of a person many years his junior. Coupled with his sharp, brown, distinctly military, flattop hairstyle, which sported only a vague sprinkling of grey flecks, it would be easy to put him in his early forties.

'Thank you for agreeing to meet me,' Hill said, with a welcoming smile.

Laura had a fleeting thought of taking issue with the use of the verb *agree* but quickly and politely replied. 'My pleasure, General.'

'Jacob Rozen has recommended you for secondment to an exciting new project. But he did fail to inform me how attractive his favourite agent was,' smiled the General, from a left-field position.

'I think we need to concentrate on the agenda, General,' Laura directed, a little offended by the General's outmoded forwardness but also, strangely, a small part flattered.

'Maybe we could take lunch in before you leave today?' Hill pushed.

'Thank you, but I'm neck-deep in a hugely important...' She was abruptly cut off.

'Yes, Operation Persiana is of great importance, but the cat and mouse games with Iran will continue on into the future, as they have done in the past,' Hill stated.

How would he know about the project, Laura mulled, not liking his dismissive manner. 'It's sounding like my new role is a done deal – may I know the details, General?'

'Of course, but firstly, I'd like to officially welcome you to our new team.' General Hill opened his top drawer and placed a thin, brown paper file in front of him, sporting a stereotypical 'TOP SECRET' stamp in red ink on the cover.

Trying not to come across as being condescending, she

25

queried, 'A step back from the digital age, General?'

'Everyone is hailing the digital age, Ms Lafayette. As you are acutely aware, governments love the digital age. The public are told it's greener, quicker, more convenient and it represents progress, so they accept the changes with little protest. But digital data is our greatest servant – it tells us what our friends and partners are doing, it gauges what the mood of the public is, it reveals what our enemies are planning and it also has the power to control, direct and influence whomever we want. It's our most powerful, non-kinetic weapon, hidden in plain sight!'

He took a moment to lean a little closer and Laura felt he was studying her reaction. 'This file may not rely on twenty-first century media and has been typed, by myself, using a nineteen-nineties electronic typewriter, but its greatest advantage is that it can only be seen by those who I choose to have sight of it. To my knowledge, you will be the third person to ever have read it, though I have since made some redactions that Rozen can fill you in on when the time's right.'

As Laura reached to take hold of the file on the desk, the General's thick index finger jabbed down to pin the paperwork. Laura guessed that some caveats were about to follow.

'Please hand me your phone, then take this file over to the sofa behind you. Read it again and again until you know it, until you really know it, as you will never see this file again. You will then return to DC and await further instructions from either me or Rozen. All of this stays between you, me and Rozen. The importance of your work re-assignment will be revealed in time and you will also come to appreciate the necessity of the fundamental changes your new project, Operation Octal, will usher in for every corner of the world.'

3

Victoria Park, London, England
15th June 2018

As Sam sat on the stern of his widebeam canal boat drinking a rapidly cooling cup of tea, he absently tracked the meandering of two white-billed coots on the wind-rippled surface of Regent's Canal. Yet another fresh, grey day in London in what could easily count as a warm day in January. This seemingly endless period of unseasonal weather lay an extra layer of oppressiveness to his mood. Though only a quarter past nine in the morning, Sam, yet again, as he had done for countless days previously, declared to himself that today was another day to cruise through on autopilot and hope tomorrow would bring a new tack with some wind in his sails.

A momentary splash from a fish, probably jumping from the jaws of a pike, caught Sam's eye, but even the thought that his life was not in such jeopardy did nothing to ease the heaviness of his depression. Try as he might to reason with logic and rationale, it rarely eased.

A last slurp of cold tea and Sam flicked the rest of his drink into the grey water. Standing up to stretch, he spotted a Canal and River Trust enforcement officer working his way towards him on his bike, punching in the index numbers of every boat into a handheld device. It afforded the Trust the data on all boat movements, allowing the organisation to see who was playing by the fourteen-day maximum stay rules and who was not.

For Sam, this checking process only served as yet another reminder of his condition. Having only taken a month to physically recover from the attack in Afghanistan, the resulting mental trauma during the past five and a half years had crippled his ability to function normally. He craned his head around the side of his boat to check the vivid yellow licence was still on display. This colour badge represented a form of exemption badge for boat owners. Useful, as Sam did not have to abide by the Trust's strict rules to keep moving his boat, but it shouted out to everyone and to Sam himself, that he had special needs. Though this grated against his pride, it had been a lifeline to not have the stress of finding new places to moor. It permitted him to stay close to the doctor's surgery he visited with annoying regularity, as well as grant him his frequent walks around Victoria Park, an oasis in an otherwise unloved region of London.

He straightened the lifebelt on top of his boat, so that the name *The Wanderer* was central to the boat's axis. The irony of the boat name was not lost on Sam, yet another reminder of his life's stagnancy. He lackadaisically ducked his head going back into his boat and caught it on the underside of the sliding hatch.

'Bollocks!' He rubbed the sore spot whilst tempering his self-anger. He had lost count how many times he had hit his head somewhere onboard.

Sam's thoughts were interrupted by his phone ringing – a rare event these days.

'How are doing, Buddy?' Tinks asked, upbeat. There had been longer and longer gaps between their conversations as each one became increasingly arduous. Sam was aware of this but he knew he was still deeply affected by his shooting a kid in Afghanistan. Therapies and friends' loyalties were not enough to allow him to operate on anywhere near a normal level.

Sam took a deep breath and tried to out an equally upbeat tone, failing miserably but still the call gave him an extra little boost. 'Oh, yeah, you know, getting by, mate.'

After one or two minutes of niceties, Tinks got to the crux of the call.

'Listen, Angel, I've got a big favour to ask.'

'OK,' Sam tentatively replied.

'Well, you know my business partner, Lenny?'

'Yeah,' Sam responded with little enthusiasm.

'He's gone and done a runner with some bird he's been knocking around with. Her husband is after him so they've gone abroad for a while to lay low. I think he went to Spain but he's not saying in case their whereabouts get back to her husband. Anyway, he's left me up shit creek as we were booked to go to Bhutan in a couple of weeks' time to train some of their government partners and contractors on some harsh environment courses.'

'Nah, nah, nah, nah, there's no way I can do that, no way,' Sam said, his pulse quickening.

'I know it's a big ask, but I'm desperate here, backing out of this contract now will incur costs and penalties, and the loss of our company reputation will probably sink us,' Tinks implored.

'There's got to be someone else, Tinks. I can barely get out of bed these days, let alone go to Bhutan to work! And I haven't got the skills to train people anyway. And I've no passport or visa. And Bhutan's mountainous, I'm unfit, two stone overweight…'

Sam was starting to feel trapped. He knew Tinks could chew up every excuse he threw at him.

'Angel, there is no one. I've asked everyone I can think of, but no one can drop their lives for nearly three weeks to help and no one else has the right skill set. Look, I know this is uncomfortable for you and I know what you've been through—'

'Uncomfortable? Uncomfortable! Not a day goes by without me seeing that dead kid's face. I'm so fucked up by it, just getting through another day is a major achievement for me. You know I've been diagnosed with PTSD…' Sam tailed off, hating himself when he felt forced into playing the victim card.

'I know, mate, I know,' Tinks said quietly in a compassionate tone. 'We've had this out before, haven't we? We can't change what happened, but only we can choose to loosen its hold on us.'

'Ha, you sound like my fucking therapist now,' Sam said, with a hint of humour.

'We go back so long, Angel. It's got to be about twenty-four years ago when you moved into your aunt's home, just over the road from us? Remember all the crazy things we used to do?'

'Yeah, mainly you tinkering around with shit and breaking it. You just couldn't help yourself – you well-earned your nickname. I shouldn't be here by rights after you "tinkered" with my bike brakes to "fix" them,' Sam said fondly.

'I fixed them properly – it wasn't my fault both the rotten brake cables snapped, and it wasn't my fault you steered into that milk float.'

'Yeah, what a mess there was, and the milkman was so

pissed off but we couldn't stop laughing, and when we said…'
Sam chuckled.

'You can't cry over spilled milk!' they both said, laughing in unison.

'Ah, good times, mate, good times.' Tinks fell silent and Sam suspected he was trying to pick his next words carefully to try to win him around.

'I really, really need your help here, Angel,' he reiterated gently but Sam thought he was starting to sound desperate. 'This could be great for both of us, not just to save my skin, but to get together again, have some more good times just like the old times. You know they say insanity is doing the same thing over and over and expecting different results? Well, you're not insane, mate, but here's a chance to maybe move forward a little. I'll be with you, all the way. You can help save people with your knowledge. These people need you, and I need you. You know all the stuff there is to teach, a refresher will bring you up to speed – we could even do that on the flight if needs be. We can get the passport and visa sorted in a day. Everything will be paid for and the contract allows for a day rate of two hundred and fifty pounds. That'll blow the socks off your pitiful army medical pension. It's your call, Angel. How 'bout it, mate?'

Sam felt pulled in two directions. 'I can't, I should be here. I've got some medical appointments coming up that I must attend—'

Tinks interrupted but with careful intonation. 'Listen to your words, Angel. They aren't you. "Can't", "should", "got to". Surely these are words you want to part with, leave behind?'

Sam thought on all that had been said. Logically, he couldn't fault it, but he was clinging to his safety buoy and couldn't let go.

'Angel, I've got another call come in, I've got to take it. I'll call again within the hour. Have a good think because we can do this, together. We're like brothers, yeah? Brothers do what brothers need to do!'

The phone line cut off.

4

South-East Tibet, China
1ˢᵗ July 2018

Tenzin Gorji reached into the inside pocket of his traditional tunic for his tin of beloved snuff. The Buddha-embossed, circular tin still kept his fine-ground tobacco fresh and dry, as it had for his late grandfather on his father's side, though dampness was rarely a major threat on the high and arid Tibetan Plateau. As he sniffed, he kept a watchful eye on his herd of yak. He blew out the dusty smoke through his mouth, creating an auburn cloud trail, and relished the flavour and the nicotine hit. Spotting one of his yak trying to double back, he nimbly stepped across to cut off her route whilst vigorously swinging his slingshot, instantly diverting the yak back onto Tenzin's desired course.

Tenzin, the most common of Tibetan names since the enthronement of the Dalai Lama, Tenzin Lotse, in 1950, was returning to his nomadic family after a day walking their herd up one valley and down the next for fresh grazing, albeit sparce. The valleys in the area were generally deep and steep sided, predominantly flanked by fortress-like, bare rock-faced cliffs, but they served to trap just enough water vapour to create an early-morning dew in the hotter summer months. This produced an amount of green growth for the yaks in these warmer summer months. The permanently snow-capped peaks in this region soared to over 5,500 metres high, but there was little benefit for any nomads to reach these heights.

Though the tint of the landscape was generally rock, it was broken by intense blue skies, lakes and rivers. Tenzin's eye was trained to see green, for this meant sustenance for the herd which, in turn, meant sustenance for his family. The only breach of these colour staples were the occasional prayer flag outposts, contrasting with their bright and multi-coloured patchwork strings of fabric, furiously fluttering in the almost permanent winds.

The thin air, the dryness and the demands of herding had honed his tall physique over the past seven years, since the start of adulthood; lean and wiry but with immense strength belying his slenderness. The harsh elements; the sun, the wind and the winter cold had desiccated Tenzin, aging him by more than a few years, though this was culturally taken as a sign of maturity.

On his return route, Tenzin commenced one of his many daily meditations, his version of a kinhin, whereby he walked purposefully whilst concentrating on breathing and balance of movement. As a practitioner of Buddhism, Tenzin believed in practices to reduce suffering, his own and those in his sphere of influence, and his daily practices helped him understand himself and the world in which he existed.

A constriction in the width of the valley guided Tenzin and his herd to a narrow strip of land which was adjacent to an equally narrow width of ice-blue stream. It frenetically tumbled down the steep incline with randomly flicking currents and eddies. Over recent geological time, the stream had cut a chase in the valley floor and had thus created small drops down to the bankside, up to one and a half metres in places. Tenzin's walking meditation, at times, took him close to the edge of the torrent, depending on the obstacles he needed to traverse. Though deep in concentration, his attention was immediately seized by a foreign object in the shallow watercourse.

Never before had Tenzin seen such a large expanse of bright orange material, let alone here, in this remote valley, wriggling and moulding on the water's surface like a giant jellyfish.

Checking that the herd was close and could be temporarily left, he set about climbing down to the water's edge and carefully waded, knee-deep, to the head of the material. Once he had grasped the silky fabric, he pulled it to the edge of the stream and embarked on hauling it in.

Going for his knife, he paused before cutting the lines at the base of the orange textile. He ran his fingers over the soft, silky material until they reached a series of strings leading upstream to something heavy or stuck because it could not be pulled in. *A parachute!* He had witnessed the Chinese military periodically using such methods to deliver supplies to groups of troops on the plateau, except they used dark coloured parachutes.

 Lifting the yards of 'chute and placing it on the ledge above, he carefully traversed up the stream, following the lines. Through the cascading water, he could just make out a spherical shape, a man-made object of some description. Plunging his arms into the frigid stream, he cradled the object, the size of a small coffee table, to attempt to lift it and gauge its weight. It moved a little but it was large and heavy. He readjusted his grip and balance of the object and lifted it clear of the water. Carefully, he walked to the bank and placed it down.

A quick glance at the herd informed Tenzin that no action was needed; they had stopped walking and were happily grazing. He spent a while analysing the object's structure, unsure what he was looking at. To one side, possibly the bottom he judged as it was on the opposite end from the parachute attachment, was a circular shallow dome that appeared to be made of a form of ceramic and which had been heavily scorched by some process. Just above this was a tarnished, metal sphere made from two halves. These had been bolted together where the two equatorial flanges met. And finally, the supposed upper end looked like a couple of steel boxes with some metallic stubs protruding from the lower box. Tenzin ascertained that the top box, which was open, had housed the now unfurled orange parachute.

Then he recalled, when he was maybe six or seven years old, his father had taken him on a trip to Lhasa to trade yak skins for tools. After trading was complete, they passed the main square which had been set up as a morale-boosting outdoor cinema for the locals. While a dozen Chinese military soldiers laid out chairs at the front for the dignitaries and military high brass, Chinese propaganda news was being broadcast on a big screen on a loop. There was a clip of footage from the Shenzhou 1 mission, the first unmanned launch of this new space satellite. Tenzin recalled the female newsreader's shrill and overzealous, upbeat voice coming from the public address system. She sang the praises of the Chinese Communist Party and the successful return landing of the spacecraft somewhere in Mongolia. He recollected the unfamiliar, tarnished, burned capsule and three large, withered orange parachutes lying on the arid ground. Tenzin had craned his neck, transfixed on the screen. He'd wanted to stay and watch but his father kept the ponies trotting, pulling their cart past and beyond the main square.

Now with a better understanding of what he had retrieved, he set about loading the satellite onto his sturdiest yak, whilst stuffing the parachute material into his tunic, allowing his arms to be free for balance and controlling the herd on his way back to the family summer encampment. He estimated the object's weight to be about twice that of the family's cast iron stove they had in their yurt, an item Tenzin had lifted many times due to their nomadic lifestyle. With another round of snuff in his system and a magnificent find to share with his family, he quickened his pace down the valley.

'Mother! Father!' Tenzin shouted, waving his hands excitedly in the air. He could see his mother, Dawa, gathering piles of dried yak dung and his father, Choden, methodically wafting a small fire to burn incense for the safe return of the livestock. They each took a cursory look up. Tenzin was still a couple of hundred metres away and they acknowledged him with a brief wave then continued with their respective tasks in hand.

Dusk descended rapidly once the herd had been accounted for and secured to their tethers for the night. As usual, the whole family congregated in the main yak skin tent for dinner and to recount the day's stories to one another. This was a cosy affair, with a total of eighteen in the family unit, counting grandparents, parents, aunts and uncles, siblings and cousins.

The meal comprised a good serving of barley and yak meat, washed down with as much yak butter tea as anyone could want. Tenzin retold the story of his day for everyone's benefit before all the youngsters turned in for bed.

'I don't know about the lump of metal really, Tenzin, but the parachute material is a valuable find,' Tenzin's mother said. 'Think of the uses for clothes, bags, accessories and prayer flags, just to mention a few.'

Choden strode out of the tent.

'Yes, Mother, I knew it had great utility and value to us. But the metal part could hold even more value. It's a real satellite... from space!' Tenzin couldn't contain his elation.

Choden re-entered the tent with his treasured toolkit. 'Come on, Tenzin, bring in the satellite. Let's see what riches it holds.'

It took over an hour to dismantle the satellite into its separate parts. Nothing of particular interest was found but Tenzin and his father suspected any real treasure would be found in the core of the football-sized sphere.

'This is it, Father, the moment of truth – let's open it.'

A throaty, aged voice spoke up from the darkest section of the tent. It was Tenzin's grandma, Norbu. Having smoked tobacco for nearly eighty years, her voice was instantly recognisable. 'You don't know what you're doing. It could contain a poison, evil spirits or worse.'

Tenzin had negated to think critically about such outcomes as a possibility, in his honest excitement to know what might be concealed in the satellite

'You're quite right, Mother, we have no idea what these colonialists could have concocted in their pursuit to control the heavens,' Choden said. 'We know the Chinese and Russians cannot be trusted, and God forbid, what if this is an American creation?'

Grandma Norbu promptly spat on the ground three times, one for each of the aforementioned countries and then announced she was going to bed. This brought an end to the evening and everyone returned to their own tents, leaving Tenzin with just his immediate family.

Tenzin silently looked at Dawa, Choden, and his sister, Rinchen, in turn and then gazed at the sphere.

'I've got to know,' Tenzin said, pulling the toolbox towards him so that he could select the correct tool to unbolt the sphere.

It took a few minutes. 'That's all the fixings removed; it's ready to open,' Tenzin declared, making purposeful eye contact with each family member. Choden returned the contact and nodded his permission to reveal its contents.

The two halves would not separate at first. Tenzin then asked his father to hold the bottom half. By partly re-screwing in two bolts on the top flange, Tenzin created two secure hold points. He applied force to turn the top hemisphere anticlockwise. When nothing happened, he increased the force. A sudden jolt told him the seal was broken. After turning the hemisphere forty-five degrees, he felt the top half of the ball become loose.

'Mother, please could you bring the lantern closer,' he asked. 'We need the best light possible.'

He lifted his piece off the bottom half. It revealed a moulded brown foam-like substance sitting like a dome atop the bottom half of the ball. Two long, steel probes were attached to the inside of the top half, long enough to have penetrated through the foam into the lower level. Setting the top half to one side, Tenzin started to break off the crumbly brown foam until the top dome was removed and he then continued to carefully prize away the foam from the bottom half. This was made instantly easier as the whole middle portion dislodged.

'Is it a kind of bowl?' Dawa asked.

'I'm not sure.' Tenzin reached in to lift it. He held it in his fingertips and slowly rotated it for all to see in the lantern half-light. Though it took on the form of a thick-sided bowl, the surface was crazed as if it had been broken and glued back together. Tenzin stared puzzling at the off-white artefact with its mosaic appearance.

Abruptly, Tenzin set it back down in the foam nest whilst gasping suddenly, his eyes transfixed on the object; Dawa rushed to his side to tend to his distress.

Choden, unaware of his son's reaction, was focussed on the

object. 'It looks like an eggshell or maybe even a skull.'

Dawa ignored Choden's comment. 'Tell me, Tenzin, what is it?'

It took a few moments for Tenzin to speak, and when he did, his delivery was frail and staccato. 'It's what I saw, it's what it told me!'

'What do mean, what did you see?' implored Dawa.

With his hands visibly trembling and a feeling of shock well established, he whispered. 'All at once, I saw me. I saw me in terms of all the bad things I have done, and not just in this life. I started to see my karma, Mother, I looked my karma in the eye.'

Tears rolled down his cheeks.

Neither Tenzin nor Choden slept much after the unusual events of the previous day. They subsequently journeyed the fourteen or so miles to the Sangye Monastery, followed by an intense two-hour meeting with Jinpa Lama and the high monks to explain Tenzin's discovery. They had been instructed to wait on the steps to the monastery whilst the elders discussed the next steps; they took this moment to rest their eyes.

A half hour later, Jinpa Lama emerged and addressed the two travellers. 'Choden, Tenzin, please, follow me.'

Passing through the temple's main prayer chamber again, they were accompanied this time by the comforting, deep sound of a throat singing chant from eight red-robed monks, who were in full Dharma prayer. Through a couple of more doorways and corridors and they were back at the sparsely decorated, wood-panelled, private chambers of Jinpa Lama, who was sitting cross-legged on an oversized, golden-tasselled cushion. In front of him was a large carved-legged table, upon which the karmic artefact was placed on its own saffron-coloured cushion.

Once Tenzin and Choden were seated on the two remaining cushions beside the table, Jinpa Lama commenced his monologue of findings and decisions.

'Thank you for your patience. This artefact is of great interest and of great importance. It is clear it possesses immense power that has yet to be fully appraised, but with any power, rightful responsibility of its custodian is imperative.' He paused to collect his thoughts.

'I have been in discussions with the most senior officials of the Central Tibetan Administration, based in McLeod Ganj, Dharamsala in India, home to the Dalai Lama. They, in turn, have been advised by the Dalai Lama himself on this matter.' His gaze did not leave the phenomenon in front of him, and his delivery was calm and measured. 'I have been instructed to impart certain details to you to concentrate your minds on the importance of the tasks ahead of us. From the memory of the elders in the Administration, it is certain that this artefact is of ancient Greek origin and there have been prophesies of its growing ability over time, however, no further information survived the hurried exiling of our spiritual leader following the Tibetan uprising in 1959.'

'Time is now of the essence. Tibetan intelligence sources indicate the satellite was a relic of the Cold War and is most likely of American origin. It landed in Tibet recently and there is increasing Chinese military activity in the area, but it would have also garnered the attention of both the American and Russian military too, with Russia's greater open-mindedness to matters beyond that which science can explain.'

Having lived an insulated but noble nomadic life, some of this detail was not fully understood by Tenzin and even less so by Choden, judging by the vacant look on his father's face. However, Tenzin was all too knowledgeable about the intent of military forces, having heard about his father's encounters and especially having seen for himself the Chinese in action in Tibet. Along with these facts and that he had unwavering trust in the Buddhist monastic network, he awaited his instructions, no matter what they entailed.

Jinpa Lama's gaze finally lifted as he looked deep into Tenzin's and Choden's eyes in turn.

'Please, listen carefully and follow these instructions with the utmost diligence and secrecy; deceiving the cunning of the Chinese fox is our upmost ambition. Failure of this plan will undoubtedly lead to consequences of great magnitude for mankind beyond contemplation.'

5

En-Route to Thimphu, Bhutan
2nd July 2018

Sam never tired of looking out of the window on a flight, tracking the aircraft's position and identifying the landmarks below; it was his favourite mode of transport and he always opted for a window seat. And the Airbus A350-1000 granted a superior view due to the larger than normal window design. To the far portside horizon, he could now clearly see the majestic Himalayan mountain range, with its snow-covered peaks, as the plane flew south-east over Pakistan, near the end of the first leg of the journey to New Delhi. With a further two-hour flight to Paro airport, Bhutan, to go, Sam periodically felt the rising spectre of anxiety as he transiently thought of his new work schedule ahead. He managed to push that notion out of his mind by reconcentrating on the geographical marvel in the distance. Before the incident in Afghanistan, he had always relished travelling, the journey being every bit as enjoyable as the destination.

Tinks sat in his economy-class aisle seat, a spare seat between them, tweaking his course notes and presentations. The past few hours on the flight had been put to effective use to reaffirm Sam's understanding of the harsh environments training he was to provide in the coming days to a group of international scientists. This group's mission was to create a new calculation basis for the gross national product of Bhutan. Tinks' brief explained that these scientists would be researching in several remote areas of the country where they would be traversing some pretty rugged landscapes, fraught with natural dangers. Hence the course had been tailored to suit the delegates' upcoming survival risks.

Taking a break from his laptop work, Tinks leaned over towards Sam and said, 'Pretty amazing, aren't they, Angel?' gesturing in the direction of the mountains.

'Absolutely breathtaking, mate. When did you say we'd have time to explore them a little?' Sam asked.

'Our first course starts tomorrow and finishes Thursday. Then we have a break, so we'll do some trekking Friday, Saturday and Sunday.'

'Now you're talking.' Sam smiled. He was savouring this new, generally lighter mood that had developed the day after he foolishly – as he thought at the time – said yes to Tinks' cry for help. It had culminated in them zipping around London getting the necessary paperwork completed and shopping for suitable hiking apparel. Though Sam knew he still had a way to go before he could declare he was 'happy', whatever that really meant, he appreciated this new feeling, albeit very modest, of purpose and belonging. A feeling where he was able to breathe deeper and welcome in the relaxation it brought with it.

Laura detested flying. Her logic understood the high efficiency in terms of time that flying afforded, however, her acrophobia was never more pronounced than when on a plane. She masked her phobia well and used the flight time to catch up on paperwork or taking an occasional fitful nap.

This was the longest journey she had ever had to make, made even longer by not flying through Russian airspace. Routing from Washington DC to Ankara, refuelling, then flying on to Thimphu but avoiding Iranian airspace, added nearly three hours to make it a gruelling nineteen-hour journey, even with the comforts afforded by the CIA Gulfstream G500 private jet. Laura had enquired of the pilots as to why they couldn't route over Russia, but was told that although possible, it could lead to suspicions, monitoring of their flight and carried the risk of sudden diversions or even instructions for unscheduled landings. Hence, the routing over 'friendlies'.

Laura stared at her computer screen and contemplated the work ahead in Bhutan. Despite not knowing what she would be doing, she still felt the buzz of excitement and she was so looking forward to it – once this wretched last flight leg was over.

Jacob Rozen sat opposite and returned his seat to an upright position. 'You still on that laptop? Don't you think you'll be best to get some rest?'

'There's still so many gaps in my understanding of this whole operation, sir.' She sat back in her oversized, cream-leather seat and looked deep into his eyes, trying to use mind-control to get him to divulge some of the detail he had been withholding.

'It was quite an eye-opener reading General Hill's file on Project Arcane and what the military was trying to achieve in the Cold War but there was scant detail on this Operation Octal. And why have we got to retrieve this satellite shell, as if we're going to march into China, trip over it and walk out with it. I don't know how I might be involved in it over the next few years and why I've been taken away from Operation Persiana at such a critical stage. When are you going to throw me a bone, Rozen?'

'OK, Lafayette, look, let's pick over some points and see if you can get a clearer image in between the lines. I can let you know a little more about the history here,' Rozen offered.

'Firstly, Operation Persiana is in fine hands and your work has been exemplary, which is why you were chosen for this new project. Secondly, I can't answer why we have to traipse across the world to recover this shell though we will have some asset support. Nor can I answer what our future roles in the project will be. But, onto what I can say,' Rozen said. He sunk back into his seat.

'In 1922, there was a small archaeological dig in northern Greece which unearthed this half shell-like artefact. It emitted some kind of energy which mildly affected the cognitive ability of anyone in its vicinity. The Smithsonian Institution got wind of this and sent their representative over to Greece and managed to acquire it from the National Archaeological Museum in Athens.'

'It's not explained why the Greeks would have given this up; look how they are still campaigning to relocate treasures such as the Elgin Marbles in London back to their proper home,' Laura added.

'Yes, you're not wrong there but we'll never know about that, probably used arm-twisting tactics, as usual. As with many finds, the Smithsonian has a system to make certain antiquities 'disappear' if need be. Some are destroyed or purposefully lost, such as the giant humanoid skeletons dumped in the Pacific Ocean in the deep trenches off Los

Angeles in the early 1900s, to support the story of evolution.'

Laura sat up. 'Whoa, I didn't know that!' Laura said.

'Look it up online, there's plenty of information since the declassification following a Supreme Court ruling a few years back. Anyway, now we had this shell with some unusual energetic capabilities and it was secretly stored and not discarded. A 1950s' military researcher who specialised in Nazi occult records and accounts, used military warrants to access Smithsonian treasures not on the official register.' Rozen paused as the Gulf stream hit moderate turbulence and the pilot announced that seatbelts should be fastened.

No sooner than the panicking Laura had haphazardly secured her seatbelt, the aircraft found smooth air once again, and Rozen continued re-finding his position in the details. 'So, this guy takes some weird electronic measuring equipment and finds the shell,' Rozen continued. 'The shell is then passed on to the "woo-woo" Project Arcane where they manage to "weaponise" it. That was just a grandiose term for them finding out that it could be used as a barometer of intention, good or bad, of those near it, by radiating different frequencies to signify which intention and to what level, for example by percentage of the total number of people being read. It's all beyond me this stuff but this is how it supposedly works. I wouldn't be surprised if some projects hired ghosts to further our Cold War aims,' he mocked, with a grin.

'I'm sure they did.'

'The higher they put this thing, the more of the local population it could read, so they hooked up with NASA and developed the project to put the shell in orbit via a Gemini rocket in 1965, so they could monitor the psyche of the Russian populous. Its affectionate nickname was the Gemini Shell.'

'It's all a bit woolly, sir. I can't see how that would have provided a strategic advantage,' Laura pointed out.

'Yeah, but it was a convergence of several factors. One, an accident at a military satellite building facility meant that the Gemini rocket, which needed more testing, did not have a payload and that the uncomplicated shell satellite, the *ConchaSat*, was ready and waiting for a ride into orbit. Two, the push for space advantage over the Russians was at fever pitch and budgets were at record high levels, so most projects got go-aheads no matter how unlikely they sounded, in the spirit of "it was worth a try". And thirdly, this original military researcher, the Nazi occult specialist, had assimilated information from numerous historical sources which indicated there was a prophesy that the shell's capabilities – namely its power – would increase as astrological time proceeded. The predictions especially pointed to an increase at the turning of the age.'

Trying to comprehend this information, she rubbed her forehead and suggested, 'You mean into this technological or digital age?'

Rozen gently shook his head and appeared a little pained; Laura wondered if he was not convinced. 'No, the astrological age. Around the time we leave the Age of Pisces and enter the Age of Aquarius. Even though this all sounds like nonsense to me, I have researched this, Lafayette, and it seems like there is a migration to a new age that's occurring right now.'

6

South-East Tibet, China
6th July 2018

Despite the recent summer rain showers, volumes of dust billowed from behind the three-vehicle convoy of troop carriers, which had now clearly diverted off the tarmacadam road from Lhasa, demonstrating that the Chinese army contingent had finally located Choden and were making a beeline for him and his precious cargo. Deciding that now was not time for a quick blast of snuff, Choden geed up his trusted Tibetan pony to gallop up the valley. He was intent on reaching the higher shaley chimney a mile ahead in an attempt to lose the army pursuers and push on to the next valley, on his way to Lhasa.

Named Akar, *White Crystal*, owing to her stunning light colouring, Choden's prize pony used her sure-footedness and resilience to skilful effect, barely disclosing any reduction in performance even following the seventy-mile trek covered since the Sangye Monastery. Taking occasional glances over his shoulder, Choden saw his hunters were gaining rapidly, and so gave Akar every signal to go flat-out. Akar responded by straining every sinew as her master demanded; the section of shale rushed into view and was just a couple of hundred metres in front.

'Crack! Crack! Crack!' The Chinese fired upon Choden but this did not deter him from his course. With the terrain that the Chinese troop carriers were traversing, the shots were likely just pot luck. No soldier would be able to take proper aim unless they were motionless.

Akar nimbly carried Choden up the chimney, slightly weaving to reduce the attack of incline to afford the quickest route up. Such endurance from a pony would be rare anywhere else in the world, but this Tibetan breed was tuned to this hostile, high altitude topography, and it earned the reputation of being the most valuable of assets over the centuries it has been revered.

Another glance back saw the army trucks stationary near the base of the chimney and the troops starting to alight. Choden steered Akar up the left-hand side as a lower protrusion of rock gave them a natural shield from their chasers' firearms. A short-lived smile manifested on Choden's weather-worn face as just a few minutes more and they would be over the ridge to continue their mission.

The unmistakeable sounds of motorbikes firing up swung Choden's cursory moment of pride to one of concern. Though he carried on his run, he knew he did not have long. A couple more shots hit the ground near Akar's hooves; he needed to make a decision – continue this now doomed mission and allow Akar and himself to be shot, or to surrender and face the consequences. As the motorbikes quickly closed in, it was a decision he made quickly, easily – the Chinese had no need to kill them both. He heavy-heartedly stopped the climb, dismounted his beloved Akar and dropped to his knees with his hands clasped behind his head.

Minutes later, Choden and Akar were back with the convoy at the foot of the chimney, with Choden a little bruised from the heavy-handedness of the troops' search of him. He felt annoyed at himself that he, a Tibetan nomad, had been caught by the abhorred Chinese military.

Two of the soldiers began tossing out the contents of Akar's pouches.

'You have secret property of the People's Republic of China. Where is it?' barked the Chinese commander in Mandarin, inches from Choden's face.

'I don't know what you are saying. I am just a nomad,' Choden said in Classical Tibetan.

A first officer stepped forward and translated in as brusque a manner as the commander.

'I have only my own yak skins for trade in Lhasa. Look. Look for yourself,' said Choden.

The commander looked at the searching soldiers, who corroborated that only yak skins, water and small rations were found.

'Shit! Decoy!' spat the commander. 'Get me HQ on the line,' he snarled at his radioman. 'And you,' he said menacingly to Choden, continuing in Mandarin whilst displaying a wicked and bad-toothed grimace, 'you will be coming to Lhasa alright, and will enjoy our Chinese hospitality!'

'So, what about this, Angel?' Tinks asked as they stopped to take a break from the ascent of the steep trail they were on just north of Paro.

Sam felt as alive as he could ever remember. Taking in deep regular breaths of the warm pine-scented air due to the physicality of the climb and the rarity of the air at nearly ten thousand feet, he drank the vista from their narrow path. They reached for their water cannisters in their backpacks.

'Just look at that view,' Sam said. The words alone did not adequately convey his feelings at what he saw. A series of steep mountains and valleys dressed in alpine forest, with random whisps of thin cloud flirting with the highest reaches, had a backdrop of deep azure sky.

Tinks placed his arm upon Sam's shoulder. 'It's great to have you here, mate, and more than that, it's great to have you back.'

Sam let out a little affirmative whimper. He could feel himself welling up. He had come so far in such a small amount of time and his current state of mental well-being was in stark contrast to that of just a couple of weeks ago. Tinks was right to push and pull him over that comfort hurdle, and now Sam was relishing the benefits of his actions. He was eternally thankful to Tinks, despite finding the physical exertion a challenge in his current state of fitness.

He breathed deeply again. 'Thanks, Tinks.' Though he knew Tinks was not after any accolade, he was sure he knew the depth of Sam's gratitude. With the success of the first training course, Sam was now very much looking forward to the remaining two still to deliver.

'How's your leg holding up, mate?' Sam said.

'It's fine, thanks. It's only the cold, damp weather that gets to it. Come on, let's get moving, else we'll not get to see this temple – it should come into view around the next ridge,' instructed Tinks, marching on up the trail.

'Nah, nah; you said that twice before,' Sam said, jokingly.

Their strides were interrupted by a familiar sound. The 'wop-wop-wop' was faint and intermittent at first, then constant as it came into view to their right from one of the side valleys. Sam recognised its distinctive signature rotor pattern and jet-like engine whine from his military service. Though a dated airframe now, they stopped to marvel at the capabilities of the Aérospatiale Gazelle at this altitude. Mid-blue in colour, as it passed at its closest point, Sam could clearly read the owning company's logo, Bhutan Heli-Tours, emblazoned on the side.

'Looks like one pilot and two tourists in it,' Tinks said.

'Yep, probably off to the temple; must be people of influence,' Sam speculated. 'I thought we were told helicopter trips were stopped two years ago for noise abatement reasons.'

The helicopter disappeared as quickly as it had revealed itself and Sam and Tinks continued their trek.

Laura sat in the middle seat in the back of the chartered tour helicopter; she could not get further away from the glazed doors of the Gazelle as it swept left and right through the valleys up and towards the eventual landing point.

'Stunning views,' Rozen declared to Lafayette over the headset.

'Yes, sir, quite unbelievable,' she responded, without taking her eyes off a random dial on the cockpit, one that never seemed to move. She held on tight to her lap belt.

As her phone plinked, Rozen explained, 'I've just sent you a photo of a friendly that might be in the area. It comes from our General Hill at NORAD – best to learn that face to avoid a friendly-fire event.' Laura looked down at the grainy snap on her phone. Though of poor quality, she thought there was a degree of instant attractiveness to the friendly face, before another high-pitched sound grabbed her attention and sent another wave of ill-ease through her gut.

Laura and Rozen put their linked satellite phones to their free ears when the expected call from the Australian CIA centre came in.

'Yes, Pine Hill, can hear you loud and clear,' Rozen responded to the caller.

'OK, sir, we will be re-establishing connection with the target in sixty seconds. Target is still expected to be in the disputed land between Bhutan and Tibet. We will then have satellite thermal imagery for the next two minutes or so.'

'Two minutes! That's why I wanted a drone,' Rozen blurted unprofessionally. Laura knew full well that operating a drone in this locale of the world was a recipe for a full-scale diplomatic or even military skirmish; this mission had to be clean and quiet. 'Quick as you can now, Mason,' Rozen directed the pilot.

Mason took a sharp bank to the portside and swiftly levelled the aircraft. Now looking through the front windscreen, Laura was equally amazed and concerned at what she was now seeing. The helicopter was travelling at speed into what was locally known as the Horseshoe; a dead end. Tree-lined and cliff-faced mountainous terrain was all she could see from left through to right, and no sign of a landing site. But to briefly distract from this great concern, her right-hand window was now simultaneously providing a stunning view of Tiger's Claw Monastery, a series of white temple buildings adorned with traditional roofs of red and gold, impossibly clinging to a sheer cliff face.

The Australian asset spoke again, 'Sir, target in sight and is now on your side of the mountain, just descending into the Horseshoe.'

'OK, keep the commentary coming, we're coming in to land.'

Sam and Tinks' trail passed over a sheer cliff, providing a gap in the forest with no trees to obfuscate their vista. They were lost for words as they took in the full splendour of Tiger's Claw, perhaps five hundred metres directly across the valley. They could just make out the trail to the temple. It looked wafer-thin as it clung to the wall of rock all the way back to the centre of the Horseshoe far to the left of them.

'Absolutely stunning,' marvelled Tinks, as he joined Sam in taking photos of the ancient miracle afore them. 'Must have been built by angels,' he added. Sam expelled a droll laugh.

Taking time to scan the route they were soon to traverse, Sam spotted the mid-blue Gazelle, just to the right of a thin waterfall, cascading down the side of the Horseshoe. It had landed on a small, level clearing nestled into the mountainside and its rotors were idling.

'Maybe the pilot doesn't want to risk a high altitude restart,' Sam suggested.

'Could be the case, but it could be idling for ages if the passengers have a good look around Tiger's Claw.'

'We'll get to it in five or ten minutes. We can be nosey and ask the pilot.'

Sam and Tinks pursued the rock-carved track once again, and it was soon enveloped in the forest canopy, sparing them only fleeting glimpses of any view. The fact they were not far from the Buddhist monastery gave them a renewed burst of energy.

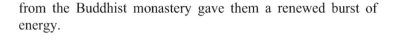

Laura and Rozen got ready to exit the Gazelle as soon as it landed on the makeshift helipad.

'Wait until the skids hit the deck,' Mason bellowed at them both, before concentrating on shoe-horning the aircraft onto the ledge, ensuring he landed nose to the mountain to gain the best view of any possible obstructions. The passengers' egress was swift as they made their way the few metres to the six-feet high chain-link fence, the only barrier at this point between Bhutan and an area of disputed land of which China had claimed ownership since 1959, when it annexed Tibet.

'Sir, target approx one hundred and fifty metres due north and closing. Satellite contact will be lost in forty-four seconds,' came the update over the satellite phone.

Dozens of small boulders lined the bottom of the fence, one of which provided the best springboard for Laura to effortlessly scale the barrier. Rozen's boulder of choice was smaller but he made quick work of clambering over despite holding the sat-phone in one hand and outwardly exhibiting sloth-like athleticism due to his ample middle-aged spread. As quickly and stealthily as possible, they traversed up a dark, twisting, narrow track, canopied by trees and bush understoreys, alongside a small but fiercely torrid stream.

'Sir, target forty metres away, and satellite connection now lost. But you appear to have company, sir. Two heat signatures about two hundred and fifty metres to the south-south-west and closing. Also, a Chinese military transport helicopter, possibly a Changhe Z-8, landed approx two miles to your north with eight heat signatures spilling out, six troops and two dogs, and rapidly coming your way.'

'Message received. Rozen out,' he whispered and hand signalled to Laura ahead that the target was just around the next bend. They both took out their Glock 19 handguns and held them at arms' length, pointing to the ground but ready to re-aim in an instant.

The rider lay back as far as he could astride his pony to counter the steep downward incline of the track, his lower back extra supported by two large saddle bags, but kept his head tilted forward which stopped his yak-fur hat from falling off.

The target came to an abrupt halt a few metres from Laura, with her gun now pointing straight at the chest of a Tibetan nomad.

'We are agents of the government of Bhutan licenced to stop and search anyone...' Laura's pre-concocted cover story was cut off by an unmistakeable 'fwoop' sound that could only have come from a silenced gun. Rozen's gun.

Tenzin made no sound as he fell off his pony backwards, thudded to the ground and rolled a handful of times down the incline towards the stream.

'What the fuck!' Laura whispered loudly through angrily gritted teeth, lowering her gun and turning to challenge Rozen.

He pushed past her, re-holstering his firearm and then started pulling the contents out of the nearest saddle bag.

'Get looking, Lafayette!' he said in a gruff voice.

No sooner had Laura put her gun away to join him in the search, Rozen declared, 'I got it.' He re-wrapped his find in yak skin jackets from the saddle bag, cradled it in his left arm and immediately started to trek back to the helicopter.

Laura followed closely behind. 'What the hell was that about? We didn't need to kill him!'

Rozen spun around to meet her, stopping inches from her

face. She could see his anger in his cold stare.

'Do I like doing that? Eh?' he seethed. 'No, no I don't, but I act on instinct and training. I've been working in the field since you were in diapers and my actions, like these, save lives and secure objectives. You've only been a proper field agent for ten minutes, so fuck you and fuck your judgements.'

He turned to continue the descent, the blue of the helicopter now visible through the foliage and the chain-link fence in clear view once again. A few steps later, they both heard the latest broadcast from Australia on their ear-pieces. They pulled out their firearms and Rozen quickly turned to Laura to assess the situation.

'So, we have a group of Chinese military coming from up there,' he said, indicating the direction with his gun, 'and two unknown heat sources approaching us from over there.' He used his gun to show her again. 'The military we do not want to see nor engage. The other two are probably just tourists, but we want no witnesses. Understand?' he whispered. '*No witnesses*!'

Sam and Tinks walked on the path in single file, focussing on the upcoming clearing, which was bathed in contrasting bright sunlight. Sam now had a clear view of the Gazelle, being about thirty metres from it. Just in front of the chopper, he saw rapid movement from behind a chain-link fence. He continued walking whilst watching a portly, middle-aged male and a younger female clamber over the fence.

Sam stopped and held his arm out back to arrest Tinks' progress and indicate something was up. He swore he saw a gun holster on the man as he ungainly dropped from the top of the fence, revealing his mid-riff. The two passengers then ran to the helicopter. It was now clear they were brandishing firearms and looking Sam's way, like they knew he and Tinks were there. The man carefully placed a woolly package in the Gazelle. Something was not right; Sam turned to Tinks.

'Don't move a muscle,' he whispered. The need to know started drawing Sam towards the Gazelle and into the clearing.

Laura and Rozen stood staring in Sam's direction, holding onto their respective open doors with one hand, their other hand tightly on the grips of their holstered guns, scanning for his intention. Sam stopped and froze, even holding his breath so as not to startle the two adversaries who were less than thirty metres away.

After several long seconds, Lafayette declared, 'Agent identified! He matches the snap we were sent.' The Gazelle's engine started to wind up and the rotors increased in revolutions. Rozen shouted, 'OK, let's go!' They jumped in but still kept a watchful eye on Sam and for any other witnesses to target.

After watching motionless for what seemed like an age to Sam, the Gazelle finally lifted off and flew out of the Horseshoe.

'What the fuck? What the fuck were you thinking?' Tinks scowled.

Sam ignored Tinks' concern. 'Let's look up that ravine, try to see what they were up to. Sounded like American accents to me,' he said. Tinks agreed.

Ignoring the clear signage on the fence warning of risk of death to trespassers beyond that point, the friends set upon satisfying their curiosity. A minute or so up the track, they found the lonesome brown pony, standing still and chewing a clump of tree leaves. Tinks looked in the pony's bags as Sam walked a little further up the track to rifle through the yak skins strewn across the path.

'This is frickin' weird, Angel.'

'You're not wrong…' Sam replied. A body shape caught his eye off the track, just a few metres down. 'Tinks!' he beckoned, scurrying down the bank. The body was in traditional dress lying on his back, and his arm was over his face. With his lips pale blue, he did not appear to be breathing. 'Hey!' Sam started to address the patient. He pulled his arm off his face and horror flooded his senses. He saw a young, tanned face and what looked like a bullet wound to the left side of his forehead.

Sam gasped and backed away unsteadily. His hands shook uncontrollably. He felt physical paralysis and a mental feeling of tumbling down a vortex, destination Afghanistan. Déjà vu. Tears welled in his eyes and he started to go into re-traumatised shock.

'Angel, Angel, it's OK, I'm here,' Tinks reassured Sam, holding his forearms, guiding him to sit down next to the stream.

Sam controlled his breath with slow intakes and watched Tinks turn his attention to the body, checking for reasons for there being no breathing. On checking the mouth, he found the tongue was causing an obstruction and quickly, Tinks readjusted his head in a backwards manner to clear the airway. Just as he was about to check the man's throat for foreign objects, the patient started breathing.

'Angel, he's alive. Hang on with me, mate.'

'But… he's shot,' Sam replied, feeling slightly more composed.

Tinks checked the still unconscious victim's forehead. 'It's OK, Angel, it's a fall wound.' He moved to the chest area where the tunic was blood-stained in the middle. He opened the garment fully. 'I'll be damned,' fell out of Tinks' mouth.

'What is it, Tinks?' Sam grabbed an adjacent tree to pull

himself upright, still unsteady.

Tinks reached into his backpack for his travel first aid kit and prepared some gauze and opened the sterile tweezers and attended to the patient's chest area. Moments later, Tinks had quickly checked the rest of the body and walked over to the now standing Sam and showed him a nine-millimetre bullet between his right thumb and index finger and a round, ornate metal tin in his other hand. The tin had a hole through both the top and bottom and light powder dropped out of the damaged area.

With a huge grin, Tinks said in amazement, 'This is one lucky mother-fucker! The bullet stopped; it just lodged in his intercostal muscle just in front of his heart. He must have knocked himself out from the fall from the pony.'

Sam eyes opened wide; he could not believe the young man's luck. 'He must have some good karma.'

Their wonderment at this karmic fortune was abruptly cut short with the sound of distant dogs barking, big dogs, coming from higher up the ravine. Sam's face morphed into critical concern.

'Trackers,' Tinks said. 'We got to get out of here – with this guy!'

They each grabbed an arm of the patient and hooked them around their shoulders. Sam operated on autopilot, following instruction from Tinks. Going down the track back to Bhutan would have been precarious without the weight of the patient, the pressure of the dogs closing in, the rarified air and Sam's semi-state of shock, but Sam knew failure would lay all three of them to bear whatever fate the owners of the tracker dogs would have for them.

Breathlessly, they dragged their invalided companion to the border fence where Sam and Tinks caught their breath and worked out how to get over the barrier. With the dogs barking getting louder and the now clear, urgent chatter of Chinese-speaking men, the Englishmen's minds were finely focussed on the last push to their perceived safety.

Tinks ordered Sam to lift the patient so that he was half lying over the fence. With Sam holding the patient's legs to avoid him falling over the chain-link, Tinks scrambled over the other side. 'Quick, there they are,' Tinks said.

Instinctively, Sam looked behind and got his first glance of their pursers and the snarling tracker dogs. Military men for certain and capture imminent. The Chinese commander shouted a demanding order in Chinese and raised his rifle towards the fleeing three. Sam and Tinks knew there was nothing they could do but surrender.

Sam watched as quite unexpectedly, the pursers stopped in their tracks and lowered their arms. Sam and Tinks were caught on either side of the partition, both holding on to their patient. Sam felt like time had frozen and was unsure what to do.

New voices started shouting, they could be Chinese but they were coming from a different direction, Sam realised. He turned to look along the barrier and saw a sea of maroon-robed and saffron-robed monks. They conversed with the Chinese military whilst at least two of them were videoing the scene on their smart phones.

Within moments, the patient and Sam were being assisted over the fence by some of the monks. Curt negotiations continued across the border to the disputed land. The monks displayed the three foreigners to the Chinese pursuers, including the contents of Sam and Tinks' backpacks, to show that they were not in possession of any objects of interest, though the Chinese did not elaborate as to what they were looking for.

'You are not carrying what they seek,' a young monk spoke to the Englishmen, in broken English, as the Chinese retreated back up the creek. 'Please, all come back to our monastery.'

He directed his hand towards Tenzin, 'We will treat our brother there.'

'What was all that about? The helicopter? The Chinese?' Tinks asked, searching for at least some understanding.

'He has been robbed of something of great importance. This is a sad day for humanity,' the young monk said

----

Laura still couldn't fathom out what it was sitting in the non-descript cardboard box that sat nestled under a spare chair on the right side of the Gulfstream. If nothing else, thinking about it was taking her mind off the endless sleepless hours ahead of her on the journey home. The shock that washed over her the time she held the Gemini Shell and the equal state the laid-back Rozen fell into after his introduction to the artefact's otherworldly power, played on her mind. She couldn't help recalling the countless bad memories the artefact branded on her consciousness, many of which she had no recollection of but to which she felt a connection, and which added confusion to the trauma. When she managed to change her mental focus, she was sickened by the Tibetan nomad's execution, right in front of her; he had presented no threat. It was torture, her thoughts digging deep into her psyche. She could not make this abate.

After sitting in silence with these harrowing thoughts, Laura checked the time on her phone, just as it flicked to nine o'clock in the morning, Washington DC time.

'Rozen. Rozen,' she gently called; his eyes blinked open from his apparent state of dozing. 'It's nearly nine am – you wanted to be woken up at nine EDT.'

He vigorously rubbed his face and then scratched his balding head in a random pattern all over.

'Coffee?' he asked, stifling a yawn. Labouring to leave his chair, he walked to the small galley area at the rear of the business jet to make them both a coffee.

Laura was still a little bemused that the return plane was not a standard CIA Gulfstream and more a top-end luxury model, with high-end fittings and trims and with subtle emblems on the bulkheads at both ends of the aircraft. Each comprised a black velvet-like inset square, sporting a gold trim, and what looked like a golden, elongated figure of eight in its centre.

Wearily, Rozen returned with their coffees, and then they conferred the checks they had made at Paro airport to ensure there was no hire trace of Bhutan Heli-Tours. He dropped back heavily into his chair. Laura thought he still looked unnerved from his recent artefact encounter, but gauged he was stoically pretending to not be affected. He took out the work's satellite phone and dialled a preset contact.

'Hello, General?' he said in a chirpy but respectful manner. He paused listening to the response. 'Yes, sir, we secured the cargo and have been airborne for about two hours now.' He paused again.

'Understood, sir.' Rozen ended the call.

'What was that about?' Laura enquired.

'I was instructed to report success to General Hill, six am Mountain Time.'

'You could have told me,' she said pointedly, still feeling disgusted by Rozen's actions earlier in the day and this feeling presenting itself in her curtness to him. 'So, what did he say?'

'He said standby for further instructions.' Rozen pouted and shrugged his shoulders, then resumed dozing in his seat.

No sooner as his eyes closed, the satellite phone rang.

'Rozen,' he answered. Laura's eyes were glued on him for

an update. 'No, it's just Special Agent Lafayette and myself. The two pilots are in the cockpit.'

Rozen looked at the phone and pressed the button to put it on loudspeaker mode, then lay it on the table between them.

'Rozen, Lafayette, I'm known as Elion,' said an old-sounding and scratchy male voice. Laura thought the accent was mid-European with certain phrases enunciated in what seemed a grand English accent. It was imparted with such charisma it would garner instant respect and attention no matter the content or context. She readied herself to scribble down notes.

'You will have several questions and many more before I finish, but my brevity is for just reason. Please do not question me and only listen. Further, do not waste time trying to locate or identify me; I can tell you this, it will be a fruitless and dangerous task,' Elion said with a knowing, low chuckle. This was followed by a short, phlegmy cough.

Taking in a deep, rattly breath, Elion continued, 'I know much about both of you, it is what I do. From hereon in, until further notice from myself or my family, you are both under cover, in a deep fashion. As far as the CIA know, you now work long-term for the existing dark project called Operation Octal, and they will not distract you, however, their resources will continue to be discretely open to you. You may be working in other places, but mainly and firstly in London; your pilots are being instructed to change the flight plan as I speak.'

With a final rasping breath, the voice continued with an intonation of glee, 'We will talk again before long, but do not underestimate the glorious part you and your new shipment will play on the long-awaited betterment and realignment of humanity.'

There was a click and the call was over.

Lafayette and Rozen locked eyes and were silent for several moments. Laura tried to comprehend the gravity and implications for both their respective lives after hearing from the enigmatic Elion. They then launched into a long discussion to try to understand what they had just been told.

7

Castel Gandolfo, Italy
23rd February 2022

'Ah, Cardinal Francis, please come and join me,' Pope Peter said, warmly beckoning his Cardinal with one hand whilst purposefully dabbing his lips with a crisp, white serviette with the other.

'Most Holy Father, thank you.' Cardinal Francis humbly bowed his head before entering the austere but impeccably adorned papal chambers of the Apostolic Palace of Castel Gandolfo, and softly walked across the flawless, ebony timber floor to the indicated seat on the opposite side of the table. The Cardinal gazed down at the exquisite parquet flooring, awaiting His Holiness, Pope Peter II, to finish his seabass supper, laid out on a splendid but small dining table, nestled next to the outside wall.

'It's always in loving companionship when we meet up, Holy Father. You wished to see me?' His trepidation and unease was reflected in the unsettled manner in which he handled his ever-present rosary beads in his right hand.

Pope Peter II methodically folded then lay his napkin next to his empty plate and promptly studied his white cassock for any food dropped, taking his time in doing this. Cardinal Francis then noticed the Pope looking into his eyes with his usual kindness. 'Francis, thank you for coming at short notice; I dearly hope I have not inconvenienced you too much. May I say, you do seem,' he paused for a second and made Francis feel he was being studied, before continuing, 'a little distracted, on edge, perhaps?'

The Cardinal awkwardly fidgeted in the ornate carver chair, desperate to disguise his demeanour, a task which was made all the harder as he knew it had already been detected by his intuitive companion. He swallowed more intensely than intended and quickly calculated his response to defuse the atmosphere. 'Please, forgive me, Holy Father, it may be because I have been working so many hours on my holy project and I fear I have not made as much progress as you would have wished for by now.' He bowed his head, projecting humility.

Whilst Francis fought to hide his nervousness, concerned he would invite even more scrutiny from his friend of fourteen years, the Pope softened his tone as he replied, 'Please, Francis, I did not mean to add to your burden.' He reassuringly tapped his beringed hand on the Cardinal's red cassock-covered arm. 'I understand our Lord has given you work that is testing on so many levels, but serving Him is what we do, there is nothing more important, however steep the climb, however unpalatable the substance.'

'Thank you, Holy Father, your words are welcome and most soothing.' Cardinal Francis relaxed somewhat though was still apprehensive of his companion's seeming ability to mind read.

'As you know, I would like to have announced some positive progress on your investigation of inappropriate liaisons with minors within the Church at the next Vatican synod. Pressure is building for insight, action and, ultimately, new direction, which is quite right.'

'Most true, Holy Father. As you know, I have always been a reformist and took pride and honour in taking on this responsibility to reshape the future of our Lord's holiest Church,' Cardinal Francis said in a composed fashion.

'Will there be significant news I can announce next month?'

'I cannot give you any false hope,' Francis replied, with undertones of regret. 'This decay runs so deep and is much complicated by the span of decades of obfuscation; I just learned this week that it would seem that two of our cardinals are still active in sheltering impropriety in their home countries. As each month passes, the trail splits again and again and thus the workload increases exponentially. To make any premature announcements would drive activities and evidence to be buried further.'

'This is such depressing news to absorb; such a delicate matter which demands action but not before the extent of the rot is established. I will not put more pressure on you and will push back any updates to the synod. The nature of this work must be taking a heavy toll on you, Francis. Is there any way I can help you?'

Cardinal Francis breathed deeply, relieved that the thorny part of the meeting appeared to be coming to a close and judging that his honesty had been well received, especially as he knew that Pope Peter had a talent when it came to reading people.

'Perhaps if I could have an additional clerical member of staff, this would greatly help, but I concur with your wish to keep the team as small and as tight as possible, due to the sensitive nature of the assignment.'

'I will give your request careful consideration and let you know shortly, however, I can see that if we do not utilise more hands, this project will be as old as me before it is completed,' Pope Peter said, with a little self-deprecating humour.

There came a long pause in their exchange. The Cardinal could sense Pope Peter was still scanning him for clues as to why he came to the meeting so ill at ease. Years ago, an outspoken sister let Francis know he had three states of being; unbefittingly sanctimonious most of the time, then sometimes he showed flashes of controlled anger where his eyes would widen and his nostrils would flare before reigning back the red mist, and lastly a state of anxiety where he would project a meek and distracted version of himself and endlessly count his rosary beads. Ever since that exchange with the sister, whom Francis had subsequently ordered to be transferred back to Greece, he regularly thought upon her words and had tried, mostly in vain, to temper these traits. Though looking a little uncomfortable with the extra weight he carried, Francis was proud of his youthful appearance, perhaps looking mid-fifties, a good ten years younger than his age, in stark contrast to the appearance of the Pope in Francis' estimation. Though Francis considered Pope Peter a friend, he was well aware it was his predecessor that had appointed him Cardinal and knew this Pope would never have ordained him.

The Cardinal had now settled to a degree but his claim that his agitation was due to his work remained unconvincing. The Pope, stroking his pointed chin and gazing again at Francis, unsettled the Cardinal once more, as he knew it was a sure sign that the Pope was assimilating information and analysing to come to some conclusions.

Cardinal Francis desperately clung to his inner voice telling him to keep composed until the Pope broke his train of thought. He concentrated on looking around the room, as if interested in the surrounding art and architecture, even though he had studied it many times before. He was taking nothing in.

Cardinal Francis knew he had not been advancing his investigation as fast or as thoroughly as was expected, and perhaps even starting to look like he was stalling the process. These were serious allegations and he estimated that the Pope would need more time to think, not to mention collating solid evidence of motives to corroborate such assertions.

Coming out of his trance-like state, the Pope changed the subject. 'Francis, I can only apologise hosting you this late and I let the kitchen staff go home early, so cannot even offer you a light supper or snack.'

Although the thirty-five kilometre distance between his monastic home, Monastero San Francesco in Cori, and Castel Gandolfo took the best part of an hour in heavy traffic, Cardinal Francis always relished the prospect of food being provided at the Palace, what with its fine dining chefs and much of the produce being hand-picked from the Palace's seventy-five-acre organic farm.

'No, no, Holy Father, heaven forfend,' Cardinal Francis dismissed, accentuated with a quick sweeping hand gesture, even though he had not eaten since lunch and with it approaching ten o'clock, a Castel Gandolfo snack would have been most welcome. A fleeting glance down the front of his scarlet cassock to the straining buttons around his midriff served as another reminder that eating less and losing weight would be of benefit to him.

'Francis, how is your dear brother, Paolo? Is he still delightful company?'

'Brother Paolo is just fine, thank you,' Francis replied with a wistful smile. 'He is still as dear to me as our gracious Lord. He recently involved himself with taking on light domestic duties at the monastery, sweeping and cleaning floors and polishing altar artefacts. Small steps of progress by the measure of some people, but positively giant leaps for dear Paolo.'

'It is by God's grace that brother Paolo is still with us and may well be the most loving and caring of His family on Earth.'

'Your kind words always humble me, Holy Father.' The Cardinal clasped his crucifix necklace and raised it to his lips giving it a sweet kiss. He quickly pushed aside the intrusive memory of the terrible rock-fall incident more than fifty years ago, which had left his younger brother with horrific brain injuries and had robbed him of a chance of a normal, fulfilling life. Thankfully, he now lived a simple life where he loved all that he beheld.

'Would you care for some water?' the Pope asked.

The Cardinal breathed deeply to arrest a wave of rising anxiety, dropping his hastening rosary bead counting hand out of view. He answered in a forced upbeat tone, 'Thank you, I would and I'd like to offer you a little surprise.' Turning to the open door to his left across the room, Francis called out, 'Luigino! Please would you enter?'

The monastic boy, just fourteen years old, quickly appeared, having been sat just out of sight in the corridor. Francis saw the Pope look somewhat surprised but welcomed the boy, perhaps wanting to save any embarrassment for him.

'Ah, my son, I was not aware the Cardinal had brought you along. Please, come, let us meet.' He carefully orientated himself towards the unexpected visitor and held out his hands.

Luigino anxiously approached slowly, rubbing his fingers into his palms, then carefully placed a jute bag on the ground, before dropping to one knee to receive the Pope's greeting. He subsequently kissed the Pope's right hand, just as he had been instructed to do earlier in the day.

'Luigino was so wanting to meet you and has been carrying out extra duties at our monastery to get into my good books in the hope I would grant him his wish to meet you, Holy Father,' explained the Cardinal.

'Of course, I am more than happy to meet any child of our Church. Please, Luigino, do stand.'

Nimbly jumping to his feet like a fawn, Luigino quizzingly glanced to his left at the Cardinal. In response, the Cardinal gave a nod of the head for Luigino to proceed. 'Holy Father, I understand that you are partial to summer fruits.'

The Pope raised his eyebrows and smiled in agreement. Luigino pulled a flask from the jute bag and held it out to the Holy Father. 'So, I have made a summer fruit compôte for you, made from frozen fruits grown last year here on the farm. It is made with cherry, raspberry and pear. I have since been told that compôte is not blended, so I am sorry that it is puréed.'

The Pope was delighted, always having enjoyed his sweets more than his entrées. 'Please, Luigino, you must join us in this out-of-season surprise. Lumpy or smooth, I am most grateful for your delicacy.'

'Thank you, Holy Father, but may I graciously decline as I fast for Lent after six pm and have renounced all sugar for this year's observance.'

'Yes, yes, of course, your dedication is noble. I might add that your politeness is also second to none. Please bring a chair and join us.'

The Cardinal assisted Luigino with the selection and helped him carry the antique chair to the table. As Francis sat down, he noticed two bowls of compôte had been poured. 'You'll join me, Francis?' Pope Peter asked.

After a brief hesitation, Francis politely confirmed what was really an order. Francis knew that the Pope would never solely eat any unofficially sanctioned food, even from a cardinal or young disciple.

The dessert was swiftly consumed and Luigino suitably praised for his culinary treat. Aware of the late hour, the

Cardinal brought matters to a conclusion. 'Holy Father, as much as I would love to continue our evening, I am conscious of the hour and the work that beckons us all from the dawn. If there is nothing else pressing, we should be on our way.'

Glancing at the mantelpiece clock, the Pope agreed, 'My, it's past ten o'clock and we are all servants of God. I will need to speak to you again tomorrow, Cardinal Francis. Thank you both for coming and it has been a pleasure meeting you, Luigino. God bless you both.' He gently tapped his forehead and chest to form the Sign of the Cross, and his two companions dipped their heads, followed suit and left the chambers.

Walking down the marbled staircase of the palatial villa towards the entrance hall, Francis asked, 'How do you feel having met Pope Peter II, Luigino?'

'It was amazing, Cardinal Francis. I cannot thank you enough for giving me this opportunity.' Luigino was ecstatic, oblivious to the Cardinal's discomfort.

'Luigino, please go on to the car outside. I need a few minutes to visit the ablutions before our journey.' He then lay his hand on his companion's forearm and enquired, 'Did you de-stone the cherries in your fruit dessert?'

'No,' Luigino vacantly replied, 'does it matter?'

'I'm sure not. Please,' and the Cardinal used his eyes to indicate it was time they parted and headed for their respective destinations.

Upstairs in the papal chambers, after having said goodnight to Alessandro, his premier chambers assistant, the Pope retired to his bedroom and started to methodically remove his papal regalia. He put each item in a pre-defined place so it would be pristine for wearing in the morning. As his brushed his teeth, a pang of indigestion grabbed his attention. Lamenting his late dinner and surprise dessert, he turned his attention to the running order of work for the next day.

'Digilogix International, hello, how may I help you?' a young male voice answered.

'Hello, yes, I was given this number to call. I am Cardinal Francis of Monastero San Francesco, in Cori. I understand my call is expected.'

'Please wait while I put you through, Cardinal,' replied the receptionist, in what seemed to be a Spanish accent, but Francis could not be sure and quickly shook away his unfocussed train of thought. Although exhausted, he needed to concentrate now. He had been expressly asked not to mention his contact by name. No doubt that name was a pseudonym anyway, but he duly followed instructions...

After thirty seconds or so, there was a soft click and a response, 'Good evening, Your Eminence. What is your report?' It was the familiar tone of an old, rasping, male voice with an abundance of charm.

'Good evening. Elion?'

'If such labelling is important, then yes, I am he,' Elion said.

'I have done as you asked.'

'Don't make it sound like this is all about me, you know the magnitude of your reward,' Elion replied.

'Yes, forgive me, but this plan has not been easy for me. I even had to eat the compôte with Pope Peter, and I am all jittery now. I had to flush my stomach several times with salted water before leaving Castel Randolfo. Oh, Lord, forgive me, what have I done?'

'Oh, enough of your dramatics! You must remember, I know you, really know you. I have seen into those dark recesses in your mind. Save your self-pity for the gullible. I told you before that the Pope had suspicions of your seedy pastimes and it was only a matter of time before he acquired proof. Did you feel any effects from the dessert?'

Flustered with Elion's directness, Francis answered with diminished presence, 'Yes, I felt quite unwell within ten minutes of finishing.'

'Good, that means it contained a good measure of amygdalin.' A rattly in-breath and cough followed.

'So, your doctor will tend to the Pope and make the right decisions?' Francis enquired.

'It is all set. So long as you added the requisite amount of fine cherry stone powder, your altar boy will attract the blame – though it will be deemed an act of ignorance, an accident, and with some extra orchestration, you will soon achieve your life's goal. We will then meet when you are Pope!'

8

Near Victoria Park, East London
25th February 2022

Sam sat in a camping chair on the back deck of the canal boat and breathed in a deep breath, enjoying the dawn-damp smell of the canal, exacerbated by the high humidity. He slowly started to gather his thoughts for the day, as fast as a seven am start would allow, pondering on both the first aid training course he was to give with Tinks at nine-thirty and the mundanities of life on the river – when the water tank would next need to be filled and the septic cassettes emptied, tasks inconveniently requiring half a day to pilot his vessel a couple of miles to the nearest service point.

Though the day was promising to be bright, it still felt cool and the sunrise glow had little warming effect. Sam's bankside mooring, next to Victoria Park, was mostly in the shadow of an early-budding London plane tree. A brisk gust of wind brought out goosepimples on Sam's bare arms and legs, and gave him the impetus to jump into a hot shower.

Taking another slug of now-cooler tea, Sam scanned across the water and towpath that his stern afforded him, and was instantly drawn to a movement on the towpath about a hundred metres away, on a curved section, devoid of moored boats. What looked to Sam like a younger, city-dressed woman with striking lengthy flame-coloured hair, was tracking back and forth along the path but with her attention fully on something small splashing around in the water. He strained to discern exactly what was going on due to the distance and the weak dawning light. He mulled over whether to throw clothes and shoes on and offer to help, but no sooner than him deciding to follow that course of action, the lady fell into the canal, with a moorhen fluttering and squawking out of her way.

'Shit,' he spat. He banged down his mug on the steel roof and leaped off the boat onto the towpath. Sprinting as fast as his bare feet would tolerate on the occasional stone and gravel surface, he swiftly approached the stretch of bank from which he saw her fall. There was no sign of her. Sam scoured the dark water, starting to doubt he was in the right section of the canal. A bloom of flame hair wafted to the surface and withdrew into the foreboding water as quickly as it had arrived. Not really knowing the canal's depth or what obstructions lurked beneath, Sam jumped in and stayed under water, frantically searching with his hands and feet. He momentarily opened his eyes, but shut them again when he realised visibility was virtually zero, especially as significant silt had been stirred up.

In what was only seconds, but felt like an age, Sam had grabbed onto some wool-like material and then resurfaced. Gasping for breath from his exertion and the cold water, he managed to orientate the woman so her limp head was also above the water and swam her the two metres to the bank. His feet and legs banged and scraped on branches, bricks and other debris as he drew nearer to the shallower bankside. Sam knew he needed to act fast.

A quick look along the towpath confirmed there was no one to shout to for help. He scrambled for a foothold in the steep bank and grasped a tree root to grab hold of at the path level, pulling himself up and out so that he was now lying along the bank's edge and still holding onto the woman's coat collar. He heaved mightily, to pull her out of the water, bringing her head to the path level. With a final movement onto his knees, Sam used every sinew to pull on the waterlogged coat and drag the unconscious body up and out onto the towpath.

With no time to regain his breath or composure, Sam started chest compressions, just as his training had taught him to automatically do. Another look both ways attested they were still on their own.

With water already seeping out of her mouth from Sam's actions, the woman violently convulsed, spluttering out water and then gasping in air. A series of coughing fits followed as her lungs cleared. Knowing she would be in shock and realising they were both shivering to the core, Sam grappled to pick up the woman and carry her to his boat.

Some ten minutes later, the woman spoke to Sam in a soft but noticeable French accent. 'Thank you, thank you, I can't thank you enough, you saved my life.' He had been focussed on getting her dryer and warm on his boat, having taken off her coat and placing her – propped up to one end of his sofa – next to his newly-stoked stove. He had covered her in a heat foil blanket, with two duvets on top. They warmed themselves on freshly brewed tea. He was transfixed by her, firstly, by how quickly she had calmly bounced back from being technically dead less than fifteen minutes before and also on account of her striking flame-red hair and matching eyes. *Could they be real, orange eyes? They must be contacts or something*, he thought.

She continued, 'I really don't know what happened – I was trying to free a bird caught up in some fishing line, then I was in that frigid water and must have gasped as I went under.'

'I just saw you fall in and rushed over – in fact, I was going to come over to see what you were looking at before you tumbled in,' Sam said.

'Look at you, you're all wet and you risked your life saving mine, how can I repay you?'

'It was nothing, anyone would have done the same,' he said, wiping dribbles of water from his hair that were running down the side of his face. 'Are you feeling OK? I'll call an ambulance to get you properly checked over.' He picked up his phone, but the woman placed her hand over it and said, 'No, please don't. It's not necessary.'

'But it's protocol in my line of business…' Suddenly, she cut him off.

'What you did today was good karma. My name is Amelie, and yours?' She stood up to stand next to him, her facial expression serene.

'Sam, Sam Angel. Look, you really need to be checked out.' He was talking but realised he was transfixed on the most amazing eyes he had ever seen. On close inspection, he could only liken her irises to two fiery suns, a kaleidoscope of yellows, reds and burned oranges, encapsulated by a soft brown outer ring.

As soon as Amelie spoke, he snapped out of his trance and felt a little self-conscious that he had been staring. 'I know my eyes are unusual, many people make comment. I just assure them they are more common amongst some of my fellow islanders in Tahiti,' she affirmed with an empathetic smile. 'I must leave now, but please could I have your mobile number, Sam? I'd like to keep in touch, if that's OK?'

She took Sam's number, thanked him again, assured him she was totally fine, and that as she didn't live far away, she could soon change out of her wet clothes. Watching her walk back along the towpath, he recalled her words about good karma. He had not heard anyone use the karma word since that fateful day in Afghanistan, and he refused to let his mind replay the events of that day. As he finished his tea, his thoughts switched to when he was eight, the day he was told his parents had both drowned in that accident. How he yearned to be able to go back in time and save them, just like he had done for Amelie. That sunken feeling of loss for them presented itself again.

Laura Lafayette left her Stratford apartment as usual at ten past six in the morning, giving herself plenty of time to commute to her office in East Hackney. Although her works-paid accommodation comprised all the things she demanded – new, clean, modern, a balcony with views and a gym and spa – she felt jaded due to such a long work secondment in London. It was coming up to four years since her jet from Bhutan had changed its flight path and she had started work on Operation Octal, soon afterwards renamed Project Octal to give it a more civilian title. She had challenged her secondment to the project several times during the first year, but Rozen and General Hill were having none of it; she would work on Project Octal until she was no longer needed.

Though quite a few changes had occurred within the project over the years, Laura was grateful that Rozen was still seconded. He was the only person she could talk to about deeper CIA matters. As far as everyone in the office was concerned, even though they were all high security-cleared, deep-state staff, they were encouraged to act as private freelance project managers, IT technicians and programmers, with the idea that they would integrate into local life better, without raising awkward questions. However, Lafayette and Rozen were the only staff sharing a private office, which made it easier to talk, if they so wished.

Elion's implication of travel to other places had never materialised and she had been working mostly seven days a week, save for a couple of weeks' holiday each year and the standard religious holiday festivals.

She had two reasons for renewed enthusiasm for work today. She was scheduled to update Elion on the project and the project was nearing its completion. A change of scene was well overdue and she longed to return to standard CIA work and help make the world a better place.

The morning walk took her through Victoria Park and along the Regent's Canal, the most pleasant parts of her commute. Often wondering what it must be like to lead a simpler life on a canal boat, she always studied the boats and occasionally stopped to speak to owners if they happened to be up when she passed by. Today was quiet along the water, but Laura couldn't help notice the attractive cream boat, named *The Wanderer,* with chrome-trimmed windows she liked, had dripping-wet clothes hung along its back handrail and what looked like wet footprints on the rear deck. She concluded that some unlucky person had, most likely, fallen in the river.

Minutes later along the towpath, she passed the modern but heavily graffitied apartment block just before ascending the steps leading to Cambridge Heath Road. With her innocuous four-storey office block diagonally opposite, Laura checked the access lanyard hanging around her neck and when she arrived at the entrance, held it up to the entry system. Chosen for its close proximity to East London Cyber City to blend in with the plethora of high-tech companies, but not really part of it, and for its generic appearance of having the façade of a residential apartment block, it was an ideal location from which to run the tech company Religix Limited, an arm of Project Octal. The building had now one of the most pristine exteriors in the area. Though having been encased in scaffolding and netting for weeks was far from ideal, having to endure considerable daytime noise as building contractors redrilled and refixed the façade cladding due to an original design fault, it was better than worrying that the cladding could fall off at any moment.

Laura selected the PH button on the lift, entered the seven-digit code and started the upward journey to the 'secret' floor. Although technically a four-storey building, a fifth floor with a much smaller footprint and roof terrace, with a view across the adjacent railway line and canal, had been added and named the Pent-House. Only Laura and Rozen knew the code, affording them privacy from everyone else on the project.

'Morning, Laura,' Rozen greeted, as she entered.

'Hi, Jacob. Fingers crossed for some good news today from our mystery man,' she replied with an exaggerated sense of exasperation. It was a close reflection of how she felt inside. Having spent so many years at Langley, she had surprised herself at how quickly she'd settled into a relatively small office environment and using colleagues first names. 'Did you get to call Eliza last night?'

'Yes, I did, thanks. Can't believe my youngest is twenty-five; how did that happen?' he responded. 'Rebekah was there with her too, getting out while she still can. And, of course, the old trout was with them.'

Ignoring the ex-wife comment, she asked, 'Rebekah's about seven months gone now?'

'Must be, baby's due at the end of April. I'm too young to be a grandfather.' Laura was not sure if Jacob was joking or being serious, but he seemed in a bit of a victim mode this morning and so she carried on working on her PC.

Laura's phone rang with an unknown number. 'Jacob, could be him,' she said, to catch his immediate attention.

'Lafayette here.'

'Good morning, Laura.' The unique sound of Elion's voice filled her ear. 'Is our dear Jacob with you and are you alone?'

'Hello, Elion. Yes, it's just us two here, up in the Pent-House. Let me put you on speaker; OK, it's done.'

'Firstly, thank you, both of you, for your dedication to this project.'

'We had no choice,' Laura whispered to herself.

'I fully understand that having devised and mastered the technique to harness the power of our ancient artefact, it was a disappointment to you that it was relocated to a secret venue at the end of last year. However, the service you and your team have provided for this project is phenomenal, and I tell you, it will change the world forever.'

Both Laura and Jacob had heard this kind of patter many times but now knew the project was coming to a close. What they did not know was how the project would be rolled out, and quite frankly, they didn't care; they just wanted to get back to their normal lives.

'I know you crave to go back to your Langley home and the good news is that the project is coming to a natural break point. For reasons I cannot divulge, we must accelerate the final elements of this stage and your secondments will thus terminate within the coming few weeks. Watch the news this morning – something quite relevant and important will be breaking in the next half hour. Also, you will be hosting a VIP client very soon. Details will follow. Viel spaß!' And in line with the other brief phone calls from Elion, before either of them could ask a question, the connection terminated.

'Well, that didn't clear much up,' Jacob snorted.

'No, but he did confirm we can go back to our old lives

soon. I've got a yearning to go and fill up on some good old swamps,' she joked in an exaggerated southern drawl, knowing swamps were not to everyone's taste.

Jacob opened up a new browser window. 'I'll stream ZUX news in the background, wouldn't want to miss any fireworks,' he said sarcastically.

'OK. But I'm wary of his last words, "Viel spaß" – "Enjoy". He usually means that sarcastically.' She briefly paused to concentrate on logging in to one of the CIA databases, 'I think it's now time to have a little dig around to find out who our mysterious man, Elion, really is.'

08:00 UTC ZUX NEWS 24 LIVE ---- BREAKING NEWS ----

'Pope Peter II is dead. This is the shocking and sad breaking news here on ZUX News 24. The Vatican has just announced the passing of the Pope, the supreme pontiff and the Bishop of Rome, the one hundred and eleventh Pope, but known to most around the world as the head of the Catholic Church. The short statement went on to say that the Chief Vatican Physician declared he passed peacefully in his sleep from a previously undiagnosed co-morbidity and was found lying in rest yesterday morning in his chambers at Castel Gandolfo. Condolences have started pouring in from leaders and prominent figures from every corner of the globe, driven by social media platforms. Pope Peter was last seen in public on Sunday when he gave Mass…'

Sam alighted his bicycle at Stratford's Westfield Shopping Centre, out of breath, peeled off his jacket and repeatedly pulled at his shirt to cool his sweating body. Although only a four-kilometre ride, due to the events that morning, Sam had left himself only twenty-five minutes to cycle to the course venue, secure his bike and get to the training room to start the set up. He knew he was running late and rushed through the large department store to the training room at the rear.

'Cutting it fine, Angel,' Tinks said as Sam walked into the room. It was said without giving offence, but served as notice that an eight-thirty start did not mean gone twenty-to-nine. Sam could see Tinks had arrived early so the pressure was off to set out the first aid kits, CPR mannequins, defibrillators, Tinks' company branding posters and set up the PowerPoint presentation. Sam noticed Tinks had his slight hobble back, on account of his war-wound and the colder winter weather.

'Sorry, mate, I've had such a day already,' he apologised, followed by, 'That leg playing you up today?'

'Oh, a bit; just one of those things. What happened with you then?' Tinks asked, apathetically. He flicked through the PowerPoint presentation to ensure all slides were present and correct. Sam went on to give a synopsis of the morning's events, which elicited Tinks' full attention.

'Jesus, Angel, living up to your name again! Well done, but you know you should have called nine, nine, nine before you jumped in; you could have both drowned.'

'In hindsight, yeah, you're right, but I guess I just thought that by the time I had run back to the boat and called, then described where I was, she may have died,' Sam replied.

'So, you going to go out on a date with this flame-eyed bird? She owes you, I'd say. It's about time you had another focus in your private life that doesn't involve conspiracy theories.'

Angel took this as a cheap shot on account of his non-mainstream view of the world. A while after that tragic day in Afghanistan, he had read and then come to believe that the whole premise of the West starting that conflict was on a stack of convenient lies which were then propagated by the media and governments alike. This had led him into researching other Western countries' conflicts, events and stances, where he continued to find a similar pattern.

'It's not like that,' he replied, letting the conspiracy comment slide to avoid a possible clash with Tinks. 'But she's got my number if she wants to make a date,' he joked.

'So what's your take on the Pope news?' Tinks asked, knowing he was poking Angel for a reaction.

'What news?'

Tinks took a couple of steps closer to tell him. 'The Pope's been found dead.'

'Shit! How?'

'They say natural causes, died in his sleep of some condition.' Tinks studied Angel's reaction and waited for some comment to dispel the official narrative.

'Wow, that was sudden. I guess he was quite an age, heart could have given out or an embolism? Strange though, they made such a big deal of him being so fit for his age and gave him the all-clear about a month ago when he tripped up those steps in front of an altar,' Sam said, thinking out loud. 'Surely they would have given the Pope a full scan and medical check over, and supposedly nothing turned up.'

'Maybe they missed something,' Tinks said, throwing in some of his logical thinking, 'or maybe something developed quickly; he was about eighty years old.'

'Mmm, but as he was such a reformer, he must have rattled a lot of cages, especially with ongoing investigations into global Church abuse and paedophilia; would've made a lot of people worried about being exposed.'

'Everything's a conspiracy to you, why do you always think there's a dark explanation for everything and not just a series of random, natural events?'

Angel felt himself getting somewhat agitated and wanting to defend his own critical thinking, he moved even closer to Tinks. 'The Catholic Church is a hugely powerful global entity and slowly but surely its wrongdoings are being exposed, whilst they suffer a huge drop in their congregations; they are in trouble. We are always being lied to.'

Angel took a breath and decided to continue. 'Look, you were there in Afghanistan, you heard all the stories, saw firsthand, our being there wasn't all what we were told. First it was all about hunting down Bin Laden, then when he melted away, it was about ousting the Taliban and installing a government that would not harbour terrorists. But really it was all about reinstating the opium fields and installing a Western presence on the doorstep of Iran and Pakistan; drugs and geopolitics. We were fighting terrorists but perhaps we were the terrorists? '

'That's not provable and you know it,' Tinks said, pushing Angel a bit more.

'No one's going to admit to it, just as no government wants to admit the Iraq wars were all about the control of oil. I'd love to see the world like you and believe everything happens by chance. It must be very relaxing, but I can't, there's something very wrong with it all and I can't ignore the evil in this world that is disguised by righteousness and hidden behind compassion.' Angel did not feel great about the pointed exchange with his best friend and boss, who was now visibly agitated.

'Yeah, evil, like a pre-adolescent boy trying to shoot us dead!' Tinks regretted the remark instantly and noted the expression of horror develop on his pal's face. 'I'm really sorry, Angel, that was so uncalled for.' Tinks tried to undo some of the damage by putting his hand on Sam's shoulder.

Just as Sam felt the familiar wave of nausea rise up from his stomach, the training room door thrust open as the trainees entered.

'And here are our trainees. Showtime!' Tinks said, lighting up his expression and clasping his hands together, something he did every time before starting a training session.

With this tension with Tinks, Sam knew this was going to be a difficult day.

9

Vatican City, Rome
25th March 2022

11:00 UTC ZUX NEWS 24 LIVE ---- BREAKING NEWS ----

'And once again, it is black smoke emanating from the chimney on the roof of the Sistine Chapel. Black smoke; so, still no Pope has been chosen in this papal conclave, which is turning out to be a modern marathon. The atmosphere of disappointment can be clearly felt here in a packed St. Peter's Square. By some estimates there are over a quarter of a million of the faithful here, reinforcing that there is still relevance to the Pope and the Catholic Church in a world turning its back on traditional religions.

'Following traditional protocol, the one hundred and twenty cardinals from forty-four countries have now been locked in the historic confines of the Sistine Chapel for twelve days, not having any contact with the outside world, just eating, sleeping and partaking in scrutinies in one of the most beautiful buildings in the world.

'I'm just checking my notes and yes, it seems we are now at a turning point in the scrutiny or voting process. Please let me take a moment to explain. The late Pope Peter II was known for, his reformist gall, and many admired him for this, and he set about the most comprehensive catalogue of change for the Catholic Church in modern history. All this in the two short years of his reign as Pope. Now, to avoid papal conclaves becoming unnecessarily protracted events, Pope Peter II reinstalled a change that Pope John Paul II made in 1996, whereby after an unsuccessful thirty-fourth scrutiny ballot, the two cardinals with the highest votes in that ballot will be put forward for an absolute majority vote.

'So, if I am correct, we should have a new Pope by this afternoon...'

Cardinal Francis anxiously took his seat at one of the long, white tableclothed-tables in the glorious splendour of the Sistine Chapel for the thirty-fifth and, possibly, final scrutiny. His mind was flitting from one thought to another; the enormity of his life's dream of becoming Pope was bearing down on him. What would he say to the world on the balcony? How should he conduct himself? He slowly lowered his head and wiped his mouth with his left hand to remove any telltale signs of one of his favourite meals, seafood linguini, although he'd not been mindful in his consumption of his luncheon. This led him to cup his full stomach and worry if he would fit into the papal robes. All this time, he was anxiously counting his rosary beads with his right hand, under the table and out of sight.

Trying to steady his nerves – there was excitement also, he had to admit – he looked heavenwards, and attempted to study Michelangelo's masterpieces adorning the vaulted ceiling of the chapel. But not even the finest religious artwork in the serenity of this magnificent fifteenth century centre of worship could calm his mind.

Aware that all but a few of the one hundred and twenty voting cardinals were now seated, looking practically identical in their crimson and white cassocks and matching biretta hats, Cardinal Francis knew the vote would start within the next few minutes. With his best attempt at projecting serenity, he looked to the other side of the chapel towards the other candidate in this run-off scrutiny, Cardinal Bankole. He instantly returned a nod of affection and drew the Sign of the Cross with his open right hand.

Francis had had many a convivial conversation with Kanu Bankole, Cardinal Bishop of Velletri-Segni, whose suburbicarian diocese was less than an hour away in Rome. Born in the Igbo southeastern area of Nigeria, he discovered Catholicism as a teenager and had devoted his life to the church. Cardinal Bankole was a conformist and a unifier, who was politically sensitive to opposing views, liked to compromise and was thus not keen to shake-up a Church that had been functioning well for so many centuries. This was in direct contrast to Cardinal Francis' stance that the Church needed a new and bold direction to reverse the waning congregation numbers and he wanted to actively market Catholicism, akin to a global business. Though both of their manifestoes divided opinion amongst the conclave members, Cardinal Francis was confident of becoming Pope, even without Elion's assistance. Pope Peter II was voted in easily and was a known reformer, so, Francis rationalised, why would this group of cardinals vote for old-style leadership and compromise?

And there was one other reason for Francis' confidence, the well-known but little talked about prophecy by Saint Malachy back in the twelfth century; the one hundred and twelfth Pope being a black Pope presiding in the end of days. *Surely some cardinals will fear the possibility of bringing such a prophecy to fruition*, Francis mused. *The world is now ready for a Pope of colour, but what of the prophecy?*

As the last of the cardinals made their way to their respective seats, Cardinal Francis breathed in and out deeply, closed his eyes, lifted his head upwards and silently prayed.

Dear Father, if it is Your will that it is my time to ascend to your highest chair, I will serve You without question and without complaint. I pray for my unknown parents who died so young and I pray for redemption for my childhood abusers, as they were troubled souls. I pray for redemption for the sins over the years and most of all, I pray for Your love and courage to continue to reside with my dear brother, Paolo. I am forever Your servant. Amen.

As he finished his prayer, he raised his crucifix to his lips and gave it a long and meaningful kiss.

An accustomed silence befell the chapel once again, as had ensued many times over the past twelve days, signalling the voting procedures were under way. One hundred and twenty immaculately dressed cardinals, in scarlet and white, now sat at six long tables, three in a line, each line adjacent to the long walls of the chapel, with a seventh head table placed in front of the steps to the altar. The orchestrating cardinals of the conclave, three scrutineers and three observers, were seated at this head table, upon which was placed a tray of small, aged, wooden voting balls, a plain timber ballot box, and a few feet along, a large, decorated golden bowl to receive the wooden balls.

The three scrutineers at the head table rose to distribute the ballot papers to the voting cardinals. The one difference immediately apparent to Cardinal Francis this time was that the scrutineers did not hand him the usual two blank ballot papers. Placed in front of him were a bible, a large, scarlet-covered writing pad, a black fountain pen and a glass of still spring water. Under the papal conclave rules, both Cardinal Francis and Cardinal Bankole were now spectators in this head-to-head ballot and could do nothing more than await the outcome of the scrutiny to see who would become Pope. Francis reckoned that the election would be close, but unlikely for the outcome to be a tie, fifty-nine to fifty-nine votes, which would trigger another head-to-head vote.

After what seemed an age, Cardinal Francis was relieved to see all the ballot papers completed and the first cardinal was called by selection of one of the wooden balls, 'Cardinal Alberto of Italy.'

Cardinal Alberto approached the altar table, stopped by the ballot box and recited, 'I call as my witness, Christ the Lord, who will be my judge, that my vote is given to the one who before God I think should be elected.' He then stepped to the ballot box and slotted in his voting slip, made the Sign of the Cross and returned to his seat. As a belt and braces approach to adjudicating the proceedings, the scrutineers marked off the vote on parchment and placed the wooden ball in the bowl.

Throughout this election process, which lasted an agonising hour and forty minutes, Cardinal Francis frantically counted his rosary beads. He used some of the time to visualise his inauguration and rehearse his reactions and public address but fought to keep at bay the list of his sins that kept barging their way into focus. Now, with just the ballot count standing between him and his lifelong ambition, he tried his best to keep composed and serene.

The head scrutineer stood and picked up the ballot box in

front of him, giving it several meaningful shakes and passing it to his colleague beside him. This scrutineer began to remove the ballots, one by one, reading out the name written upon it. The vote was dutifully checked and recorded on parchment by the third scrutineer, and subsequently the ballot paper was passed to the nearest observer cardinal, who held a large darning needle threaded with a length of scarlet twine, knotted at one end. Once recorded, each ballot paper was threaded onto the red cord.

After one hundred votes had been announced, it was still seemingly neck and neck. Cardinal Francis noticed Cardinal Bankole trying to catch his eye, perhaps to show solidarity in their joint situation, but Francis' gaze was promptly redirected to fix on the altar table. He still furiously thumbed his rosary, so much so that his whole body noticeably rocked as every bead passed.

The count concluded and, as had occurred many times previously, murmurs of anticipation rippled through the chapel.

'It is my holy duty and an honour to announce,' the head scrutineer said, standing to deliver the result, 'that Cardinal Bankole has been elected the one hundred and twelfth Pope.'

As the Sistine Chapel exploded into rapturous but dignified applause for the new Pope, Cardinal Francis nostrils flared uncontrollably, his eyes widened and he took in a sharp intake of breath. The anger that coursed through him was nothing like he had experienced for many, many years. Through his rage he had failed to notice he had broken his rosary string, with the beads cascading and noisily bouncing around on the marble floor. Worse still, he failed to detect that his unbefitting reaction was being witnessed by an increasing number of cardinals.

'The results tallied at fifty-eight votes for Cardinal Francis and sixty votes for Cardinal Bankole,' the head scrutineer concluded and a second round of applause followed.

Francis wrestled with his anger as soon as he was aware that was fast becoming the centre of attention, and promptly joined in the applause, even giving an affirmative nod and smile to Cardinal Bankole on the opposite side of the church. He decided to attend to collecting the beads at a later time.

The conclave observer holding the string of threaded ballot papers walked over to the log burner temporarily installed for the election, and with the assistance of a member of chapel staff, threw the ballot papers on the fire along with a cartridge comprising potassium chlorate, lactose and pine resin, which burned together to produce a white smoke.

Within a mere second or two of closing the burner's door, the chapel's bells rang out and Cardinal Francis heard the distinct roar of hundreds of thousands of devoted Catholics in St Peter's Square expressing their pleasure at seeing the white smoke, signifying the conclusion of the selection of a pontiff for their Church.

Cardinal Bankole was graciously greeted by his fellow electors, like a sea of scarlet punctuated by flashes of white, all gushing with heartfelt congratulations.

Having witnessed a few moments of cooing, Francis knelt next to his chair and started picking up his rosary beads. A member of Vatican staff, who had been waiting on the conclave endlessly for the past twelve days, began to assist, but to give himself some physical room, Francis kindly asked if he could collect those that had rolled to the centre of the floor. The more he analysed the outcome of the conclave, the more confused and annoyed he became. He had been assured of victory in the election, or so Elion had led him to believe. A wave of nausea washed over him when he thought of the deed he had been tasked with to poison the previous Pope, thus setting up his favourite altar boy, Luigino. An overriding thought replayed itself in his head whilst he resisted a surge of anger bubbling to the surface. *Elion has played me; I need to speak to him, urgently, and give him a piece of my mind.*

'Cardinal Francis?' Cardinal Bankole enquired.

Craning up his head, from an all-fours position, Francis used the back of his chair to stand up.

'Holy Father, such a close conclave, but the Lord has chosen wisely,' Francis said, with as much sincerity as he could muster. He held the new Pope's right hand in both of his and lowered his head to kiss it.

Cardinal Bankole smiled. 'You are most gracious, Cardinal Francis. We will meet up again very soon to push forward His work,' he said in his distinctively smooth West African lilt, 'but first, our congregation calls. It would be my honour, if you would accompany me now to the Room of Tears to watch the process of ordainment?'

Francis had the briefest moment of aversion to this gracious offer before accepting, and they both promptly made their way out of the chapel's grand hall.

In the hall in St Peter's Basilica leading to the grand central balcony overlooking St Peter's Square, Francis watched the new Pope, accept the canonical election as supreme pontiff and subsequently change into his papal regalia in the Sistine Chapel's Room of Tears, though, in contrast from usual reaction, there were no tears from Cardinal Bankole, only joy. The Master of Papal Liturgical Celebrations asked which papal name he was going to assume.

'Leo, I have decided upon the name Leo. Not only is it my birth sign, it reflects the courage I will need by my side for my Papacy, that of a lion,' Kanu Bankole warmly replied, with a broad, white-toothed smile, locking eyes with Cardinal Francis. Turning his attention back to the Master of Papal Liturgical Celebrations, he said, 'I think I am right in saying that there have been thirteen Leo's before now?'

'Yes, Holy Father, Pope Leo XIV,' the Master

subserviently bowed his head and disseminated the chosen name to everyone else in the hall.

Protodeacon Cardinal Jorge Sanchez stepped through the gap in the opulent rouge curtains, which separated the Room of Tears from the papal balcony and Francis enviously witnessed the gathered congregation's roar of delight. 'Dear brothers and sisters,' he said and waited for the crowd to settle. 'We have a new pope!' and with that the crowd's roar became deafening.

Pope Leo XIV could not contain his happiness and beamed what would become his trademarked broadest of smiles as he made his way towards the balcony. As he neared, he could feel the electric atmosphere in the square. Francis was surprised when he stopped and then slowly turned to him and solemnly confided, 'Finally, I can now exact my plan for humanity.'

10

Lisbon, Portugal
29th March 2022

The Church of Santa Maria Maior stood like a sentry in the historical centre of Lisbon, just a stone's throw from the banks of the River Tagus. Inspector Manuela Ferreira parked her patrol car on the ancient, cobbled area in front of the twelfth-century Lisboan cathedral, inside the police-taped cordon and next to the two other police cars already present.

'Ooh, I could do with one or two pastel de natas from that bakery,' Officer Afonso Costa said to his senior, pointing at the shop. 'I haven't had any breakfast yet, and it's gone eight am.'

'Not now. You're always thinking of your stomach, Costa,' Ferreira replied, as she unbuckled her seatbelt, thinking how Costa was already overweight and did not have the fitness that was ideal for his police role. Being able to chase after suspects was still a central role for law enforcers, in her mind, but she resisted making comments because the culture now dictated that to express such views was tantamount to bullying, hate speech or something similar. Having worked her way up to the grade of inspector over twenty-five years, in what was mostly a man's world during that period, she did not fancy throwing away her career over a fat-shaming comment.

She looked at Costa and thought how he could be so much more than the second-rate, overeating police officer he chose to be. About the same age as her son, she was despairing of the younger generation and how glibly they threw away life chances. She thought of her son sitting at home after having been released on bail on charges of theft of two hundred euros in cash from the bank branch in which he worked. Now off work pending the trial, he maintained his innocence, much to the consternation of Manuela Ferreira.

She peered into the rearview mirror and adjusted her ponytail band, before the two officers exited their car and strode up the half-dozen wide stone steps leading to the church's impressive main entrance, with its imposing series of concentric arches and enormous, venerable timber doors. Showing their credentials to the police officer on duty at the entrance, they made their way into the cathedral.

'It's been ages since I've been in here, Inspector. I think I was a kid and loved the echoes,' Costa said, proceeding to give out a loud whoop. He smiled, listening to the acoustic wonders the cavernous nave provided.

'Cut that out, Costa. Decorum! Not only is this a sacred place, there's a possible serious crime scene to see here.' Ferreira was in disbelief she was having to tell this twenty-year-old how to behave.

Looking all around and scanning the high vaulted ceiling, Costa asked, 'Can you tell me more about the crime we're investigating?'

'Look in front of you, at the far end, behind the altar. The photography flashes should have given you a clue where to look,' Ferreira said flippantly. *What the hell do the youngsters get taught in police training school these days?* she thought.

'Can't really see, the altar's a bit in the way. Oh, is it something to do with that framework and crucifix behind it?' Costa asked, naïvely.

As they ascended the altar steps, it was understandable to Ferreira why the Commissioner of Police had sent his best inspector to the scene.

They were presented with a scene more suited to the Medieval Ages with hints of biblical horror. To the very rear of the semi-circular area behind the altar, stood a large wooden cross. It was mounted on a mechanical jack which had raised the cross about three feet from the marble floor. In front of the cross, a black, metal frame stood with three crossbows set within. Two were mounted just about six feet up and were spaced out to about the same measurement. The other crossbow was set low down, just a inches from the floor. The triggers of all three crossbows were connected by cables, and they led to a collection of cogs and pulleys set near to the base of the cross, on the left-hand side. Also attached to this mechanical hub was a vertical steel pole, which had the ability to rotate from its base, over to the cross.

Crucified on the cross and dressed in his crimson and white cassock, Cardinal Celestino Pinto exhibited a gruesome and bloodied sight. Ferreira knew him from childhood days, having been brought up in the parish of the Church of Santa Maria Maior. He was a well-respected and loved Lisboan, dedicating his life to the Church and the community it served.

A crown of thorns sat on his head and blood trickled down his weathered face. Both his hands and one leg, just above the ankle, were spiked by black arrow-like bolts from the crossbows, with his wrists and ankles bound to the cross by way of wide-buckled restraints. To the Cardinal's left flank, a long, vertical steel pole was connected to a wide-blade sword, which had been pushed into the holy man's side by the mechanical rotation of the steel pole.

Costa looked only mildly concerned, whilst Ferreira bowed her head and made the Sign of the Cross. She tried not to retch. Noticing that Costa was so composed, she redirected her focus to the scene more closely.

'What do you make of this death, Costa?' Ferreira asked, testing to see if her colleague could think laterally.

'It looks like he put on the thorned crown first, then affixed himself to the cross. The crossbows then fired by the cogged timer, pierced his hands but only caught one leg as his legs were not crossed over. Then the crossbows firing triggered the other cogs to turn to lift up the cross, whilst also pushing the rod, with the sword attached, over and into the side of the Cardinal. I can also see that the sword went through him and out his right side.' Costa was devoid of any emotional reaction.

'Well done, Costa. Good analysis. So, what do you suspect is the cause of death here?' she asked.

'It's quite obvious really,' he said convincingly, as if he had this one covered. 'Suicide. This guy, possibly for some religious reason, set up this elaborate system to crucify himself, maybe a move for martyrdom or publicity. And it is Easter in about three weeks' time. Or perhaps he's a paedo and wanted to punish himself in a nasty way?' Costa offered as an insensitive afterthought.

Trying to keep calm from Costa's maverick last statement, she responded, 'Well, we don't know his background at the moment, but just looking at what we have in front of us, do you think this frail old man had the physical capacity to build and erect this clockwork crucifixion apparatus? Look at him and then look at the size of the cross? Don't you think that odd?'

'Maybe he was stronger than he looked. Maybe he had

some help?'

'OK, but does anything else here lead you to believe this was perhaps not a suicide and in fact, a murder?' she queried.

Seconds passed before he bluntly replied, 'No.'

'Look at his restraints, two on his wrists and two on his ankles,' she guided. She looked at Costa as he thought.

A few more seconds passed and he vacantly replied, 'And?'

'Yes, don't worry, I'm probably overthinking matters. I don't think we're of any use here now.' They started making their way out of the cathedral with Ferreira realising that Costa had mostly met her expectations with his crime-solving abilities. Once in the open air, she suggested, 'Why don't you go to the bakery and get those pastel de natas you were after, if you're still hungry after that horrific scene?' She felt sure the visuals just witnessed would not have had any negative effect on Costa.

'Great! Thanks, Inspector. Do you want anything?'

'No thanks. I'll be in the car,' she replied.

Once in the car she immediately called the Commissioner.

'Ah, Ferreira. Do you concur that the death of Cardinal Celestino Pinto was a suicide, too? That's the word from the two detectives who visited the scene before you,' the Commissioner asked.

'No, sir, it's a murder scene,' she asserted.

'How so, Inspector?'

'Apart from the fact that this frail-looking, elderly man would not have had the visceral strength to erect such equipment, how could he have buckled up all four restraints himself? It's an impossibility. Three, yes, but not four. There is at least one other person involved.'

The phone line stayed silent for some moments. 'I think to call this a murder is the wrong analysis, Inspector. There may well be a third party, who was involved or coerced into helping him, but I've just been informed that a suicide note has been found, and I also received a whole load of information on this man. It looks like we have another bad apple in the Catholic Church and his misdemeanours were about to become public knowledge. A strong motive for taking his own life.'

'I don't see it that way. We should not close down the murder avenue, sir.'

'This is your case now, Ferreira. It looks like a clear-cut case of suicide.'

'But, sir...' she was cut off before she could further remonstrate.

'Suicide, Ferreira. Suicide and your son goes free. If you pursue the murder route, your son goes down,' the Commissioner said.

11

Northern Europe
30th March 2022

09:00 UTC ZUX NEWS 24 LIVE ---- BREAKING NEWS ----

'More specifics on the death of Cardinal Celestino Pinto have been released by Lisbon Police Department which highlight the most bizarre and horrifying suicide ever investigated by their detectives. If the reports are accurate, Cardinal Celestino Pinto appears to have crucified himself in a highly elaborate and gruesome manner. Strangely, the death occurs less than a week after Pope Leo XIV was inaugurated. Rumours abound of a twelfth-century prophecy which foretold of a black Pope in place at the End of Days of the world, the biblical Apocalypse, but social media fact-checkers have been quick to dismiss this suggestion as "misinformation" and remind media users that conspiracy theories have no basis in fact and only serve to do harm.'

Cardinal Francis stared without focus over his new pince-nez glasses, through the sizeable window of the private jet. He thumbed his rosary beads. As he adjusted his posture in the oversized and sumptuous leather seat, being careful not to create any worse creasing of his black suit complete with black shirt and religious clerical collar. He mulled over the breaking news of the death of his Lisboan friend, Cardinal Celestino Pinto, refusing to accept that he would have ever taken his own life. Validating thoughts churned through his head. *Celestino was here until God called for him. He lived and breathed to help others so he would not have taken his own life, and especially in such a gruesome manner as self-crucifixion. He was infirm, how could he have exacted such an end?*

Now taking in the views of the northern extent of the Swiss Alps, from an altitude of over forty thousand feet, Francis thought of an unusual comment Celestino had made after Pope Leo had been inaugurated. Whilst gently holding Francis' forearms and seemingly concerned for Francis' mental health, Cardinal Celestino Pinto said, 'This time God chose Cardinal Bankole, but you will have your time. I do worry for you, my friend, but remember, suicide is a crime, like murder, in the eyes of our Lord.'

No, Celestino did not take his own life, he must have been murdered, Francis uncomfortably concluded of his close friend.

'Would you like another coffee, Your Eminence?' the immaculately dressed air steward asked. His patterned, beige waistcoat and crisp, white shirt, perfectly matched the interior of the Bombardier Global 8000 business jet.

'How long until we land, Felix? I don't want to rush it or waste it,' he warmly replied, dipping his head and looking over his spectacles to fully appreciate the attractive young man before him at close quarters.

Glancing at his watch, the steward replied in a faintly Germanic accent, 'About thirty minutes until we land at Luxembourg, Your Eminence.'

'Not long then, but time enough. Yes, please, to coffee, the same again,' Francis responded. Gently reaching out and upwardly cupping Felix's forearm, he said, 'Oh, there is one other question you may be able to answer.'

'Certainly,' the dark-haired steward replied.

'That emblem.' Francis pointed to the front bulkhead of the airplane. On the textured, mottled light-brown wall to the right of the cockpit entrance, lay an embossed golden icon, perhaps two feet in height, in perfect proportion with the vertical surface in which it was incorporated. It was contained within a black velvet-like inset square with a gold trim. To the layman, it might seem to be just the number eight, but Francis recognised it was more intricate than that. It had a three-dimensional quality, an ever-changing thickness as was present in calligraphic practice. The icon was made up of dozens of fine slivers of gold giving the appearance of a solid yellow, metallic emblem. To Francis, who had been surrounded by art and insignia for as long as he could remember, this apparently simple piece of artwork had deeper significance, but explanations eluded him at this moment.

'It looks somewhat familiar but it is surely not just a number eight. Please, Felix, could you tell this old soul what it signifies?'

Felix glanced at the emblem and explained, 'That is the insignia used by Mr Rotzburg, but I'm afraid I do not know what it represents, Cardinal Francis.'

'I'm sorry,' Francis asked, queryingly. He let go of Felix's arm. 'Who is Mr Rotzburg?'

'You may know him as Elion.' Cardinal puzzled this over while Felix turned his attentions to making coffee.

'I'm very thankful for such a swift transfer from the aircraft, Captain. The weather's atrocious here,' Francis said, trying to hide his concern for flying in the helicopter with such poor visibility. He brushed down his clothing from the sharp soaking they had received on alighting the business jet. The plane had landed only minutes before at Aéroport de Luxembourg and subsequently taxied to the private apron, well away from the public terminals. Even Felix's efforts to shield the Cardinal from the rain with a large golf umbrella failed to have the desired effect.

'Please, call me Carlos,' the captain replied in a distinctly Spanish accent. 'We do get some heavy showers spawned from the Belgian Ardennes region at this time of year, Your Eminence,' Carlos replied, fleetingly glancing to his right to make eye contact with his VIP passenger. As Francis exhibited his apprehension by anxiously thumb-counting of his rosary beads, Carlos continued, 'But we'll be out of the storm in one or two minutes and we have the best navigational aids on this craft. We're flying north-west into the wind, so will be in clear air very soon.'

'Thank you for your comforting words. I'm not ready to meet my maker just yet,' Cardinal Francis quipped, with a forced titter. 'It's strange, but I haven't even shown anyone my passport yet.' After pausing for breath, he continued, 'Does Elion, or – Mr Rotzburg – own this helicopter, Carlos?'

making small talk whilst suddenly remembering to clear his glasses of the raindrops they carried.

'Yes, this is one in his fleet.'

'Fleet,' Francis repeated, *this man must have substantial wealth*. He silently berated himself for an obvious observation. Anyone owning aircraft such as these must have significant wealth. He scanned the helicopter's interior briefly, but failed to find another fine insignia such as the one he had witnessed on the jet.

As the rain quickly cleared, the vista afforded from the ample windows of the Eurocopter Hèrmes EC 135 became both panoramic and lush. This was the first time the Cardinal had visited Luxembourg and he found the swathes of pasture interspersed with large forests and smaller copses, with scant few built-up areas to be seen, very appealing.

'So, Carlos, how long do you expect our journey to be?' Francis asked.

'Not long now, maybe four minutes. We're just about to enter the valley we'll be following to the château.' He pointed out the valley entrance.

They flew up the valley, following the meandering topography of the land and the shallow river below, the sides of the valley, a couple of hundred feet high, becoming steeper and rockier with every fast mile travelled.

Again, briefly pointing with his right hand, Carlos highlighted their destination. 'There's the château, Your Eminence, straight in front of us.'

Francis marvelled at the four-storey Gothic castle, with its countless turrets perfectly capped in individual, conical-fashioned, grey roofs, connected by walls, both flat and curved, and which were punctuated with numerous windows and a supporting a myriad of medieval-style chimneys. Perched tightly atop a light stone cliff, the rock face and château seamlessly merged from one to another, as if the castle walls had morphed out of the cliff face itself.

'What a magnificent castle. I'm so lucky to view it from the air – I bet the views from its balconies are divine,' Francis declared.

'Actually, this is the only way to access it,' the pilot explained. 'It's effectively surrounded by cliff or escarpment on all sides with the River Holz almost creating a full three hundred and sixty degree moat around the base. There are no roads or tracks in the vicinity.'

'So it's like a fortress.'

'Yes, a natural fortress. Mr Rotzburg owns this valley and much of the land beyond, so uninvited guests cannot get within ten kilometres of here without having their progress intercepted.'

Francis found the use of the word 'intercepted' a little unsettling, but concentrated on the experience as the pilot swooped the helicopter up the cliff, leap-frogging over the tall wall of the castle and gently setting the helicopter down on the spacious, grassed courtyard secreted within the Gothic masterpiece.

'Welcome to Château de Holzer, Your Eminence,' the pilot said, as the rotor blades slowed to an idle. 'Richter is just coming across and will accompany you into the château.'

Dipping his head to once again look over his spectacles, Francis thanked Carlos for a smooth and safe flight.

'Your Eminence. Elion is ready to see you now in the grand library – please, would you follow me,' Richter announced in a measured meter and calm tone. Francis followed Richter, leaving a good two pace gap. A slight but sprightly man, dressed in classic butler apparel, Francis could not pinpoint his age. Anything from his sixties to eighties, it was hard to discern. The Cardinal was struck at how fit the butler appeared, seemingly gliding across the polished hardwood floors and up two grand staircases with no change in speed.

'What a magnificent château, Richter,' Francis said, breaking the silence as they walked some distance from the reception hall to the grand library. 'Have you served here for a long time?'

'Yes, Your Eminence, I have,' Richter replied in a mid-European accent that Francis suspected could be a local accent.

'How long has Mr Rotzburg owned this incredible castle?'

'For quite some time, Your Eminence.' Francis got the message that Richter was not into chit-chat and chose to remain silent from this point on and take in the glory of the rooms and halls they traversed.

Before long, they arrived at a set of finely detailed, carved double wooden doors, extra wide and around four metres in height. Richter held both wrought iron handles and let out a little grunt as he pushed them down, releasing the doors from their stasis and also, Francis suspected, to alert occupants that someone was about to enter. A second later, Richter pushed both doors inward to reveal another hall with imposing, high vaulted ceilings and a multitude of windows to the far side.

As Francis stepped in, he was greeted by the vision of a library of such splendour it would favourably compare to some of the best he had seen in the Vatican. The towering walls were adorned with dark wooden shelving, from floor to vaults, crammed with historic-looking books and binders. To the far right stood an excessively large leather-topped desk, with an antique desk chair behind. To both the left and right of the hall hung two steep ladders on runners, affording access to every shelf. In the middle of the room, taking up most of the space, was an expansive Persian rug. Upon this dark red, mottled carpet were three oversized, dark green leather couches arranged in a horseshoe and which faced an imposing stone fireplace and hearth.

Richter checked around looking for his employer. He turned to the Cardinal and beckoned him to take a seat near the blazing fire. He then walked past the large table towards one of the sets of windows through which the sun was streaming. From a distance, the windows looked nothing other than that, windows, but Richter turned a black handle and pushed open a concealed door that led to a stone balcony and proceeded to walk out. Francis removed his pince-nez and craned his neck to see if he could make out anyone there, but the balcony extended far beyond his line of sight.

Francis spent the next few minutes gathering his thoughts of the events of the past weeks and months and how best to give Elion, or Mr Rotzburg, a piece of his mind. His thoughts were interrupted when Richter re-entered the library.

'Mr Rotzburg is ready to receive you now, Your Eminence.' And with that, Francis made his way out, putting on his spectacles and checking his pockets to ensure he still had his rosary beads. Stepping onto the balcony, Francis started to feel ill at ease. A light sweat formed on his palms. He glanced at the views across the river, valley and hills, but his attention was taken over by this increasing presentation of anxiety, which led him to take out his rosary beads and start thumbing them as he approached a set of varnished garden furniture. There were two chairs, one empty and someone sat in the other. He could not see who because the chair had its back to him. Both chairs were separated by a slatted table and a substantial, cantilevered parasol shading all of the furniture. Francis could now see the grey hair of his host but was taken aback by the contiguous presence of a blood transfusion trolley, with a bag of reddish liquid suspended high above.

'His Eminence, Cardinal Francis Antonio Ballerini, Mr Rotzburg.' Francis stepped around the chair, expecting to see an ailing venerable man, and held out his hand to greet his host.

'Your Eminence.' Elion took his hand and for a moment he was locked in a grip while Elion looked him squarely in the eye.

'It's a pleasure to finally meet you, Mr Rotzburg,' said Francis, unsure about the stocky man seated before him. His impeccable demeanour and strength of greeting were at odds with his appearance, exacerbated with his being connected to a drip line. His pale, mole-ridden skin was almost translucent. The skin on his hand felt cool, smooth, and his fingernails looked like sharp talons. Richter directed Francis to sit opposite and poured refreshments before gliding away.

Francis recognised the familiar rattle of breath and the gravelling – almost rasping – voice. 'Please excuse my not standing to receive you,' Elion said, dipping his head slightly. Before Francis could reply, Elion got straight to business. 'Do you know why I have brought you to my home, Cardinal?'

'No, not really,' Francis weakly replied, not ready for such directness from this man, whose strong presence and vigour defied his chronological appearance. To counter his host's directness, he said, 'I'm guessing it has to do with me not becoming Pope after all the assurances you gave.' This was a line he had rehearsed and he was relieved to have said it so soon.

Elion's eyes widened a touch and whilst quickly leaning forward, starting to strain the drip tube attached to the crease of his left elbow. He pursed his lips and almost hissed his reply, 'You have misinterpreted what you call "my assurances", Your Eminence.'

Slowly sitting back in his chair, he recomposed himself and continued, 'If we are to get what we both want, I need to provide some background and context to our crossing of paths. I make no apology for my curtness, as you can imagine, my biological clock has been ticking for far longer than yours, so that makes my time here more precious. It is why we will make the most of our fifteen-minute meeting.'

Francis went to protest. *Such a short meeting when I've travelled so far!* But Elion raised his hand, gesturing him to hold his thought. Francis then took a sip of coffee. 'You see, my business is people, people of all sorts, levels and backgrounds. Your rise within your church came to my attention and I knew you would have jumped at the chance to become Pope, as would any cardinal. So, our plan didn't quite succeed but our business does not have to stop there.'

Elion paused to take a couple of deep, noisy breaths. He nodded to let Francis speak.

'I don't quite know where to start. I feel you coerced me to poison Pope Peter, God bless him, and frame one of my monastery boys! Who are you, Mr Rotzburg, or is it Elion, and how do you know me?' He pointed at the drip and the bag of red infusion. 'And are you unwell?'

'I am not unwell, thank you for asking. I am more youthful than you can imagine,' Elion said. Waggling his connected tube, he smiled wryly, 'This is what I call my elixir of life! The fountain of youth, you could say.' He paused and Francis felt Elion was reading the confusion on his face. 'Yes, I am known by many names, but labels are just that. As you have asked, let me formally introduce myself. My name is Maximilian Adelino Zelig Frederick Rotzburg III, but many know me as Elion, derived from the Ancient Greek word Helios, meaning Sun. Others call me Der Puppenspieler, though I do not attach myself to being called the Puppet Master; far too pedestrian and finite a name in my estimation. I'm sure I am called all manner of things by all manner of people, but you should only be concerned by the nature of our relationship, and not my tags.'

Elion turned to study the transfusion bag and gave it a swift squeeze, before continuing, 'How and why I know you is my business, but let's say I've been watching over you for many, many years – a guardian angel, of sorts. How is your dear, simple brother, Paolo?' Elion asked rhetorically and immediately carried on, 'Who do you think saved you from your rightful fate following your jealous rock attack on Paolo, fifty-two years ago? Yes, yes, I know what really happened, Francis. You were a bitter and twisted young teenager and you panicked when Paolo said he'd seen you sodomising that younger, innocent choir-boy.'

Colour drained from Francis' face. The hidden truth was laid bare to him. He slumped back into his cushioned chair. 'But I, too, was abused in that monastery, right from the age of five. Carrying on the cycle was the currency of hierarchy, it was the only way I could claw back some control. I was so afraid of what might come from my brother reporting me, I had to stop him.' He tailed to a whisper, then shamefully looked down at his fingers counting through his rosary beads.

'I knew that establishment was a cesspit of inequity, but I saw the potential in you,' said Elion. 'I saw someone who'd go to the ultimate length to save your own skin, someone who'd try to murder their own sibling to keep a secret, just that, a secret. So, I made sure you were protected and encouraged to pursue a greater calling within the Church. I laid your path for you, and now you are a Cardinal.'

During another quick pause, Francis fidgeted in his chair before Elion resumed speaking. 'Now, "coerced", you say?' He leaned in again, fixing his stare with his cold, grey eyes on Francis. You suspected Pope Peter might know about your filthy penchant with young boys, so when I let you know that he actually suspected you, there was only one course of action for you to take. The other would have been your suicide, but you are far too egoic and self-centred for that to have been entertained. I probably know you, your family and connections better than you know yourself – that is my business and I am so damned good at it. Just look at you now, thumbing through your beads with your sweaty palms, alluding to a spiritual practice but really it's just an anxiety crutch. Your pince-nez are just for show, probably to make you look more authoritative and older than your sixty-five years of age. I'd wager they are clear glass without prescription as you possess twenty-twenty vision judging by the way you've handled your coffee cup.' He gently sat back again.

The Cardinal grabbed the arms of his chair, finding himself stifle the urge to flee to avoid sitting with all these truth-bombs detonating around him. He was disturbed at how Elion could read him so well.

'I didn't invite you here to assassinate your character. I am aware you have a deep and true wish to reform your ailing Church. You believe in it and many of its values to your core. This is an admirable and wholesome part of your being. This is why I called for you. So, the plan for you to be Pope failed at the last hurdle, a failing I have now fixed to ensure no repetition, but sadly too late for us now. However, I can offer you the next best arrangement.'

'Why do something for me? Am I now obliged to work with you or for you? And what failing did you "fix"?' Francis asked, satisfied with his more composed delivery.

'I want to let you know that if you ask me a direct question and I answer it, I will only speak the truth. I live a life where I can keep this solemn vow. You lost the papal vote effectively by one vote. And before you calculate that that one extra vote would have produced a draw, I had contingencies in place had there been a re-run. So, I had put in place every reasonable precaution to ensure you did not lose the papal vote. But the vote was lost. Not because of you, but due to direct defiance of my authority. I warned Cardinal Celestino Pinto not to work against me but he poorly decided to ignore my advice.' Continuing with his mesmerising stare, Elion executed the end of his sentence, 'And this led to his unfortunate suicide.'

'You murdered my friend, my colleague!' Francis exclaimed in a raised voice, ripping off his glasses. 'You...' but he was quickly cut off.

'Enough! Save your sermons for the weak and empathetic,' Elion asserted with a fierce wave of his right hand. Pointing at Francis with his clawed right index finger, he said, 'You are so quick to judge when *your* house entertains murder and abuse of minors. This is business, it is not personal. He knew who he was dancing with and he chose his own fate. If he had followed as agreed, you'd be meeting me as Pope.'

Glancing at his Breguet Marie-Antoinette Grande Complication pocket watch, a watch of such exquisiteness and history the likes of Francis would not have had any knowledge of its existence, Elion concluded, 'Our time is nearly up. Regarding your other question about being obliged to work with me – the answer is no. However, if our business relationship parts here and now, I caution you that I cannot guarantee the Vatican investigation into the circumstances surrounding the passing of Pope Peter II will not be reopened if new evidence surfaces.' Then with an unveiled grin, he continued, 'Similarly, I cannot guarantee that your perversions will not come to the attention of higher authorities.'

Now the cards had been laid bare, Elion progressed to the incentives on offer. 'If you decide to continue our cordial relationship, I offer to realise your dream of rebuilding your Church with renewed global power and influence, with you, not Pope Leo, at the epicentre of reform. Just like I explained to Cardinal Pinto, I advise you to work with me and to never cross me; it never ends well for my foes.' Elion smiled and continued in a quietly sinister tone, 'It's now time for you to choose, Your Eminence.'

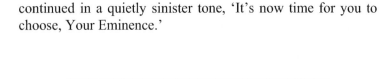

Who the hell does Elion think he is and how does he know so much about me? How has he known me for years? Why wouldn't he tell me about this project he wants me to be involved in? Why only allow a fifteen-minute meeting? These questions, amongst others, had swirled around Francis' tired but discombobulated mind ever since leaving Château de Holzer. Frustratingly, no answers presented themselves. Francis managed to compartmentalise the uncomfortable truths about his past that Elion had laid bare in their meeting, a skill of self-preservation he had developed over the decades.

'Your Eminence,' Felix announced, attracting Francis' attention. 'We land at London City Airport in less than ten minutes. Can I ask you to fasten your seatbelt?' He collected a cup and saucer and an untouched plate of fine quality biscuits from his table.

'But, of course,' he replied. 'How long before I get to where I'm supposed to be going, Felix?'

'Maybe fifteen to twenty minutes, depending on the lunchtime traffic.' This was good news, Francis thought, as he was weary from the early start and now the unexpected journey to London.

'Mr Rotzburg?' Richter awaited his boss's acknowledgement as Elion unplugged himself from his drip and blotted away the small amount of blood that leaked from where he had pulled out the needle. 'I have Shetty from CentSec on the secure line for you. She says it's quite urgent, sir.'

CentSec was Elion's very own international security company that he had setup in the late fifties and now operated in over ninety countries worldwide. It provided services mainly to government agencies but also to the largest corporations. Shetty headed an arcane department that expressly worked on matters concerning Elion's areas of interest, and took information feeds from all sources possible, including its clients.

As his boss reached out to receive the satellite phone, Richter ensured a clean relay of the phone, having previously been accidentally cut by Elion's sharp, pointed nails on more than one occasion. 'Ah, Shetty, was my hunch right?' Elion enquired of his Head of Global Security Operations.

'Yes, sir,' Shetty replied with her crisp, Asian accent. 'Your agents started searching for trails leading back to you on February twenty-fifth, and used all tools at their disposal.'

'Excellent work. How much do you think they know?'

'Our intel up until today indicates they were probably very close to tracing you.'

'So bugging their office has confirmed the risk I was concerned about?' Elion asked.

'Yes, sir.'

Elion ended the call.

'Richter, get me Lafayette and Rozen. Once I've told them to expect a visitor, I'll need to speak with Sweeps to clear up another mess,' Elion ordered, as he passed the phone back to his faithful assistant.

Taxiing to another private hanger at London City Airport, the Cardinal then seamlessly transferred from the Bombardier to a waiting black, Mercedes saloon car, with overly-smoked rear windows. He was then swiftly transported in a northerly direction.

It had been in excess of twenty-five years since Francis had visited London, then by special invitation of the Archbishop of Canterbury, and he recalled a whistlestop tour of many London churches and cathedrals, some of which were in the East End. 'How East London's changed since my last visit,' he said to the driver, studying the new, eye-catching architecture that now had dominion in the places where once drab, pollution-stained Victoriana had stood.

'Just a couple of minutes away now, Your Eminence,' boomed the thick-set driver.

'Thank you,' he looked over his pince-nez at the driver before mulling over the questions this visit might answer.

Laura looked frostily out of the fifth-floor windows, arms tightly folded and lips pursed, still not totally comfortable with the height of her workspace, but more used to it from the years of working in her office.

'This is absolutely ridiculous,' she vented, following Elion's latest call. She looked out of the window but aimed her remonstration at the captive Rozen, who had his head down, working. 'Not only have we been pulled away from proper intelligence work, but Elion wants us to sell his batshit-crazy project. It's not what I'm about, nor the CIA.'

'Come on, Laura, chill. We're on our final weeks on this project, maybe days, then this office shuts down and we get to go home. Let's just do what he asks, don't question and move on. I've only got eight weeks left before I retire and sip piña coladas all day long on the Gulf of Mexico coast,' he jokingly reminded her.

Laura knew Rozen was right, but she just felt frustrated that over the past twelve months, first the whole technical core of Project Octal had been relocated to an 'undisclosed location for security reasons', and this had been followed by a haemorrhaging of her staff from over seventy down to five, leaving them rattling around in the near-empty building. She had forged great working relationships with many of her staff, but they had been either transferred back to their originating agency positions or had been relocated to this 'undisclosed location' for security reasons. Moved to the same locale as the technical apparatus, she presumed. Part of Laura's reaction was due to her feeling somewhat put out by not having been asked to relocate with the project she felt she had nurtured, with great skill, dexterity and discretion.

Her moment of reflection was checked by the arrival of a black, stretched limousine pulling up on the double yellow lines near the front of her office block.

'I think our guest has arrived – I better go and greet him,' she grumbled.

'So, my dear Laura,' Francis continued, putting down his pince-nez glasses, with which he'd been fidgeting for much of the meeting, and taking back his phone that Laura was handing to him. 'This miracle system you have been explaining to me has now been set up on my phone in an app, and I can try it out for myself?' he said, giving out a little laugh of incredulity.

'Yes, Your Eminence, as hard as it is to believe, everything Lafayette has explained is the goddamn truth,' Rozen interjected, instantly rueing his insensitive choice of adjective, and adjusted the rolled up sleeves of his white shirt.

From behind Francis' shoulder, Laura pointed to an icon on the Cardinal's smartphone and encouraged him to open that app. As his index finger approached the icon, he slowly and gleefully read out its name typed below the graphic, 'The Divinity App! *Lo adoro!* I love it, I love it!'

As The Divinity App opened, a simple off-white screen display appeared with the app's title at the top and a stylised graphic of a fingerprint in the centre of the page. 'So, I just...' Francis intuitively moved his finger towards the fingerprint reader on the phone.

'That's it, just hold one of your fingers on the reader until...' Laura confirmed the Cardinal's instinct. He held his finger to the reader and after a short moment, the screen flashed a bright white with a bold, green tick symbol, indicating the fingerprint had been read. This was followed by the fading in of a symbol already familiar to Francis; an intricate three-dimensional, figure of eight-like emblem, exactly the same as the one he had seen on the front bulkhead of the private jet he had flown in earlier that day. The only exception was that the symbol was in silver and not gold. On closer inspection, the Cardinal could see the graphic starting to slowly re-colour in gold to the right of its top centre and continue to do so, sweeping quickly along the top right.

'Ah! A timer?' he asked.

'Yes. It'll all turn gold quickly – it usually only takes a few seconds to complete.'   The design turned solid gold and the Cardinal, with fixed eyes and suspended breath, awaited the next information to be displayed:

****

The Divinity App

Name: Cardinal Francis Antonio Ballerini

Born: Rome, Italy on 23/Jul/1960

Karmic Score:

-871,237,544

<u>Help</u>
<u>Donate</u>

****

For countless seconds, Francis sat unmoving with a fixed expression of self-disgust.

Laura backed away from the Cardinal as soon as she saw the karmic result and moved to the other side of the desk to stand by Rozen. During the app quality assurance efforts on the small sets of test subjects, she had never seen such a high negative karmic number. She felt an instant wave of ill-ease wash over her as she slid into her chair. As strictly instructed by Elion, at the point of their visitor receiving their karmic score, Rozen and Laura stayed silent and waited for the Cardinal to break the silence. Laura casually glanced at her computer monitor to ensure the web camera was still streaming and focussed on the Cardinal. Knowing the whole meeting was being watched by Elion added considerable pressure to the proceedings. *Once this meeting is over, I can, at last, go home*, she thought, consoling herself.

Now holding up his hand to indicate no-one was to talk, Francis' expression gradually commuted from one of self-loathing to that of wonderment at the simple page of information before him. He was acutely aware of Laura watching him with analytical precision, which propelled him to break the silence.

'If this program is as it appears, and is not trickery, as you have assured me, then it is nothing short of a miracle. A God-given miracle!' He looked heavenwards and with two fingers raised drew a cross in the air. He lightly closed his eyes, smiled and breathed deeply, as if he was in the presence of a divine entity. 'There is no doubt, I will take the proposition back to the Vatican and the Holy Father, and I will recommend we agree to all your terms and proceed to allow this miracle to start transforming the world.'

'We will ensure all contracts and guides are forwarded to your office, along with the non-disclosure agreement you signed earlier,' Laura replied, trying to round up matters.

'Thank you, Laura,' Francis replied, holding her gaze for a moment longer than she was comfortable with, 'but I do have a few questions, I hope you understand?'

'Yes, of course,' she replied professionally, but inwardly dying to finish the meeting and get on with the next chapter of her life.

'You're saying every wrong I've done in life accrues a kind of debt in karma?' Sam slowly summarised to Amelie, as they sat awaiting delivery of their second expressos at an outside table of the Temple Café, on Cambridge Heath Road, East London. This was the latest of a string of regular meet-ups they had arranged following Sam's saving Amelie's life. This was the first where they had stopped for coffee, as previously they had walked around Victoria Park and along Regent's Canal. He was unsure of the nature of the bond they were forming, the likes of which he had never experienced before; full of love and compassion but totally platonic, direct and fulfilling in so many ways. There was never any discussion of trivia, such as the weather or the latest news events; Amelie would greet him and he would be taken in by her captivating but unworldly flame-orange eyes and be asked how he was and how he had been since their last get-together. This would lead to deeper chats about his life and beliefs. When he asked her similar questions, her answers were short, albeit perfect, always satisfying him that she had led a blessed and content life, and said with such conviction and serenity, he had no doubt that all her words were true.

'Yes, this is how the universe works, good deeds and good thoughts are positive, not just for us but for all creation. The opposite is true for bad deeds and bad thoughts. In reality, it is quite a simple measure of account,' Amelie explained.

So many questions swirled around Sam's mind and he struggled to select one. 'Who decides which are good deeds and which are not?'

'Simply put, it is the universe that decides, but our inner

guides know which is which. Beyond that, it just gets very complicated.'

'In what way? How do you know this for a fact? Where did you learn this? What does bad karma debt mean for us? How bad must mine be, especially after my shooting incident?' The myriad of questions came out almost simultaneously, and he winced with the everlasting pain that accompanied his last.

'Ooh, so many questions, Sam,' she said, empathetically. She glanced at her wristwatch, 'but I really must be making a move now as I have an upcoming appointment. When you get back to your boat, search for a book called *Karma Calming*, it might help you understand the concept better.'

Sam's reply was delayed by their espressos arriving. 'Thank you,' he replied, as he then mirrored her standing up in readiness for her departure. 'Please let me know when we can do this again,' he said, hopefully.

Giving Sam a friendly kiss on each cheek in true French fashion, she reassured him she would be in touch soon and turned towards the city centre. With his mind swirling from the conversation content of the past while, he sat embracing the gloriously warm spring weather and sipping his coffee, wondering whether he should drink Amelie's as well. Paying the bill, he grabbed his medic-trainer's backpack and headed north towards home, along Cambridge Heath Road to intersect Regent's Canal, some ten minutes' walk away.

All three stood in unison and Laura, Rozen and Cardinal Francis said their polite goodbyes and Laura took it upon herself to show the Cardinal down to the street. She pressed zero and the lift smoothly lowered them down to the ground floor.

'Laura, do you have many colleagues working on this revolutionary project and can I meet any?' Francis enquired.

'There were quite a few but numbers are classified, and now the project has reached this stage, many have moved on. As it's late, everyone has left for the day, so it's just Rozen and me here now.'

'That is a shame. It would have been a pleasure to have met and thanked some of them personally,' he replied, but as he did so, looked at Laura in such a way as to unsettle her. When added to Laura's knowledge of his karmic score, she shuddered with revulsion and prayed that the lift would hurry so she could get rid of this man.

'Cardinal Francis has just left the building and is walking back towards the limo,' the limousine driver, Edmund Richards, reported.

'Message received.'

Richards was employed for his loyalty and robotic-like reliability to do as he was asked; nothing more, nothing less. Having made the phone call, he exited the car and opened the door for the Cardinal, who approached on the narrow pavement.

'My glasses!' Francis said, with a heavy look of concern. He double-checked his pockets. Unable to find then, he turned around and headed back to the office block.

As Richards closed the limo door and waiting for the Cardinal's return, he noticed a young man in his early thirties, with a sizeable backpack, walk past.

Laura had been reading and replying to text messages in the foyer when the Cardinal reappeared at the glazed front door. As she pressed the door-release button, Francis stepped back to allow it to open and found his path checked, bumping into a young man with a backpack.

'Oops, sorry,' Sam apologised to the Cardinal. He had put his hands on the man's shoulders to soften the collision.

'I am sorry, please forgive me,' Francis said, with genuine warmth.

Laura held her gaze at Sam as he walked on, trying to ascertain whether this was an innocent accident or part of a more nefarious agenda, vigilant at all times instilled by her field agent training. Quickly deciding there was nothing of concern here, she enquired, 'Hello again, Cardinal. You're back so soon. Can I help?'

'Ah, yes, I'm so sorry but I left my glasses on your desk.'

'Oh, yes, the pince-nez glasses. If you're OK to wait here, I'll get them for you.'

'You're so kind, thank you.'

Laura left the Cardinal, as the main door shut and the heavy lift lobby doors closed behind her.

Four hundred and forty-four miles away from Cyber City, CentSec's Sweep's mobile phone connected to the number he had dialled. Once the line was open, he brought up the keypad on his screen, steadily keyed eight, eight, eight, eight, and finished the call.

The controlling Raspberry Pi computer corroborated the code instantly, signals were sent through every loop to every detonator buried in the cladding of the five-storey London building. Milliseconds later, the detonators sent charges to their respective explosives and almost in unison, the expansion of materials created what appeared to be one huge explosion to the front and rear of 521 Cambridge Heath Road. Glass, masonry, steel, rubber seals and insulating materials were ripped from the building's façade and strewn across the street to the front and the railway line to the rear. The accompanying shock wave propelled the materials over a hundred metres from the office block and blew out windows of neighbouring properties and adjacent cars alike. Car alarms sounded and the air in the street was thick with particulate dust, billowing away from the epicentre of the explosion.

Sam opened his eyes and was greeted with a close-up view of a dusty and rubble covered paving slab. A familiar muffled sound accompanied by high-pitched ringing was his next realisation, followed by heavy, dull aches in both his hands and right cheek, which was pressed to the ground.

'What the fuck! Not another IED?'

As his brain collated the sensory information sent from his body and picked up from surroundings, and he remembered what he had been doing just seconds before the explosion, he got up onto all fours and realised he had been in an explosion of some kind, not a casualty of another IED.

Awkwardly shuffling to his feet, not helped by the improperly positioned and weighty backpack with which he was saddled, Sam coughed up particles of debris and blinked heavily to clear dust from his eyes. He surveyed the vicinity to further understand the situation and gauge any other risks. As he looked back along the road he had just moments before been walking, he saw it had been transformed into a disaster scene. Scorched and battered windowless cars lined both sides of the avenue. Copious amounts of glass and rubble were liberally scattered over the area and an office block he had just walked past, stripped of its outer cladding, had exposed the blunt ends of its concrete floors. Random   areas   of reinforcement bars were also on show where the encasing concrete had been blown away. Pockets of smoke rose from small fires and smouldering debris in the road and on floors of the building.

Unsteadily picking his way across the pavement rubble, he spotted the now not-so-black suited older man he had just collided with lying on his back, moving his arm to shield his face. A few metres beyond the man, Sam spotted another casualty lying next to the now-unrecognisable black limo. He was motionless. His training led to him prioritise his attention – he made his way to check up on the moving first casualty.

Laura calmed herself with deep breaths after having been thrown against the rear lobby wall and hitting the back of her head. She started pushing away elements of the ceiling which blanketed her. Bewildered and soaked from the active sprinkler system, she freed herself from debris and managed to open the foyer door and was greeted with what she could only compare to the carnage she had seen in her urban war training manuals. Through the dusty landscape and beyond, where the front glazing used to separate the reception from the outside world, she saw a backpacked man in his thirties seemingly frisking another man lying on the pavement, building rubble burying his legs. Field agent training kicked in and she unholstered her firearm and trained it on the movement in front of her.

'Armed agents – don't move or we'll shoot,' she

commanded, in the plural to appear more numerous.

She saw the man look skywards as streams of dust and grit fell on the Cardinal's face, emanating from a loose section of façade above. He swivelled his eyes to look at Laura, and he replied, agitated, 'This man is injured and in danger from falling debris. Either I try to assist him now, or he dies in front of us. It's your call.'

Laura swiftly scanned the area again, trying to ascertain any new threats. Whilst she wanted the Cardinal to be taken to a safe area, she first needed to mentally rerun events that had happened just before the blast and cross-reference them with her CIA training. A random guy with a large backpack happens to bump into her client and then the whole building explodes. *Was this man here by coincidence or was he part of the current threat?* Quickly, she concluded he was probably of low risk at this time. 'Proceed with your assistance, but if you pose a threat, I will shoot you,' she commanded, with emphasis on the last four words.

Sam carefully and nimbly lifted off the masonry pieces from the Cardinal's legs, walked behind his head, jammed his hands under his armpits and dragged him into the building's foyer.

Laura still aimed her gun at Sam's upper torso but her empathy for the situation had started to overrule her training. Against protocol, she made safe and re-holstered her firearm and went to pick up the Cardinal's legs at what remained of the building's entrance. Without any further warning and with a loud grumbling sound, the precarious concrete cladding slab broke free from its final tether and smashed onto the pavement, a few feet or so from the doorway. Laura leaped back from the threshold and the new danger.

Sitting on the damp, debris-covered floor, Francis slammed his eyes shut and turned his head to mitigate the effects of the dust and grit thrown up by the slab.

Sam caught his breath from the narrow escape then left the building to check on the other nearby casualty he'd seen.

'Are you OK, Cardinal?' Laura asked with concern.

'Yes. Yes, a bit battered and bruised, but I believe I'm OK,' he responded, slowly blinking his eyes clear.

Sam returned. 'The other guy next to the limo is dead. There was no saving him,' he said solemnly.

Looking to Sam, Francis empathetically said, 'That's so very sad to hear, my son. But see, you saved my life, there's no doubting that – what's your name? I'll need to have your details.'

'Sam, my name's Sam. Anybody would've done the same,' Sam said, modestly. He looked sharply to Laura. 'But perhaps not with a gun pointed at them!'

'Sam, I'm sorry,' she said. 'In my game, it's common practice to suspect everybody until you're sure they're no threat.'

'What kind of game are you in?' Sam asked, wiping a cocktail of sprinkler water and dust from his eyes.

As he asked, and although he was dusty and dishevelled, Laura thought there was a familiarity about him. She found she was rarely wrong when she had such hunches, but another thought barged its way into her mind; she needed to check on Rozen. 'I'm Special Agent Laura Lafayette, CIA,' she said, holding out her hand, then wondering why she introduced herself including her first name. She had never done that before. *Very unprofessional,* she thought. Shaking hands, she continued, 'And thank you for your actions saving the Cardinal's life.' Subsequently, she continued to rifle through her memory. *Where do I know Sam from? Think, Laura, think!*

Laura's internal dialogue was again interrupted by sirens wailing and the appearance of two uniformed police officers, who enquired after their well-being.

'We are OK, though the Cardinal here will need assistance

for multiple cuts and bruises,' Sam reported. 'There's a guy next to the limo out to the right, but he, unfortunately, was killed outright.' One of the officers attended to Francis whilst the other radioed for additional help.

Laura stepped up to Sam and, having seen he was medically trained, asked, 'Can you come with me? I need to check up on my colleague on the fifth floor.'

'Sure – is there anyone else in the building?' he asked as they picked their way through the lift lobby and up the first flight of stairs.

'No, it's just the two of us here.' She glanced at Sam. 'What's your surname, Sam?'

'Angel, Sam Angel,' he replied and looked at her from the side more closely than before. Laura was aware of Sam's lingering look but wanted to work out why he seemed familiar to her.

A few more stairs up, she took the opportunity to study his face, albeit from the side. Her eyes widened momentarily as she finally made the connection. *Bhutan!* she shouted in her head and retraced the salient points from that trip. She said nothing and decided she would discuss it with Sam once she reunited with Rozen. She was not sure what his reaction would be to this connection or his links to that slimy General in NORAD – the same guy who had labelled Sam a 'friendly' four years previously.

Peeking through the fire-glass window into the fourth-floor main office, Laura found it unrecognisable, with no cladding left to the front and rear, a mist of spray in the air and broken office furniture and glass tossed all around the floor. Ascending the final set of stairs to the fifth floor, or Pent-House, they nimbly traversed the lobby. Laura pushed ajar the door to her and Rozen's office, the door half-hanging from its hinges and with the access control panel drooping from the adjacent wall.

'Jacob!' she screamed and ran to her colleague. He was sitting in his swivel chair next to the now missing windowed wall. The whole left-hand side of Rozen's face and torso was a mix of blood, lacerated skin, glass and shrapnel, and this horror was exacerbated by the contrast to his white shirt. He gave a vacant, lifeless stare. 'No! Jacob!' she cried. After she forlornly checked his neck, she fondly whispered, 'You only had two months to your retirement.' She gently stroked his eyelids closed. 'Your girls are going to be devastated,' she said.

'I'm so sorry, Laura. This is so shocking. Must have been a gas leak or something,' Sam said in empathy.

Laura located then carefully righted her office chair. Lowering herself onto it and pushing away the shock and grief she had experienced in the past few minutes, mulled over the possibility of a gas explosion.

The sudden moving of her team to an unknown location, the fact that she and Rozen had been working on an immense project – one with the power to change humanity – the mystical shell-like object, the mysterious Elion who she now knew by his proper name but seemed like a ghost and fell between gaps in the systems she had access to, and now this explosion, which happened to involve Sam whom she had last seen in Bhutan. While she analysed, Sam watched but remained quiet. 'Gas explosion, you say. There is no gas supply to this building,' she said, quizzingly.

The glint of a delicate object caught her eye on the wreckage on the floor in front of her. She reached down and picked it up. 'Pince-nez glasses. The Cardinal's glasses. He obviously did not need his glasses for any ocular correction. Glasses he doesn't need but came back for.'

She took a sudden intake of breath and Sam witnessed her eyes filling with energy as the threads started to coalesce. Her eyes darting up to look up at Sam, she realised, 'Of course, this was meant to be a summary execution of Jacob and myself, dressed up as an accident. The scaffolding up for ages, all that drilling, it wasn't for fixings, it was to plant explosives.' She studied the glasses in her hand. 'The Cardinal had left, but came back for these. He'd left them on my desk. He was meant to live, and we,' she said, looking at Rozen, 'were meant to die.'

Instantly, Laura squared up to Sam, and pointed her firearm at him. This time it was aimed at his face.

'Who are you really, Sam? I had a feeling your being here outside this building was more than a coincidence, and I now know you have something to do with all this.'

Sam lifted his hands in submission and watched her intently but Laura remained vigilant to any defensive moves he might try.

'What the fuck? I have told you the absolute truth! I was walking to my home, my boat is just up the road from here. I didn't ask to be caught in this explosion and I didn't have to help the priest, but that's the type of guy I am,' he protested.

'Who are you? Are you military or work for a government agency?'

'No,' he said uncomfortably. 'I-I'm ex-forces, but I'm a first aid trainer now.' His voice was starting to waiver and Laura saw Sam's demeanour rapidly descend as he began to tremble.

'OK, ex-military, now we're getting somewhere. If you have nothing to do with this shitshow, then what the fuck were you doing up that mountain in Bhutan, in 2018?' Laura interrogated, watching Sam like a hawk for any telltale signs that would contradict his words.

Sam's eyes defocussed and flicked left and right, as if he was searching his memories. Then, with a sharp inbreath, 'Fuck! You? And Ro-Rozen? You were in that helicopter?' he asked, nervously.

'What's your connection to NORAD?' she demanded, staring deep into his eyes. She stretched her gun fingers, then regripped the gun, checking the safety catch was still off.

Stepping back a half pace, conceding that Laura was in total control of the situation, Sam pleaded, 'Look, I know nothing about NORAD. Please, you're freaking me out – I was just walking past and...' His chest tightened and he heaved, struggling to take in enough air.

A few tense moments elapsed then Laura lowered her gun but did not re-holster it. She judged he was no immediate threat and, in fact, had visibly shrunk back into himself compared to the confident man on display only minutes before. At the same time, she also acknowledged that the head blow she had suffered may have made it possible that she was misreading the situation now.

'OK, let's say you're telling the truth, but we still need to talk because for someone to innocently happen upon a CIA operation on a back-of-beyond mountain, a third of the way around the planet four years ago, may be possible. But to then happen upon the same operation when its building was just blown up, killing two, including a damned decent CIA agent, is more than just chance.'

Sam slowly rubbed his eyes and forehead with both hands. He remained silent for a moment before responding. 'What the fuck am I involved in, Laura?'

18:20 UTC ZUX NEWS 24 LIVE ---- BREAKING NEWS ----

'Reports are coming in of a massive explosion in the north of

Cyber City, in London's East End. Social media posts talk of widespread damage to windows and cars for hundreds of metres, a five-storey building that is missing its entire front façade and severe disruption on many rail services from Liverpool Street station. There are no reports of injuries as of yet and the London Fire Brigade is citing a gas explosion as the cause of the blast.'

12

Castel Gandolfo, Italy
11th April 2022

'Francis, please come in and take a seat,' Pope Leo invited with an open palm, directing his guest to the seat opposite him.

Francis smiled and walked across the papal chamber to take the seat, incredulous that fate would present this early-morning meeting as an almost carbon copy of his last meeting with Pope Peter. Thumbing his rosary beads to temper his unease, Francis bowed and kissed Pope Leo's hand before sitting down.

'How are you now, Cardinal? I called for you to see you for myself – it is a miracle that you look so much better than when I saw you just after your terrible time in London.'

'Yes, thank you, and with God's grace my injuries have nearly healed, Your Holiness,' he said, touching his scabs on his forehead. 'And I am back to full duties and have been able to attend to the needs of my beloved brother, Paolo.'

'It was a great shock to be given the news of your involvement in that explosion, magnified by the fact that I was not aware of your being in London,' Pope Leo said, starting to delicately probe his Cardinal's actions.

Francis felt some of the tension he carried dissipate as the nature of the meeting seemed to concentrate on London and not on any resurrection of investigations from the previous Holy Father. 'Yes, it was such unfortunate timing to be caught up in that incident. I still pray for the families of that poor American office worker and the limousine driver who died in the blast,' he recalled, sympathetically shaking his head.

'Quite so, and we must thank God that no one else was taken – at another time, it could have been such a different story. Can I ask what you were doing in London, Francis?' asked Leo directly.

'Of course, yes. Indeed, I was planning on discussing these matters with yourself in the coming days, once some paperwork had come through,' referring to the contracts and initial trial data that had been delayed by the explosion. Francis proceeded to present The Divinity App opportunity for the Church, having practised this pitch many times in the past days, being careful to tread lightly around Catholic Church principles and explain how revolutionary it would be for the Church, its flock and even humankind.

Pope Leo listened intently, barely blinking as he gave his full concentration for the next ten minutes. As the Cardinal finished his presentation, the Pope was silent and indicated he would need a minute before responding, moving his gaze towards the window.

Francis' excitement gradually gave way to anxiousness as each second of silence joined the previous. He looked down at his hands and started to count his beads again.

'Thank you, Francis,' Pope Leo said, breaking the long silence but only to replace it with another, though shorter, one.

'I hear your details of this project, which does sound quite extraordinary, and I hear your passion for it and this Church.' He paused again.

Pre-empting that his Pope was about to turn down this golden opportunity to serve Catholicism, Francis began to fret because he knew Elion would be insistent the project would run. Feeling the pressure of the moment, he hastily geared his mind towards what more he could say in order to convince His Holiness.

'This venture,' Pope Leo continued, 'appears to be a chariot-like gift galloping from the heavens, one that glistens and spreads joy and righteousness over God's Garden. However, gifts can be interpreted differently depending on one's perspective and convictions in life.'

He held up his hand to arrest Francis' urgent interjection. 'You must understand that I have a vision which I have started to work towards in my Papacy, one which will be glorious in its unity of deep divides and in its powers of healing. This can only be achieved with the mind driven by the heart. Technology has a place in this world, but when it comes to faith, spiritual progress has an essence far more subtle and far finer than any technology we possess. And I have some other deep reservations.' He stopped to gather his thoughts, allowing Francis the opportunity to apply pressure.

'But Kanu, this has the ability to unify, to heal and to progress spiritual practice across the globe. It doesn't get better than this, you must surely look past your resentment of the technology of smart phones.' Francis' delivery was both curt and undiplomatic. Both hands gripped his rosary with fervour and he could feel heat build in his cheeks.

'Please, do not take this personally,' Pope Leo said. 'We all have different ways, and acceptance of these differences allows for emotion to be controlled. I cannot make argument against the benefits you mention, but these have not been proved.'

'I have seen the results of an initial controlled test conducted in a small maximum-security prison in Romania last month. Within days the outcome was phenomenal. Most prisoners, in an environment known for its hate and violence, changed their behaviours to those of peace, love and harmony. "This Divinity App is game-changing" was how one of the prison wardens described it.'

'That may be so, maybe in a climate as intense as that it works well, for it is untested for the wider world. Then there's the fee you mention, starting at one billion dollars a quarter and increasing thereon in. You know that I recently ordered the Holy See to transfer all financial assets to the Institute for Works of Religion to start a full audit, as the Church has many financial irregularities; this is not a time to be seen to spend so ostentatiously. Also, the mysterious fabric upon which this app has been built, this magical stone of sorts, it seems perhaps a little beyond belief – how can we trust the intention behind its power, assuming it really possesses such power? And then there's the biggest, thorniest issue that springs to mind, of which you have failed to once mention.' He leaned in towards Francis, 'Do you, a seasoned Cardinal and a devout, lifelong follower of the faith of the Catholic Church, believe in a principle so incongruent with our faith? Do you believe in reincarnation?' He delivered this bombshell argument like an arrow piercing a balloon.

Composing himself, doing his best to portray a calm and rational demeanour, Francis replied, trawling from a stock of pre-prepared responses. 'It is not based on reincarnation but karma, a divine force of teaching where improper acts are countered by God's will and loving acts are rewarded by His glories. The Divinity App is not looking at anything other than a person's one and only life on God's Earth.

'What you are describing is a spiritual philosophy but not

that of accepted Catholicism. I cannot see any way of sanctioning this app, especially due to this issue of karma.' Pope Leo sat back in his chair, indicating the subject was now closed.

Wanting to at least leave the meeting with a chink of light and not a firmly shut door, Francis continued, 'I understand, Holy Father, and do accept your position on this matter, and I must say that I had my doubts at first but those fears allayed after some days of contemplation.'

He knew he exaggerated but he felt that floating this little white lie was justified. 'But before we turn our backs on what could be a humanity-changing moment in our history, I ask of you to at least consider setting up a meeting, as soon as practicable, with the Council of Catholic Theologians and Scholars, to see if an acceptable interpretation can be reached with regard to the matter of karma within the context of this app in our faith?'

After a short deliberation, Pope Leo agreed. 'It is sometimes useful to test and retest our belief systems, and I do consider myself as an accommodator for the greater good of the Church. However, I am such a long way from being able to give my blessing to your proposal, I doubt you will ever be able to secure it. As you know, Easter Mass is upon us at the end of the week, and with my diary so very full, it will be quite some weeks before I could convene a Council meeting.'

'Thank you, Kanu.'

'On another matter, I will need an interim update on the ongoing investigation you are carrying out into abuses. It seems to be going very slowly, but I'll expect a report by the end of next week. Is this agreeable?'

'Of course, Your Holiness,' Francis said, thankful he would have time to flesh out the report, on account of his lack of progress on the matter.

After some closing pleasantries, Francis left the papal

chambers. He descended the grand staircase satisfied, on the one hand, that he had managed to avert a straight no from his friend, Kanu, but on the other, beginning to feel ill at ease with Elion's short deadline to get the green-light for the project. And more to the point, what would he expect if he couldn't get the go ahead. Quickly, he chose to compartmentalise these intrusive thoughts and directed his driver to take him back to Monastero San Francesco in Cori so he could spend quality time with his brother, Paolo. Perhaps also, some time with his favourite altar boy, Luigino, he thought to himself, with deviant intent.

13

Monastero San Francesco, Cori, Italy
18th April 2022

'Thank you all kindly for your presence here this morning at our humble Monastero San Francesco.' Peering over his pince-nez perched on the bridge of his nose, Francis, dressed in the full scarlet and white regalia of his position of Cardinal, greeted the journalists before him. Taking a moment to absorb the situation in which he found himself, he scanned across his elevated table, individually looking at each of the dozen microphones afore him, the journalists jostling for position to capture his every word, each microphone wrapped with its owning broadcaster's acronym.

Before continuing his presentation, he looked across the hall and caught the eye of brother Paolo, standing at the back of the plain monastery hall, usually tasked to offer canteen facilities and occasional local civic meetings, but today converted into a global press conference centre. Connecting with Paolo provided Francis with a necessary reminder of the importance of what he was about to do. Refocussing on the near-capacity media crowd, he couldn't help but marvel at the masterful organisational power Elion could wield, with arranging such an international press gathering in mere days. *Time to proceed and push aside egoic worries of speaking to an ultimate audience in, perhaps, the billions*, he thought, thumbing his rosary beads, as ever.

'When we contemplate the history of our species, it is a sad reflection that, oftentimes, our most important events are gauged by periods of dark times; battles, wars and world wars, the development of weapons, state injustices, assassinations, colonialisms and enslavements, natural disasters and man-made disasters. But, seemingly, our history is only briefly punctuated with positive events for humanity, such as the discovery of antibiotics or the global awe generated by mankind first setting foot on the moon.' Francis took a moment to pause his monologue for effect and to make sure he had the full attention of the crowd of international journalists.

'Today, I want to explain how the Catholic Church will give each and every soul on God's holy planet the opportunity to be part of one of humanity's positive punctuations in the continuance of our history.' After another short pause, 'May I humbly present to the world The Divinity App – God's technological tool for the betterment and advancement of humankind!'

Instantly, two large panel televisions, placed either side of Francis' position in a portrait orientation, flicked into life with the app's splash screen. The reporters began to fire urgent questions at Francis, questions which blended into a cacophony of indistinguishable noise as the photography flashes fired like lightning. Laying down his beads on his elm desk, Francis raised his arms and slowly oscillated his hands up and down to calm and quieten his hungry congregation. Once he had succeeded in restoring calm to the hall, he said, 'I understand you, quite rightly, have many questions. Let me explain what The Divinity App is and how it will benefit all of us.

'The Divinity App is one of the simplest but most powerful apps ever created, a gift from our Father, Son, Holy Spirit and Mary, Mother of the Church,' Francis started, whilst gently air-drawing the cross in front of him with his right hand. 'This app measures one's karmic score, the sum total score of all the sins we have accrued in our lifetime.'

The vertical screen changed display again to provide a demonstration of the simple layout of the app. Francis resumed his presentation, referring to the screens, 'Once the app has been downloaded and installed on a phone, one logs in with a fingerprint scan and almost instantly, the app will show a screen like this, the main score in the centre, and below, this smaller number which shows the difference in karmic score since the last login. This is displayed in green and front-loaded with a plus sign to signify the amount of karma worked off by good deeds. It will show a zero in black if there is no change, or will show in red, front-loaded with a minus sign followed by the change of increased karmic score. I hope this explains the workings of the app sufficiently; it is that simple.'

Holding up his hands again to hush the media, he continued, 'It is the Catholic Church's assertion and prediction that once one sees one's karmic score, and how even seemingly small, kind-hearted gestures will reverse the growth of karma, one will try harder and harder to improve one's score. Now, everyone sins to one degree or another, this attribute unfortunately resides in the current human condition. But as humanity starts to work for the good, to unify with our fellow brothers and sisters, sins and evil will recede and as humanity ascends, our world will return to the original biblical state of Eden. This is my solemn hope and prayer and will herald possibly the most significant punctuation for good in our history. Thank you.'

The monastic room erupted once again into riotous shouting, the reporters squawking in unison like starving fledglings demanding to be fed their answers from their adopted religious parent. Francis pointed to a young Hispanic-looking journalist sitting directly in front of him, chosen for the convenience of his location and due to Francis' finding him attractive.

'Hello. Juan Lopez, Mexico News Nacional. Your Eminence, when will The Divinity App be available, how much does it cost, how did the Catholic Church create it and how does it actually attain the karmic scores?'

Francis made a note of the four-headed question. 'OK. I am told it is available right now from all major download sources and it is free. There is no cost to people for tools of God, but there is a donation link on the app for those who want to pay a little or offer a recurring donation. We have seen even the act of giving money to good causes reduces one's karmic debt. On the question of its creation and the exact technology powering the app, I cannot make further comment on that, other than myself and the Catholic Church assuring you that it is God's hand at work providing these scores.' Francis pointed to the reporter on Lopez's left.

'Gillian Doherty, Ireland News Network. This app sounds amazing but is it too good to be true? You were tasked by the late Pope Peter, God rest his soul, with running an internal investigation into allegations of sexual abuses within the organisation – are you still working on this and can you give us an update to the progress made? Also, what is your view on the black Pope prophecy?'

Francis immediately squirmed in his chair at the surprise

second half of the question. 'All I can do is leave it to you, and anyone else who tries this app, to see for yourselves how it works. You will be the judge but I am confident you will find it a wonder of God. On the matter of investigations, until any ongoing inquiry is completed, there cannot be any discussion or updates made public. The black Pope prophesy is just a fairy tale, spread around in a time when skin colour was a very big issue.'

As the sea of hands erupted once again, Francis looked to his right, to the side of the hall and made eyes at the monastery's curator, Lorenzo. Lorenzo stepped forward and brought the conference to an abrupt close.

11:44 UTC ZUX NEWS 24 LIVE ---- BREAKING NEWS ----

'So, in an extraordinary press conference which concluded just ten minutes ago, one that was hastily organised here at the picturesque Monastero San Francesco, about twenty-five miles southeast of Rome, Cardinal Francis Antonio Ballerini has addressed the world to announce the release of The Divinity App. Heralding that this Catholic Church-approved app will change humanity for the better, everyone with a fingerprint-access smartphone will be able to access this app for free and monitor their karmic debt, a score of the total amount of sins they have perpetrated in their lifetime. Now, we will be joined by Professor Ian Trail from the Union School of Theology, in London, to help us understand what The Divinity App is all about, but just before we go to the Professor, we are hearing reports of internet outages relating to the unprecedented demand for downloading The Divinity App – more on this as we get it.

'So, Professor…'

Pope Leo muted his television set, inwardly raging at the blatant insubordination shown by Cardinal Francis.

'Father Fabian,' he turned, speaking to his personal secretary who had rushed into Kanu's quarters some fifteen minutes earlier to switch the television on to watch the renegade press conference. He sat next to the Pope on the sofa watching the proceedings. 'It is with regret that I must ask you to notify the Ispetorre Generale of the Gendarmerie Corps of Vatican City State to arrange to collect Cardinal Francis and bring him to the Vatican as soon as possible. And please also make arrangements for my return to the Vatican with immediate effect. Thank you.'

'Thanks for meeting me, Tinks,' Sam said, delicately lowering two pints of Guinness onto the table of the pub-boat moored on the Hertford Union Canal, in Stratford.

'No problem, Angel. Always happy to see you when you are buying the drinks,' Tinks said, chuckling.

Ignoring the usual banter they would have over who put their hand in their pocket more when buying rounds, Sam said, 'Probably only got time for one drink as I'm meeting up with

Amelie at five back in Cyber City.' He looked at his phone clock. 'As it's three thirty now, I've got about forty-five minutes.' After clinking glasses and saying the obligatory 'cheers', Sam continued, 'I needed to show you something. Did you see that Cardinal giving that press conference this morning to announce the launch of The Divinity App?'

Tinks grinned. He picked up his phone and tapped the screen. 'Oh yes. And guess who managed to install that app on his phone?' He showed the app and his karmic score of - 78,618.

'So you managed to get it? I read that the download centres are still creaking and crashing under the demand load.'

'I tried loads of times, but I guess just got lucky. Have you tried, Angel?'

'Nah, nah. I think I'll let the guinea pigs try it first and I'll think about it later.'

Letting out a scoff of a laugh, Tinks replied, 'Might have guessed, you think it's some plan to control us or kill us.'

Sam took another gulp of stout. 'Well, the safe and effective solution to the covid-19 pandemic didn't work out so well for countless people and the real toll is still to be determined. And now some random people have a copy of your fingerprint. Sometimes I do envy your faith in the integrity of all these people in positions of power.'

'If everyone was like you, nothing would progress through lack of trust,' Tinks said matter-of-factly.

'Trust is hard-earned and easily lost. Anyway, what do you think of the app?'

'Hard to say, but every time I have logged in after purposefully carrying out a small but good act, like when I helped a guy push his broken-down electric car to the side of the road about an hour ago – I think he'd run out of 'lecky – I get a plus sign and green score to the value of karmic debt worked off. If nothing else, and even if this is all a joke or a scam, people will genuinely try to reduce their karmic debt by way of being kind to others. Social media is buzzing with people's good acts and resulting reductions in karmic score.'

'But don't you think it's all a bit far-fetched, science fiction-like? No one knows how the scores are worked out. It's some secret.'

'Look, all I know is that I can see good coming from this. And, fuck me, after the years of shit from wars, pandemic and economic woes, we're all overdue a happy break from problems,' Tinks concluded.

'Yeah, I can't argue with you there.' He took another couple of gulps of beer and Sam got to the point of their meeting. 'Funny coincidence though, because I wanted to talk to you about that cardinal who launched The Divinity App this morning.' Sam dipped his hand into his small backpack and pulled out a letter. He handed it to Tinks.

The weight and quality of the paper indicated to Tinks that it had been sent from an organisation of importance. He unfolded the letter and was immediately attracted to the golden motif letterhead, promoting that it was from Monastero San Francesco in Italy and connected to the Vatican.

Getting a little closer to Tinks and pointing to the letter, Sam said, quietly, 'It's a letter from the very same Cardinal Francis you saw this morning on TV, who is the very same Cardinal Francis I gave first aid to in that Cyber City bombing a couple of weeks back.'

Tinks carefully read it. 'So, he wants to thank you in person for almost certainly saving his life, but am I understanding him right in that he wants to discuss the possibility of awarding a business contract to us?' Tinks' eyebrows were raised and eyes widened in anticipation of confirmation of the bonus news.

'Absolutely,' Sam replied, with a wide smile. 'And it gets better still. I called the Cardinal's secretary to double-check this was genuine and to get more detail. The Cardinal has given us a couple of dates to choose from and his office is paying for our airline tickets. We will be put up for a night at his monastery and, if there is a gap in the Pope's diary, he will arrange a short audience with His Holiness Pope Leo XIV for the two of us.'

Tinks' jaw dropped at the magnitude and honour to not only have a solid business relationship with the Vatican but to also be in the presence of Pope Leo. 'You know I'm not a religious man, Sam, but fuck me, if you excuse my French, this is mega. I don't quite know what to say other than thanks, Angel. You're living up to your name again.'

'Look, I'll ping you the dates and details and we'll go from there.' Finishing his drink, Sam stood up and shook Tinks' hand. 'I'll leave you to mull over the business opportunities, but I'm off to meet Amelie now.'

Just as Sam turned to leave, Tinks reached out to hold Sam's forearm. 'This Amelie, is she your bird now, or something? When am I going to meet her or even see a photo of her?'

'It's not like that with her. There's something so very special about her, I can't explain the feeling, but it's not what you think. I do love her, but it's like a love for a close family member,' Sam said, shrugging his shoulders. 'I'll try and get a snap of her so you can see how lovely she is.'

'Hi, Sam.' Sam rose out of his pavement chair as Amelie greeted him with a friendly kiss on his cheek. 'I'm sorry I'm late. Thank you for getting me the coffee.'

'It's always a pleasure to see you, Amelie. I still can't

believe how stunning your eyes are.'

'You're very kind, Sam,' she calmly replied and then sipped her coffee. 'I just wanted to see you to ask if you had an opinion on The Divinity App?'

A little taken aback by this direct question, he replied, 'I'm not too sure, really. I've just seen it in action on a friend's phone – Tinks – you know, I've mentioned him before. He says it's causing quite a positive stir from social media reports.'

'But what is your gut feel?' she enquired.

'I don't trust it and the Catholic Church has been mired in controversies for decades. But the idea of working on one's karma to lower one's karmic debt, seems an outcome to be lauded,' he concluded.

Amelie watched Sam with her full attention before finishing her drink. She took a cursory look at her phone. 'I do apologise, Sam, but I have to be somewhere else now; I'm so sorry for such a short get-together, but I would like to leave you with one thought upon which to ponder.'

Disappointed in the brevity of their chat, but understanding of her need to go, Sam leaned in to help him concentrate on her next words of wisdom.

'The Divinity App measures karma and allows for reductions in karmic debt through the measurement of good deeds and their likes. Do you think the divine karmic system would take into account one's intentions when carrying out actions or do intentions not matter?' They stood up almost in unison, and she leaned over to kiss Sam goodbye. 'Put another way, Sam, if good deeds are carried out just to reduce one's karma debt, surely the intention is egoic, a means to an end, instead of guidance from the heart. See you soon, my friend,' and with that she left.

Sam sat down and thought about what she had just said. *Is she right that without a loving intention behind our acts, do such acts not lower karmic debt, or maybe just not as much? Or perhaps people may start to do good things for wrong reasons, such as to lower their score in this app, but then soon may start to do them for the right reasons?* The complexity of his thoughts made his brain hurt but his attention was soon diverted by the waiter appearing.

'Can I get you more drinks or maybe the bill?'

'Just the bill, please.'

Sam again tried to pick up on what Amelie had said, but felt fatigued with the subject. He paid the bill and as he grabbed his backpack to leave, the waiter said, 'I'm sorry you were stood up. Hope to see you soon.'

Sam looked at him confused. 'I wasn't stood up, my friend was here.'

'Oh, right, sir. I didn't see you with anyone. I guess I must have missed them?' the waiter replied in puzzlement. Sam left, baffled by the waiter's words.

14

Tiger's Claw Monastery, Bhutan
22nd April 2022

Tenzin had devoted nearly four years to monastic life in one of the most amazing feats of construction anywhere in the world. The monastery at Tiger's Claw was built, stone by stone, over three hundred years before, with the closest town a thousand metres lower in elevation and over ten miles away by narrow, gravelly tracks that clung to sheer mountainsides. It was a deed of dedication of the monks of the day to complete the monument in just a fifteen-year period.

Even on a special day, such as this one, Tenzin followed his routine, starting with an hour of dawn meditation, then scripture study, before making himself a sweet milk tea. Mahayana Buddhism was the most widely honoured practice in Bhutan and as it had originated in Tibet, Tenzin had been following this path since he was old enough to talk.

In the corner of a storage room, he had made himself, with permission from the *Khenpo*, the abbot of the monastery, a *kwoon*, where he was rapidly developing his skills in Kung Fu. He would allocate two hours to this discipline, aided and guided by Chun Tong, a monk who had sought refuge at Tiger's Claw just months after Tenzin's arrival. He was about thirty years Tenzin's senior but having attained his fifth degree in Kung Fu years before, when he was living in his native Hong Kong, he was super-qualified to train anyone in the discipline.

The rest of the day usually comprised prayer, chanting and throat singing, performing rituals of honour to bodhisattvas, cleaning, crafting sacred Buddhist ornaments and strings of beads, monastic repairs and maintenance, a single meal of the day and perhaps his favourite session, learning English. He was also on a weekly rota to journey into the nearest town, Paro, to offer blessings to townsfolk, take a selection of the monks' crafts for sale and to collect food and provisions to return to Tiger's Claw.

But today was different. Tenzin reached into the pouch of his maroon robe and took out his snuff-box. He felt blessed as he gently caressed his right thumb over the tin's surface, feeling the half-repaired bullet dent that had been left following the unprovoked attack on him by the Americans. *Having this little vice saved my life*, he thought. He instinctively felt the scar on his chest. Although traumatic at the time, Tenzin came to understand that events happen for a reason and he considered them lessons in life, opportunities to analyse one's actions and oneself, a contemplation of the realm of cause and effect. He felt no anger towards those US agents, in fact, he empathised with their lack of mastery over their own thoughts and actions. Occasionally, he created thought-forms in meditation to stream love and light in their direction.

As requested for ten o'clock sharp, Tenzin made his way to the *Khenpo's* small office, which doubled as a private meditation room with its own Buddhist altar and accompanying ornaments. The dark wooded but intimate space was filled with the familiar and pleasant aroma of burned sage, with undertones of generic floral notes that came from years of burning incense sticks. Tenzin sat on a cushion at a low table, the nearest position to the door, whilst the abbot completed his own closing ritual at the altar.

He stared at the solitary wax candle flame placed in the middle of the evergreen oak table until the *Khenpo* was ready to address him.

'Tenzin. Thank you for your punctual presence; our honoured guest is no distance away now. He has been seen ascending the path just opposite Tiger's Claw,' the *Khenpo*, addressed by the monks as Khen Rinpoche, explained. Tenzin noticed the *Khenpo* sat next to him, a place that was not usual for his status instead of his usual position at the head of the table, just afore the altar.

'It is with such esteem that I have been chosen for this meeting today, Khen Rinpoche,' Tenzin humbly offered.

'I have only met him once, but I still recall the energy of that liaison,' Khen Rinpoche started to reminisce, but he was halted by a knock on the office door followed by Chun Tong opening the door just enough to poke his head around.

'He is here,' Chun Tong said, with uncharacteristic exuberance.

'Please, show him in,' Khen Rinpoche replied. He and Tenzin quickly rose to their feet.

Chun Tong stepped into the room and dipped his head, ushering in the guest and his two colleagues. 'Please, this is Khen Rinpoche and Tenzin Gorji. Khen Rinpoche and Tenzin Gorji, this is His Holiness, the Dalai Lama, and his entourage.'

12:00 UTC ZUX NEWS 24 LIVE ---- BREAKING NEWS ----

'The top stories here on the midday news of ZUX News 24 continue to be dominated by the ongoing, unprecedented effect The Divinity App is having on societies across the globe. In another extraordinary move, the mobile operating-system companies have, minutes ago, released a joint press release, a first for these technology giants, to show that The Divinity App has now been downloaded in excess of six hundred and fifty million times onto mobile devices in just under four days. They go on to say that the call for their app shop services has never seen such demand and they are working hard to increase capacity as there appears to still be a significant amount of demand.

'Social media companies are also reporting they are increasing capacity on their platforms due to a surge in usage, with users reporting their experiences of using The Divinity App.

'Further, sales of smartphones have also seen a steep increase, with many outlets temporarily running out of stock. Although we are still to hear any comment from the Pope, last night, the President of the United States of America said, before boarding his helicopter from the White House lawn, "It kinda looks like peace and harmony is breaking out around the world. Long may it last!"'

'So, Tenzin, we share the same first name, you know,' the Dalai Lama said, with a reassuring smile. 'I have been told that you sought refuge here at Tiger's Claw after you were attacked bringing your find, the satellite, here?'

Tenzin smiled and nodded. 'Yes, I was bringing the shell, as instructed, from my family home in Tibet to this monastery, but I was chased by the Chinese military and ran into two American CIA agents, who decided to shoot me and steal the artefact. I recovered here and I was kindly offered refuge by Khen Rinpoche, on agreement I could have occasional leave to sneak back into Tibet to see my family and give them any money I earn,' Tenzin explained.

'This is a story of courage and the ascendence of a joyous, young man.' The Dalai Lama commended Tenzin on his journey. 'Before I discuss the reason for our rendezvous, I'd like to explain to you the significance of this "shell" you recovered. It is what was once considered a mythical relic from ancient Greece. Its mythical status was secretly corrected once it was found to be a real object back in 1922. Of course, the Smithsonian managed to acquire it and hide it until the US military used it in a secret project back in the Cold War. But what might be of interest to you, Tenzin, is that it is, in fact, not a shell but a skull!'

Tenzin's jaw dropped and he barely blinked as the Dalai Lama divulged all that he knew about the skull.

'Now, we did not know what those CIA agents, or their bosses to be more accurate, had in mind for the skull, but when there is such superpower interest in an ancient bone, it is only a matter of time before any power it possesses is harnessed for purpose of gain.' The Dalai Lama proceeded to explain the emergence of The Divinity App and his conclusion that the control of the Greek skull's power was the only explanation to facilitate such a programme.

'So, Tenzin, we come to the point where I explain how you can help.'

'Yes, yes, please let me know,' Tenzin said, gently pressing his hands together into a prayer position.

The Dalai Lama took a moment to finish his second cup of sweet milk tea and thanked Chun Tong again. 'Tenzin, of course, everything we have discussed today must remain between all six of us in this room.' Everyone nodded in unison.

'As Buddhists, we are known for our passive nature and our abilities in meditative practices. But as the astrological age currently passes into a new one, that of Aquarius, energies become unstable, here on earth but also in the spirit world – the oneness to which we refer. As the saying goes, "as above, so below", there comes a time when our limited effect on the oneness needs complementary energy rightfully expended on the physical plane. This is what our time now calls for and it is so that our Buddhist Council, this week, agreed to build a network of Buddhist defenders to help counter and frustrate some of the negative energy, the evil that is growing and taking advantage of these unstable times. Our defenders will be selected for their moral righteousness, balanced psyche and ability to physically function well in a deteriorating and sometimes rotten, global society. You, Tenzin, are called to be our first defender and, with all our support, will be tasked first to recover that skull artefact once again. It is the Council's conclusion that the human condition is not yet ready for the knowledge and power the skull brings and has a highly likely potential to ultimately create human misery and suffering beyond contemplation.'

The energy in Khen Rinpoche's office matched the tension portrayed by the Dalai Lama's monologue. Everyone present clearly understood the gravity of the situation.

'Tenzin. Before this old man descends back to Paro and to

160

its slightly thicker air with the help of my two carers here,' the Dalai Lama said, playfully gesturing with his head towards his team, 'will you selflessly accept this most important of roles I offer you today?'

15

Mount Cheyenne, Colorado
23rd April 2022

'Special Agent Lafayette. I'm due to meet Chief of Staff General John Q. Hill,' Laura told the reception's staff duty sergeant at the Cheyenne Mountain Space Force Station, formerly known as NORAD/USNORTHCOM.

She still had extreme reservations about this meeting, not to mention it had cut her convalescence short after her new boss had authorised a month off following the traumatic ending to the London project. Since returning to the US and having gone through the standard debrief for such situations, she had spent the past two and a half weeks in a charming timber holiday lodge in the De Soto National Forest, in her native Mississippi. She knew De Soto well, having grown up thirty miles away in Hattiesburg, so returning there had felt like coming home. She was transported back to her joyful childhood camping trips with her parents, hiking, cycling and improving her swimming skills from her mother, a retired national swimming champion, and honing bushcraft skills and survival techniques with her father, a US Navy SEAL and the first African American Mississippian recipient of the Navy Cross since the Second World War. As always, she made a pilgrimage to the De Soto site where her parents had been shot dead in an unsolved shooting incident, just after her twelfth birthday.

Laura's break was punctuated when she had flown back to Washington DC to attend Jacob Rozen's funeral, in nearby Delaware. It was such a difficult trip. Aside from meeting his grieving family, especially his eldest, Rebekah, who was due to give birth any day now, she had also grown so very close to Jacob on Project Octal, and had even forgiven him for executing the mounted Tibetan on the Bhutanese border. Explaining the work-life events and tragedies he had endured when decisive action was not taken, helped her understand why he had acted the way he had. However, she still did not agree with his actions that day.

Putting down the phone, the reception officer reported, 'Ma'am, the General will be with you shortly. Please take a seat while you wait.' He gestured in the direction of the grey, corporate-looking sofas. 'Please help yourself to coffee, Ma'am.'

Laura decided against a coffee but took a seat and surveyed the cavernous reception area. The monolithic blast door looked an amazing feat of engineering but it also represented the fine line between life continuing as normal whilst open and a possible cataclysmic scenario if it had to be closed for good reason. It was also effectively the dividing point between this artificially carved command centre, bristling with military service personnel and technology and the natural beauty and wonders of the Colorado landscape, just a couple of hundred metres away.

She was dressed in her favourite, tailored, dark blue skirt

suit and crisp, white blouse and she quickly felt her hair to ensure it held a neat ponytail. She then checked her blouse was buttoned up to the penultimate buttonhole. As she confirmed this was so, she moved her hand to the second button. Although the General was one of the last people she wanted to see at this time, she remembered his manner from before and momentarily decided to unfasten this button. She remembered a training mantra branded into her mind to utilise every method at her disposal to achieve her goals, but then reversed her decision and quickly rebuttoned her blouse, full of confidence that she did not have to stoop to using such a base tactic for this meeting.

As she waited, her mind raced with all the points she wanted to raise with Hill. She found she harboured, quite uncharacteristically, a good deal of anger and resentment around Project Octal.

'Ms Lafayette, so pleased to meet you again,' General Hill said. As before, he was impeccably presented in full military uniform and briskly approached Laura, his hand extended for a customary handshake.

'General,' Laura responded with a polite smile. She shook his hand – no confusion this time as to how to greet him.

As they both started the long and convoluted march to his office, Laura tentatively and quietly enquired, knowing they would not be able to talk in detail until they were in the security of his suite, 'I do hope our meeting does not portend any similarity to the events to which I have been subjected since our last meet up, nearly four years ago.'

'Yes, you have seen some unusual times,' Hill understated, though delivered with a hint of empathy, she felt. 'I'll reveal our agenda in my office, but as you have come so far today, and at such short notice, and in the circumstances, please let me accompany you to lunch afterwards.'

Temporarily surprised again by the General's forwardness,

Laura thought that more time to get to know him could only be of benefit. She was sure she could verbally hold this frisky military man at bay, if needed. And there would be a lot of other service personnel around in the mess hall, she told herself. 'Sure, General. That would be most welcome.'

Holding open the door to his office for her, he said, 'That's awesome, Special Agent. I know this great little place in downtown Colorado Springs; it's almost on the way back to the airport, so it's a win-win scenario.' He had a lively look on his face.

Laura took her seat opposite the General, realising she had just accepted what could be construed as a lunch date with this brash, but charming, older man. She took some solace in knowing that the General would have to behave in public, especially if he was in full military regalia.

'Firstly, please accept my condolences for the loss of Head of Special Operations Jacob Rozen. Not that I knew him really well, I know he was a good man and you had a solid working relationship going between the both of you.'

Laura looked above Hill's head to the new Space Force plaque, showing that much had changed in the world, as well as in her life, since her last visit here, in 2018. This moment also gave General Hill time to admire her appearance.

Refocussing on Hill, she replied, 'Thank you, Rozen was a lovely man and the best agent.'

'Now, there's no easy way to say this, Lafayette, but this is all to do with Project Octal. You may have seen the news about The Divinity App this week?'

'Yes. Such a strange project to have been involved in.' Laura felt the urge to vent but followed her instinct to stay calm, initially. 'I never thought for a moment it would have been used in any wide sense and certainly not being licenced to the Vatican for most of humanity to use. And whilst we're on the subject, and please excuse my language, General, but what the fuck? – I did as I was asked, we produced this weird-shit app, which, by the way was not in my job description, working in the CIA, then just as it's effectively completed, this elusive Elion asshole murders Jacob. He would have murdered me too if I had not been, just by chance, in the protection of the stairway core.' She felt completely out of character being this livid. She was shaking.

Sighing and pursing his lips, Hill explained, 'OK. Look. You have good reason to react this way, I'd be fucking agitated too in your position. The short reason why you and Jacob were targeted was because you disobeyed orders. Elion told you not to try to find or trace him. He gave you a clear instruction, at the beginning of your joining Project Octal. He is not a man you go out to find, he's one that will find you when he wants you. I understand you found out who he is, but you left footprints all over the CIA tools you used.'

'Yes, tools I am cleared to use and they are there for use by CIA agents. How does Elion fit into the CIA? Is he some kinda super-agent?' she asked, flippantly.

'You see, there you go. You're asking questions that are above your pay grade.'

'With respect, General – that's bullshit! This fucker targeted CIA field agents for termination. We were ratted out by the CIA and left exposed to this treasonous act. Left hung out to dry. Am I still a marked agent? Perhaps Elion's got access to our drones and will erase me in a phantom style?'

'OK. OK,' Hill lifted his palms towards her, implying a full surrender to the barrage of questions fired at him. 'This is just between you and me, Lafayette.' The General inhaled deeply and sat back in his chair. He was careful to pick his words carefully, leading to a staccato delivery, 'Elion is an enigma. At this time, he is arguably the most powerful person in the world. Presidents, Prime Ministers, Secretary-Generals, Dictators, they all answer to him. It's been this way for decades and others in his bloodline before him. He holds an extraordinary position in society. He is an enigma, for many reasons, but he is not the enemy. We work with him to achieve certain goals that suit him and us alike. When he wants to work with us, we do not say no. The last time we denied his request was back in '41, when Franklin D. Roosevelt headed an isolationist America, and refused to enter World War Two. Months later, on December seventh, Pearl Harbour changed all that, brought about by Elion assisting the Japanese.'

'So you're saying the world's structure, our hierarchy, has a higher, arcane layer, playing the world like a game of chess?' Laura tried not to sound incredulous.

Hill pursed his lips and communicated the merest of nods.

'So Jacob and I were just a couple of expendable pawns that needed to be extinguished to protect this man?'

'I wouldn't phrase it quite that way, but it's a fair analogy.'

'Jeez, and if the world's not complicated and crazy enough,' Laura vented, feeling her blood pressure raging.

'I need you to put what happened in London behind you. It was not personal, it's the way Elion works to protect his business and to benefit his partners,' Hill offered. He brought out a paper file from the bottom drawer of his desk and placed it in front of him. It was marked 'BEYOND TOP SECRET' in bold red ink.

He opened the file. 'Although he sent a clear message to you, Elion does not now have you in his sights for termination, I have his assurance. He never lies.'

'Ooh, he's my hero,' Laura sarcastically interjected. Hill smiled momentarily.

'Remember your trip to Bhutan, near Tiger's Claw Monastery?'

'Yes, quite unforgettable,' Laura replied in such a manner that Hill did not know if she was referring to the stunning landscape or the unpalatable events of the mission.

'Well, we managed to get an informant into that monastery and yesterday we received some intel.' Hill quickly referred to his notes. 'It seems that the Dalai Lama has tasked a young monk to seek and recover the shell or skull artefact that you and Rozen intercepted. You are now tasked to find and neutralise this monk.' The General paused, awaiting Laura's initial reaction.

Laura's face dropped, agog at her new mission. 'You must be kidding! I've been nothing but loyal. I've been bombed, bereft and bewildered and not even completed my convalescence. And you want me to go kill a monk!' But then she stopped. Loosely looking at the file that was upside down to her, she spoke slowly as her thoughts formed each sentence. Hill stayed quiet and watched her intensely. 'No, wait. It's Elion that wants me to kill a monk, isn't it?' she said. 'Kill the monk, protect the artefact, protect the app. What's with this Divinity App? It's certainly not about getting people to act better even though that's what it appears to be offering. What are you, or are *we*, should I say, getting from the bargain?' she demanded.

'From our point of view, data. Simple as that. Petabytes and petabytes of data,' Hill admitted. 'Project Octal was symbolic of an octopus and the reach of its eight tenacles.'

'All this just so we can cajole and control people? This is so wrong,' she said, disbelievingly. 'I didn't join the CIA to do this to people, I wanted to make a difference. I wanted to show to myself and my beloved parents that I could use my talents to make this world a better place. My God, what's this all about?'

'What is done with all this data is not our concern. We are asked to facilitate it and once collated, we deliver it, and we move on the next order. Ours is not to reason why, you know that. You *are* making a difference and I'd wager no other agent could have satisfied Elion's orders like you did,' Hill said, attempting to bolster her up.

After a brief moment of quiet reflection, Laura asked, 'I guess the President is in on this? And you said a little while back "From our point of view, data". What other points of view are there?'

With a little chuckle, Hill replied, 'The President spends most of the day wondering what he had for his last meal! Other points of view, well, the Vatican is getting massively positive exposure strengthening their religious position in the world, not to mention a huge boost in revenue for the Church.'

'And Elion? What's he getting out of this?'

'That's a great question, but one to which I have no answer,' Hill replied honestly.

'Why me, General? Why does Elion want me on this manhunt?'

'He knows you. He knows you well and he knows your level of commitment and loyalty, other than your faux-pas in trying to trace him. Also, you are in up to your neck in this project; he doesn't need to run the risk of divulging all this sensitive information to any other agent.'

'OK, suppose I do take on this neutralising,' she said deliberately using unemotional CIA language. 'Where will I find him?'

'That's not clear at the moment, Ma'am.'

'If he's after the skull, surely I just go there and wait for him? Where was the skull moved to?' *It was a reasonable question*, she thought.

'That's not clear at the moment, Ma'am.'

'So you don't know where the monk is or where the skull is! Is this Mission Impossible?' she asked, facetiously.

'I know it sounds crazy but info will come through and it will be relayed to you promptly. I wasn't understating what I told you last time you were here that Project Octal would usher in changes to every corner of the world.' Changing the subject abruptly, he continued, 'Come on, let's get out of here and have lunch. This place does the best line in Cajun cuisine – I hope you're hungry.' Hill locked away the paperwork and stood up to leave, seemingly having switched off the subject and his mind's eye already choosing from the lunch menu.

Laura started towards the exit, but then stopped suddenly close to General Hill. She looked him square in the face and asked, 'You said Elion knows me. You said, "He knows you well". I don't really know him and certainly not well.' She looked deep into his eyes, searching for any signs to belie the truth. 'I've spoken to him on the phone maybe twenty times, spread over a period of three years. How does he know me well, General?' Her gaze was intense.

General Hill did not flinch nor reveal any tell and gave the same deadpan response he had given many times in his career, 'That's classified, Special Agent.'

16

The Vatican, Rome
24th April 2022

'You've been elusive for the past few days, Francis, according to the Ispetorre Generale of the Gendarmerie.' Kanu got straight to the point. 'You've been conducting more press conferences, which I have watched with displeasure. You have been travelling to these different cities on a private jet that seemed to evade the authorities – is this correct?'

Sitting in the papal office in the Vatican, with its walls adorned with priceless artworks, Francis let out a faint sigh. He realised he had been so close to being Pope and utilising this room as his office. He sighed jointly in preparation for his answer. Though the office was over two hundred metres from St Peter's Square, they could both hear the noise of the faithful congregation awaiting ten o'clock Mass, to be held in an hour's time. Special measures had been put in place to accommodate the crowd of unprecedented size that had gathered.

'Yes, and no, Your Holiness. An organisation offered the jet for the tour but I had no idea it was invisible – to the authorities and not the naked eye, I mean,' Francis said, trying to bring a bit of levity to the conversation.

'How dare you undermine the Church's authority, my authority, by releasing this app! Tell me why I should not defrock you right here and now!' Kanu shouted, his forehead veins becoming visibly prominent.

Francis had predicted this response and had prepared his defence. 'Holy Father. Please let me explain,' he started in a very calm manner in stark contrast to his companion. He even made sure he did not fiddle with his rosary beads. 'When we last met, you agreed to give the project some thought and to let the Council of Catholic Theologians and Scholars consider its merits, and I knew this could take weeks or even longer. However, soon afterwards, I was contacted by Religix and pressured into making a decision, otherwise the app would be rebranded away from karma as the central core and offered to the world of Islam, instead. I was shown plans of how the app would be changed to focus on the Islamic beliefs of destiny and fate, as the language of karma would not be tolerated in the Muslim faith. I was also shown documents from the highest spiritual leaders of Islam showing their interest in the project, subject to many caveats.'

'So you just took it upon yourself to press ahead with this maverick plan?'

'You know I have been a devout follower of Catholicism all my life and it breaks my heart to see the ever-increasing decline of our Church. So, yes, in perhaps a moment of rashness or maybe in a moment of clarity, I launched the app.'

'Are you saying you were forced or even coerced into your actions, Francis?'

The Cardinal took a moment to consider his answer. If he

blamed someone else in Religix, or even Elion, he may gain some understanding from Kanu. But if he did side with His Holiness' supposition of coercion, Elion would be sure to exact retribution upon him. 'No, Your Holiness, I acted from my heart for the good of our congregations and beyond.'

Before the Pope could respond, Francis quickly unfolded a piece of paper and said, 'I have here the latest news, if you would allow me to proceed?'

Pope Leo's anger had subsided and he gave Francis the opportunity to continue making his case.

'You will have seen on the news the worldwide trend of people committing acts of kindness to their families, their friends and even strangers. It has been declared the biggest and quickest positive global change to our society in history, and the number of downloads of the app has just surpassed one billion, nearly as many as Catholics there are estimated to be in the world. The Catholic Church is receiving daily positive media exposure around the globe and it is expected that today, being the first Sunday after the release of the app, there will be record Catholic congregations, if the numbers in Asia and Australasia are anything to go by. Just listen to the congregation outside, record-breaking they say. The Clerk of the Holy See reports we have received over four hundred million dollars in donations and subscriptions this week alone. And finally, I saw a report saying that many international law societies had recorded an influx of people changing their wills to include gifts to the Church. And all this, Holy Father, in just one week. Think where matters may take us in a month or a year!'

Collecting his thoughts, Pope Leo sat back in his chair and turned his head to gaze out of the window in contemplation. Francis couldn't help but hear the congregation cheer, chant and roar. *It sounds even louder and livelier than when Kanu celebrated his popedom*, he thought.

'Thank you for your explanations, Francis. At this time, the app does seem to be having a tremendous and positive effect on the world and on our Church, and my hands are now tied from trying to withdraw the programme from the populace, the Genie is out of the bottle, so to speak. I do have many reservations with The Divinity App, none less than the misguided intentions behind the masses doing good deeds to lower their debt, as opposed to following their hearts at all times. However, I am not convinced you have not been coerced and you have admitted to taking a monumental decision without authority; this is a very serious situation. We do not have time now, for I have Mass to prepare, but we also need to discuss your investigation into Church abuses, which seems to have stalled.'

The Pope leaned forward and solemnly continued, 'So, it is with extreme regret, Cardinal, that I herewith suspend you from most of your official duties in the Church, pending a synod hearing, to be convened as soon as possible, to discuss your actions and your future in the Church. You may still wear cardinal regalia and still attend to your monastic duties but alongside your curator at all times. Francis, I suggest you use your time to fully prepare for saving your career and life's work.'

13:00 UTC ZUX NEWS 24 LIVE ---- BREAKING NEWS ----

'It was the largest congregation for Mass at St Peter's Square in the Vatican City ever recorded, with over three hundred thousand people squeezed into the plaza and an estimated further five hundred thousand packing the surrounding streets. Huge crowds were expected following the stellar effect The Divinity App has had on the world, and the Vatican authorities were quick to install live feed screens and public address systems beyond St Peter's Square so that no one missed Pope Leo's Mass.'

'So, come on, mate, who is this Amelie? Bet you still haven't got a photo of her?' Tinks toyed with Sam as he checked the wall-mounted television screening live coverage of a Chelsea v West Ham United Premier League match whilst taking another swig of stout, in what had become their usual drinking hole, the floating pub.

'Look, I've told you all I know, there's nothing else I can say,' Sam replied in resignation.

'If she's your bird and you're banging her, I'm your mate, let me know. I'm beginning to get seriously worried about you. You're not having some mental episode again, are you?' Tinks asked, unsympathetically.

'No!'

'Then what is it? You save her life, you become friends, you see each other now and again, but only briefly, she talks like a sage, she has amazing eyes, no one else has seen her, you won't take a photograph of her, so what I am to make of it?'

'It's not for you to make anything of it, Tinks. Stop tinkering,' Sam added to lighten to atmosphere. 'Anyway, I did try to take a photo of her.'

'Let's see it then!'

'It didn't come out.'

'What? What do you mean? How could it not come out – were you using an old camera with film?'

'The camera app just wouldn't behave properly. Don't know why. It's fine now. Anyway, we're here to relax and watch the match, not for you to interrogate me.'

'I know, I'm sorry but I'm just concerned for you. I know what you've gone through and wouldn't want you slipping back down that path. Aside from work and us going out now and again, you don't seem to socialise with anyone, except this Amelie. You don't have a partner and don't have any real interests other than picking holes in the news. I mean, it's not as if we can do anything about the news stories anyway,' Tinks said.

'I can't help having different perspectives on world events from you and everyone else that just watches or reads the news and laps up everything they are told as gospel. I don't know what's really going on but most of the media stories seem to be just that, stories,' Sam countered, but he knew he would not make headway as they had had similar conversations in the past.

'Why does everything have to be a conspiracy theory? Why do you think that way? Is it because these theories provide a more exciting reality compared to the humdrum of life, Angel, or do they give you an excuse for your life not turning out the way you thought it should have?'

'Nah, nah, it's not that,' Sam said, preparing to give a fuller explanation. 'It probably all goes back to my dad. He was obsessed with Antarctica. He was a Professor of Geology and he wanted to gain more knowledge about the untouched continent.' Sam opened up about his parents and Tinks let him talk. Sam remembered Tinks had once tried asking about his parents back in Afghanistan, but Sam had not been ready to open that box back then.

With a vacant stare as he recalled memories, Sam continued, 'He was sure there were geological marvels to be discovered and he planned for him and Mum to get out there when a research opportunity arose.'

'What did your mum do?'

'She was a hydrologist, you know, a kind of water specialist. She was interested in Antarctica from her specialty point of view but wasn't so fussed about going there because she disliked the cold. She always opted to spend holidays in the sun, hence we used to drive to the South of France most summers. Anyway, as Dad absorbed all he could about Antarctica, he came across increasing evidence that there was more to the place than just ice and penguins. He first read tales and interviews from Admiral Byrd – I've still got the books – and his adventures on the seventh continent, especially the last visits with the US Navy. They really grabbed Dad's attention. I remember Dad's eyes lighting up when he told me he'd seen old, declassified photos of expeditions, with small mountains in the background that were almost perfect pyramids. They were in some London university library vault, meaning there was a whole lot of history to find down there on the continent. Then I saw his frustration when the next time he went to look at the photos, they were gone and no one there knew of them, let alone their whereabouts. This just fuelled his enthusiasm to go to Antarctica and explore for himself.'

'Wow, that sounds really quite something. So did they get to go to Antarctica?' Tinks asked, his attention fully absorbed.

'Yes,' Sam replied, deadpan. 'I don't know the full details of exactly where they went, but it was in early 1998. I was only eight. All I know is that they went to further a research project, ultimately under the wings of the British Military, as the continent has been controlled by militaries ever since Admiral Byrd's last expedition in the '50s. The project assignment was hundreds of miles inland from the South

African side of the land mass.'

'Is this where they died, Sam?' Tinks asked, delicately.

Looking into his pint, Sam nodded. 'All I remember is that two senior officers came around to my auntie's house. She was looking after me for the duration of my folks' contract, and when she answered the front door, I heard the conversation because I was walking down the stairs at the time and then I went and stood next to her. I guess I was so shocked at the news because the only thing I remember focussing on was that one of the officers wore a pair of brown leather gloves when the weather was really warm, and that didn't seem right to me. The officers said they were sorry to report that my parents had drowned in an accident in Antarctica.'

'What? Drowned in a frozen wasteland?' Tinks asked.

'Yeah, go figure. Minus fifty degrees Celsius and hundreds of miles away from the sea and they managed to drown in water? And it gets weirder. As the days and weeks passed my auntie and I were trying our best to come to terms with the news. Then, firstly, she received a short letter from my dad, which was written weeks before his death but really didn't say much, like a postcard, but it read strangely, like he wasn't thinking straight.' Sam paused to stretch his neck. 'Then she received more government letters and updates that just didn't add up. The death certificates were eventually sent and said they both died of hypothermia but then my auntie received a very reasonable government payment each month, even though my parents were contracted to a civilian company, not the government, which Auntie always said was odd. And the strangest thing of all was the correspondence from Buckingham Palace where the Queen said she was so sorry to hear of their accident and offered both of them posthumous MBE honours.'

'Hypothermia? So, you don't know if it was an accident in water or an accident outside in the cold, but that doesn't indicate they drowned. That is so weird, Sam. Where are they buried?'

'Your guess is as good as mine. Well, that's not quite true. We had a funeral service about three months after they died. My auntie was expecting their bodies to be shipped home, but instead we received their ashes. The explanation given was that their wills expressed their wish to be cremated, so the state took care of it.'

'So your auntie didn't even get to see your parents before they were cremated?'

'No. Really convenient, isn't it? So going back to your original question, what's happened in my life leads me to be suspicious of most things. It was probably losing my parents that led me into first aid. Subconsciously, maybe I just want to save my parents. And now, it's knowledge I have and will continue to use to help other families not get the same news.

'It makes sense, mate. I'm so sorry to hear what you've been through, and from such a young age.'

'So, returning to what we were talking about, I'm not going to be able to convince you, just like you can't convince me that there aren't dark elements behind various goings-on, such as that evil Afghan war, that still haunts me, and The Divinity App. The news is just cock-a-hoop about the app and there are people like you hypnotised by its glamour, who are using it, then telling everyone about how good you've been. At best it's an ego boost and at worst, it could be a catastrophe for everyone.'

Tinks shook his head. 'Wow, Sam, I can't see it being that bad.'

'OK, Tinks. Tell me, what data can the app access and take from your phone?'

'I dunno. Can't be much, it's from the Vatican, the Catholic Church. And I haven't got anything to hide anyway.'

'That's your answer? OK, it's from the Catholic Church so

must be good? The same Church that has been mired for decades in rumours of child abuse, which used to be called conspiracy theories, to then have many priests outed, moved aside or jailed for these crimes, and you blindly have faith in their motives! And not having anything to hide is no reason for companies and governments to take personal data. If you had nothing to say, would it be OK to lose your right to free speech?'

'I think you're going a bit too far there,' said Tinks, smiling.

'I know, but it's good to challenge each other's beliefs. I'm not trying to insult you. From my findings, the Catholic Church does not run, or even own, The Divinity App; it's a company called Religix, registered, why of course, offshore in the Cayman Islands, so no information can be found on the company. For all I know, that app is accessing every piece of data on your phone and what it deems useful to some far-flung country with dubious data protection legislation and nefarious intent. Take that video clip app, ClipTek. Government after government started banning its top spy agencies' staff from having the app, like at the Pentagon and GCHQ, et cetera, demanding it be deleted for national security reasons. Most people think it's a fun video clip app when in fact it is spyware dressed up as a fun video clip app. The Chinese are funnelling data for their own ends.' Sam paused. 'Sorry, I'm going off on one.'

'That's OK, mate. I just choose not to see the world that way, it would be a shit world if I did.'

'Fair point,' Sam responded. 'By the way, how is your karmic score going?'

'Yeah, not bad, still going the right way, but I've noticed in the last day or so that when I carry out a good deed which is almost identical to another one, the amount of debt taken off has lessened. Maybe, all acts are not equal,' Tinks surmised.

'Perhaps. Or maybe it's the app that's changing?' Both Sam and Tinks looked at each other and broke into a smile, then laughed in unison.

17

Brooklyn, New York
12th May 2022

Tenzin unfolded his paper map to double-check he was still on the right street for Kaz's School of Kung Fu. He felt confident considering this was his first trip to another country, other than when he had sought refuge in Bhutan, and despite being dressed in unfamiliar jeans, T-shirt, sports hoodie and trainers. Not only another country but the United States of America, a country he had heard so much about. Tenzin was comfortable not prejudging this country, taking the view that every person is an individual and has a right to be respected as such.

'Please, may I speak to Kaz?' Tenzin asked the reception guy in good but accented English upon entering the school.

'Who's asking?' came a sharp reply in a local accent.

'My name's Gorji. He is expecting me, I have been told.'

The receptionist looked him up and down, marched to the front door and threw the lock and bolts closed, followed by flicking the open sign to closed. 'Follow me.'

They made their way back through the premises, entering a sizeable, well-lit, mirror-clad hall, hosting a kickboxing ring in one corner, punch bags, weights and barbells, and two Mok Jong wooden training dummies. Four people vigorously trained in two pairs in a clear area. The floor was also fully padded. Tenzin was impressed with how these facilities were so professional compared to his beloved makeshift *kwoon* back at Tiger's Claw Monastery.

Finally pushing open a black, steel door to the rear of the *kwoon*, they took seats either side of the well-worn, scratched and chipped wooden desk.

'OK, Gorji, we can talk safely in here. I can tell you, I'm Kaz; how can I help?' Tenzin had studied his contact as they made their journey to this office. Although short and middle-aged, Kaz was heavily built and would undoubtedly be a force to be reckoned with if anyone were to tackle him. Even his gait gave the impression that he was magically rooted to the ground, as if he commanded an additional gravitational pull. His black sash was complemented with four gold bands, denoting he had attained the fourth degree in the Kung Fu discipline. Tenzin was ungraded and was therefore in the presence of a superior technician, so would treat him as such out of full respect and refer to him as *Shifu*, meaning 'Teacher'.

'My elders said that I should start my search for an artefact with you, *Shifu*. I have also been advised to make my enquiries in person, to reduce the risk of electronic interception of my communications.' Tenzin continued to explain his original adventure finding the skull and how he has been informed that it is pivotal in the workings of The Divinity App.

'I trust you because I trust the source who set up this meeting, but I'm not sure how useful I can be to you,' said Kaz. 'As you've been told, I worked for the Smithsonian for over twenty years at the beginning of my working life. I was quickly promoted once and then promoted again, and I found myself the head custodian at a secret storage location. This location was on a huge military base in Nevada, Area 51. You've probably heard of it?'

Tenzin shook his head, deciding against explaining how sheltered and remote a life he had led up until recently.

'Well, it's a world-known military base. Anyhow, this warehouse was huge,' Kaz explained, leaning forward and using his arms as a kind of measure of scale. 'Man, it was several football pitches in size and *all* underground. All sorts of shit was kept there, but there was also a secret lower level reserved for items of extra-special interest. These items were not officially recorded and were assessed by top brass as to whether they were kept for some future use or marked for destruction. Even before this facility was created, there were stories of the Smithsonian buying and stealing artefacts from around the world and hiding them, or getting rid of them. Bones of giants that were found in North America, which were loaded onto ships and then tossed overboard in the Pacific Ocean, a dozen miles out to sea off California. There used to be old newspaper articles reporting on these kinds of bones, but over the years, these stories were erased from libraries and living memory. Now such stories are classed as fantasy or conspiracy theories… Sorry, I digress. I was working in the stores long after the skull was taken by NASA in the sixties, but I worked with people who talked of it and its supposed powers. Quite some freaky shit!'

Tenzin nodded, his heart racing when he recalled his encounter with it.

'The rumour at the time was that although it was used in a NASA project, there was a secret Mister Big behind it all. From how I remember the gossip went, he had these sharp, long, claw-like fingernails. Strange the things you remember, huh?'

'So where does that leave us, where can I look for the skull, *Shifu*?' Tenzin asked.

'Yes, this doesn't help you much, does it,' Kaz concluded. He craned his head to view the CCTV screen. A police car was pulling up outside his shopfront. 'Strange,' he said, turning back to Tenzin. 'OK, I still have contact with lots of people, people on the inside of agencies but on the outside of life, if you get my drift?'

Tenzin shook his head.

'You know, nerds, geeks, hackers, et cetera. Anyway, a couple of them are sure they have traced the return traffic of The Divinity App to a server.' Kaz passed over a piece of paper with the suspected location written upon it.

In the alleyway directly behind Kaz's school, Laura Lafayette took up position next to the nearest galvanised, wheeled trash bin. Unholstering her gun with her right hand, she squeezed the radio talk button. 'Agent in position, time to knock on the front door.'

Laura had flown in from DC on a CIA private jet as soon as she was informed of the monk's arrival in New York. These details were a little tardy as the target had entered the country on false documents and his entry did not set off any alarms at immigration. It was only when a belated message from the informant in Bhutan was received by General Hill that Laura was told to act.

Whilst she was on the short hop to New York's Floyd Bennett naval airfield, just south of Brooklyn, and a mere six miles from her target's likely location, she planned her raid. Though Hill had made it clear she was to act alone to reduce possible exposure of the covert operation, she was able to call on the NYPD for subtle assistance. Having looked at the target's destination venue, she arranged for a squad car to make a routine call to the premises, in the hope of flushing out her target to the secluded alleyway at the rear of the building. Gleaning the target's phone number from the intel, she managed to get her supporting agency to triangulate his position and have that relayed to her in real-time.

The front door bell was frantically rung and Kaz turned to the camera monitor. 'I don't know what's going on out there, Tenzin, but I don't like it. I suggest you exit now by that door.' He pointed to the rear fire escape furnished with a quick release push bar. 'Good luck, my friend.'

Tenzin stood and bowed his head and curled his hand into a fist, then gently punched his palm. It was a sign of respect, gratitude and departure. As Kaz left to deal with the police, Tenzin read the note, stuffed it in his pocket, and dashed through the emergency exit.

Laura peered over the bin, which was overflowing with rubbish, and heard the release mechanism engage on the other side of the alley. A door opened. She decided to hold station until the door closed behind the target, also eliminating a possible escape route back into the building.

A tall, young Asian man took steps towards her. Barely eight feet separated them when she pounced.

'Stop! Special Agent Lafayette. You're a under arrest. Don't move,' she commanded. She had already decided not to immediately assassinate him; she would think of how to neutralise him after she had spoken to him. *He may possess crucial intel,* she thought.

Fearfully, Tenzin did as he was told and stood still.

'Put your hands up where I can see them,' she ordered.

Tenzin obeyed.

Laura took a step closer, training her gun on the centre of his chest. 'Are you Tenzin Gorji?' she asked.

He slowly nodded his head, trembling.

Laura was attracted to a corner of white paper sticking out of his jeans pocket. She reached for a set of handcuffs with her left hand.

He slowly lowered his right arm towards his pocket.

'Keep your hands up or I'll shoot,' she commanded, but Tenzin continued.

As he tugged on the piece of paper he said, 'You can see I'm not armed, and not a threat.' With the paper in hand, he slowly moved, offering the note to Laura.

She knew she was acting outside the parameters of her training, but sensed he was not threatening. She reached for the note with her left hand, which also held the set of handcuffs, and kept the gun steady in her right hand.

She momentarily looked to the left hand as she pincered the scrap of paper between her thumb and index finger.

Before Laura could refocus on her target, Tenzin struck with the speed of a viper. In one smooth move, he grabbed her left hand, pulled her towards him just enough to strike down on her right wrist, knocking her weapon out of her hand. With a swift crouching movement, he swept his right leg out and across and took out his would-be arrester's legs. Laura fell to the ground, managing to slap her arms down and hold her head up to reduce any impact to the back of her head. Tenzin kicked her gun under the nearest trash bin before nimbly making an about-turn and sprinting down the alley like a gazelle.

Dejected and shaken, Laura picked herself up, dusted herself down, found the scrap of paper and retrieved and re-holstered her gun.

When she got to the front of Kaz's *kwoon*, she noted the local police officers were waiting by their response unit.

Before they could ask her anything, she said, 'Thanks guys, but he scarpered before I got to the back door.' She then jumped in her agency pool car and drove off before the officers could make any sly comments.

Laura took several minutes to replay what had just happened and decide on how to report it. She called General Hill.

'General? Lafayette. I missed the target by just minutes, but I have a lead as to where to intercept him next. I always fancied a trip to Italy!'

18:29 UTC ZUX NEWS 24 LIVE ---- BREAKING NEWS ----

'In summary of the main news items. With over 2.5 billion downloads in less than a month, The Divinity App has broken a plethora of internet records and looks set to raise the bar even further. Demand for the app has increased in rate ever since it was finally endorsed by Pope Leo XIV last week, laying to rest any speculation that the Pope was at odds with this titan of apps. And social media is still awash with good news and unity in praise for this 'programme from heaven', as one popular hashtag labels it.

'In separate news, authorities from many Western countries and beyond have reported a recent but dramatic increase in sectarian violence on followers of minority religions. It is something that is being monitored, but ZUX News 24 has been assured by official sources that these events have no correlation to the extraordinary usage of the Catholic Church's Divinity App. In fact, such links have been unanimously declared misinformation by government media, both traditional and social alike. Social media companies have announced a ramping up of actions against those who spread such disinformation, and dissenters are being branded enemies of the newly formed, virtuous social order.'

18

Over Corsica, En Route to Rome 23rd May 2022

'Thanks again, Angel. This contract opportunity could be the making of us. The potential is enormous,' Tinks said, in between sips of lager and enjoying views of the evening sun lowering in the sky, which provided a backdrop to the Corsican landscape.

'It's lucky circumstance that's brought us to this point, Tinks. I just did what I thought was right at the time and this has been the result. It's fate,' Sam said, modestly. 'You got all the preparatory notes collated?'

'Yep. All ready to lay out what we can do for any size of operation,' Tinks replied, contented.

'Good evening, this is Captain Jones here from the flight deck,' the captain said. 'As you may have noticed, we have just started our descent and now we are over the Tyrrhenian Sea, but it seems we there is developing weather between us and Rome's Fiumicino Airport. Air traffic control has decided to divert all flights to Pisa – ' Captain Jones ended her broadcast abruptly as the Boeing 737 dropped like a stone and lurched to the starboard.

Chaos ensued on the aircraft as it hit clear air turbulence, losing hundreds of feet in a handful of seconds. The plane banged heavily as it reconnected with more stable air, arresting its apparent free-fall. Passengers screamed and overhead lockers flung open, discharging luggage, personal possessions, drinks and snacks. They were strewn over the cabin after having hit and ricocheted off the ceiling. Two cabin staff and two passengers lay injured where they had landed.

The flight deck intercom bonged and the seatbelt signs came on. The third cabin crew member answered the call as a priority, knowing it would be the captain. 'Cabin status, please,' Captain Jones requested.

'It's carnage back here, Captain. And it looks like we have four persons injured. Two men have got up and are caring for two of them,' the steward replied.

'How badly are those injured. Can you tell?'

'No, I've not had a chance to get to them, but at least one looks unresponsive and there's blood smeared on the ceiling as well.'

'Thank you, Ryan. Please assist the injured and report back when you can,' Captain Jones calmly commanded.

'Francis?' said Lorenzo, curator of the Monastero San Francesco in Cori, gently gaining Francis' attention.

Irritated with the interruption from his note-taking, in which he was building his defence for his upcoming hearing, he looked up from his candlelit writing desk and his attention was drawn to a corner of the office where Elion's team had installed a cabinet-sized server, something to do with The Divinity App, he was told. Naturally unhappy about its placement in his monastery and even though he had placed a blanket over the front of it, it still infuriated him that he could make out the flashing of a plethora of small green and red LED lights through the material. He locked eyes on his curator and invited further communication by raising his eyebrows.

'I've just heard from my nephew, Luca, the one who works in air traffic control?'

Francis nodded.

'He let me know that all flights into Rome have been diverted, so your guests will be sent to Pisa. He reckons that by the time the backlog of extra arrivals has been processed, your guests will end up being taken to a local hotel and will therefore not arrive until sometime in the morning.'

'Thank you, Lorenzo. That does help me as I am in my flow at the moment. I shall see you at breakfast. Sleep well and God bless you.'

'God bless you too, Francis.'

'This is Speedbird 354, PAN-PAN, PAN-PAN, PAN-PAN,' Captain Jones broadcast the international urgency signal to Rome's air traffic control. 'We have a medical emergency, one seriously injured passenger with a suspected spinal injury and three others with minor injuries following clear air turbulence. Request to continue heading to land at Rome FCO and not reroute to Pisa, I repeat, not reroute to Pisa. We see a gap in the weather giving us an acceptable landing window, over.'

'Roger, Speedbird 354, that is copied. Maintain this frequency. Standing by for information. You are cleared to proceed to FCO. Runways 16L and 16R both available. Emergency response teams have been notified.'

'Everything's OK, please remain seated,' Ryan explained to passengers as he made his way to Sam and the injured passenger in the aisle.

'OK, Ryan, it's imperative that we keep this guy as still as possible. The makeshift head restraint should keep his neck aligned but someone needs to support it until the paramedics arrive,' Sam explained. After confirming that this middle-aged passenger lying along the aisle, had a high probability of having spinal injury, Sam and Tinks braced their patient as well as possible, to avoid any movement, by using an inflated lifejacket to create a horseshoe support, from one shoulder, over the crown of his head and down to the other shoulder. Sam then sandwiched the lifejacket between his knees, locking the man's head still. Tinks restrained the patient's legs to keep his spine in line.

Ryan was looking very shaky and Sam spotting that shock was taking a hold of the steward. 'Now, Ryan, you've been brilliant,' said Sam, trying to stop him sinking under the strain, 'but I need to know from your captain if I'm alright to stay positioned like this until we land? We mustn't let his head move.'

Ryan nodded and went to speak with the captain.

A minute later, the deathly silence in the cabin was cut by the bing-bong of the public address system. 'This is Captain Jones again. As you are well aware, we hit rare but heavy, clear air turbulence, but everything is well with the aircraft and we expect to be on the ground in Rome in around nine minutes' time. We know that the cabin is in a mess and there are injured passengers and crew on board, but we will have further medical assistance as soon as we touch down in Rome. Please be aware that there are two passengers in the aisle, who must not be disturbed until the medics are on board. We appreciate your continued calm in this difficult situation and will give you further instruction upon landing. Thank you.'

The wipers were going ten to the dozen and the wheels whooshed as the car drove through a mini-river of stormwater. Tinks found himself squinting through the rental car's windscreen, helping him focus on the road ahead. Frequent flashes of lightning lit the sky.

'I've never seen a storm quite as intense as this one, mate,' Tinks declared.

'Me neither, but then I've never been to the tropics proper; I hear they get some tremendous ones there.' Sam checked his phone map again. 'Cori is just a few kilometres ahead.'

'It's just gone ten. We're a bit late, shame there was no car for us at the airport.'

'As we said, they thought we'd be in Pisa by now. Still, we'll meet this cardinal soon – the app man,' Sam joked.

'Do you reckon he uses the app?' Tinks mused.

'Who knows. Maybe all priests and cardinals have avoided it, you know, because of…'

Tinks cut Sam off. 'Yeah, yeah, yeah. You can't tar them all with the same brush.'

'You should try opening your eyes, Tinks. It's now being reported back home that the app is rewarding users who speak or act against non-Christians or those without the app installed.'

'I think you'll find that to be "misinformation",' Tinks said with confidence.

'Just because the ZUX News calls it that, it doesn't mean it's true. Look at all the reports of people having their social media accounts frozen or deleted just because they're now speaking out about the app as being a tool for inciting violence and disharmony, the exact opposite of that which it claims to support.'

'OK, OK,' Tinks said, condescendingly. 'Ah! Cori!' He pointed at the town's sign as they drove past.

'All I'd say is take a look at the non-mainstream media; there are tons of proven examples. The app's a total scam. It's a karma con,' Sam finished, pleased with his piece of oral alliteration. 'Take the next on the right and the monastery should be at the top of the hill, right in front of us.'

They parked up and ran alongside the perimeter stone wall, their raincoats held over their heads to afford a little shelter from the torrential rain. They ascended the steps from the pavement to the car park in front of the monastery and ran toward what looked like the main door. The two-storey monastery's façade was mostly rendered but aged and patchy in places and it had segmented, stone arch supports over the doors and windows. Sam thumped hard on the venerable door as hard as possible, but due to how solid it was, and the level of ambient storm noise, he did not have confidence he had been heard. After banging again, Sam looked along the front of the building and saw that it became a wing to the right. It not only had a first-floor balcony, which would provide them some shelter from the rain, but a chink of light emanated from a small pair of closed shutters at ground level.

'We might have luck here,' Sam said, hopefully, as they were finally out of the worst of the weather. Discarding his drenched coat, he knelt to peer through the crack between the shutters. He moved his head from right to left to scan a warmly lit room, which he guessed was located in the basement. It had just a few religious wall adornments, a writing chair and desk and a wing-backed, leather chair, which was positioned with its back to Sam and sat on a crimson rug adjacent to a roaring fire.

'See anything?' Tinks asked, impatiently.

'Not yet, it looks like a basement office.' Sam's attention was attracted to a movement on the rug. 'Hang on...' Adjusting his head to get the best view possible, he determined that it was not a rug at all, but what could be the lower half of a cardinal's crimson cassock. He saw the gentle rise and fall of the material, then a sudden movement whereby Sam saw a left forearm appear and slam down on the arm of the chair. There seemed to be a string in the hand, like a necklace. Sam could not believe what he was seeing – he was not sure at all – and he kept quiet until he had more evidence.

'Well?' Tinks demanded.

'Shhh!' Sam abruptly replied. The cassock started to move much more now, rising as if a helium balloon was being lifted up into the red fabric, until the cloth finally dropped to the floor, revealing a young teenage boy wiping his mouth, on his knees in between two seated legs of whoever was sitting in the wing-backed chair.

'Fucking hell!' Sam seethed, as he recoiled from kneeling, but in doing so, allowed his foot to flick out and catch the shutters. He leaped to his feet, shocked and sickened. 'There was a fucking boy giving some man a blow job!'

Tinks dropped to look for himself. It took him a couple of seconds to get the right position to scan the room, before declaring, 'Bullshit, Sam!' Tinks rose back onto his feet and got close to Sam's face, 'There's no one there, what are you trying to do?'

'I tell you, God's honest truth, it was some fucking paedo down there in a red priest's outfit. He had some necklace or beads in his left hand, sick fucker,' Sam responded curtly.

'You're fucking seeing things, Angel. All that freaky shit in your head, you're seeing things. Don't you fuck up this meeting, Angel. Don't you dare. This could be the big one for me!'

'Ah, there you go! It's all about you! I set up this meeting for us, but now it's just for you. Thanks, mate. I'm not here to fuck up the meeting, but I know what I just saw and I'm not making it up.'

The sound of large steel bolts sliding cut through the now receding storm and interrupted their argument. Picking up their soaking coats, they jogged towards the noise coming from the front door. It opened and a frail old man dressed in black and holding an umbrella, peered to the right and then to the left towards them.

'My name is Lorenzo. I look after the monastery,' he said.

'Hello, it's Angel and Taylor from England. Sorry, we're a bit late,' Sam replied.

'Oh, but we were told you were not coming tonight. Not a problem, let me show you to your quarters.'

19

The Mediterranean Sea, off South-East Coast of France 24th May 2022

'General Hill. I want an update on our hide-and-seek issue with Lafayette and the monk,' Elion rasped.

'Yes, sir,' Hill chirpily replied, even though he had just been woken in the middle of the night. 'Well, Lafayette has set up base in a village near Rome. She is on the lookout for Gorji and is ready to act on any intelligence we can supply her with. Gorji has some good people working with him, he's like a ghost,' Hill reported, uneasily.

'This is not what I want to hear. It seems with all the resources at the Americans' disposal, you still fall short. I can tell you that Gorji is already in Italy, and my security team expect he will appear at his destination later on today.' A quick wheezy breath, then Elion continued, 'Now, if your lady asset has some spare time this morning, I have a quick job for her. She's well placed for what I have in mind.'

'Thank you, Cardinal, thank you for your time this morning. We'll put together a proposal and have it to you within the week,' Tinks said with pride.

'You are more than welcome, my child. It is only a little recompense for the kindness and skilfulness you showed me back in London, Sam Angel,' Francis said, with genuine gratitude.

'Like I have said, I was on autopilot, anyone would have done the same,' Sam said.

Sam and Tinks left for the airport, more than the tiniest bit disappointed that an audience with the Pope had not been possible, but Tinks was simultaneously bubbling at the prospect of tendering for such a large and lucrative first aid training contract. Sam was very aware that this contract could propel Tinks to develop his company into a large multi-national company but he couldn't hide his reservations.

'What a sick old man,' Sam uttered.

'Even if you did see what you said you saw last night, there's no proof it was Cardinal Francis,' Tinks postured.

'He had the same rosary beads in his hand this morning and the only adults we saw were him and the curator. The man gave me the creeps.'

The rest of the short journey back to Fiumicino Airport mostly passed in silence. Tinks planned elements of his contract and Sam mulled over what he had seen and what he really wanted to say and do to the Cardinal.

The friends found two chairs airside in the airport. Tinks sat down in a surprisingly quiet area for a major airport and started assembling his contract tender on his tablet. With forty minutes left before boarding, Sam wandered off to buy coffees.

As he passed the information kiosk en route to the café, he noticed three figures having an animated interaction on the other side of a heavily-tinted set of doors, clearly adorned with no-entry signs. Two were uniformed and the third seemed to be a lady gesticulating impatiently, but he continued walking.

A minute into queuing for coffee, Sam heard the public address system.

'*Bing-bong.* Please would Sam Angel come to the information desk, Sam Angel to the information desk. Thank you.'

Perplexed, he complied and walked back to the kiosk and addressed the member of staff.

'Hello, I'm –,'

'Sam Angel?' Laura asked, holding up her CIA warrant badge, assisted by two uniformed officers.

Taken by surprise, Sam turned quickly towards her. 'Yes, I'm Sam… Wait! It's you, from London, that bombing. Laura?'

'Yes, Special Agent Lafayette, if you don't mind. Look, I need you to come with me.'

'Where? Why? What's this about?'

'I can't talk here. There's an interview room through that door,' she said, pointing it out.

They calmly walked towards the door when a child playing with an A-frame advertising board, pushed it a bit too hard and it collapsed to their left. Laura and the two officers took a reactive glance round, but Sam had other ideas. He ran as fast as possible through the nearby duty-free shop, hooking his loose arm through the second backpack strap to secure his bag as he moved.

Laura took off after him, followed by airport security, who radioed for assistance as they ran. He sprinted through the shop and out of a far side exit. Spotting a member of the cleaning team unlock a service door, he barged past the worker and disappeared down a featureless, narrow corridor.

'Stop, Angel!' Laura shouted down the corridor.

Sam turned left at the end and headed towards a glazed double door. Spotting a large green button on the wall to the side, he whacked the button and the doors opened inwards. Crossing the threshold, he appeared to have come out at a disused gate. In front of him were rows of empty seats. To his left was a glass wall, through which he could see several security guards running towards the gate, behind him he could hear the frantic squeaking of Laura's running shoes. To the right was an aircraft boarding bridge. He had no choice. He turned right. He passed the unmanned checking station and ran down the gentle incline of the ramp. He approached an elbow in the bridge. Straight ahead of him, a horizontal red rope created a weak barrier to a set of built-in descending steps. He had a choice to go down them or else take to the right and carry on down the bridge. Under pressure to escape, he took the easier path and continued to the right.

'Angel. Give up! There's nowhere to go,' Laura shouted, still trying to catch up with him.

Sam's pace slowed as the light at the end of the tunnel grew larger. He could see there was about a ten metre drop down to the apron. If he jumped, he would break his legs. He knew the game was up, so he raised up his hands and turned to face Laura, who was brandishing her gun.

'OK, now turn back around and put your hands behind your back,' Laura commanded. He did as he was told and was handcuffed.

In the interview room, Laura ordered the security detail out, leaving just the two of them in the room.

'That wasn't smart, Angel. You knew you would be caught,' she stated.

'Maybe. I should have gone down those stairs and taken my chances on the apron,' he said, rueing his decision. 'But when I saw you, I just panicked. The last time we met I found out I was possibly caught up in some shit. Then it cooled off but now we meet again, I didn't like the idea of having a chat with you. What's up this time?'

'To be honest, I don't know. I had orders to find you,' she looked at her watch.

'Someplace you've got to be?'

'No. Actually, someplace *you've* got to be. We have a few minutes, so what have you been up to, Angel?'

'Nothing. I've just come over to Italy by invitation of Cardinal Francis, you know, the guy we saved in London.'

'More like you saved him. I had my gun trained on you at the time, I seem to remember,' she credited him but frowned and then rubbed her forehead. 'First you were identified as a friendly in Bhutan, then a suspect in London and now being called for from high up. I can't work it out,' she mumbled to herself.

'High up? What are you talking about?'

Looking at her watch again, she said, 'OK, time to go. Come on.'

'Go where?' Sam vainly protested.

'Elion, everything is falling apart. I'm having to defend your actions to save my position as Cardinal, the word on the ground is that The Divinity App is creating increasing social tension, division and even violence and I'm not sure if my visitors last night saw something they shouldn't have,' Francis blurted out with some embarrassment.

'Firstly, at the least it was *our* actions you're having to defend, but in reality, you took your decisions with my assistance,' Elion said. 'Secondly, there is nothing wrong with the app, it is all going to plan. Thirdly, your sickness damages people all around you, damages your Church and damages our relationship. I have decided to remove you from the chess board for now.'

'Wh-what does that mean?' Francis asked, deeply worried. Was his life in danger?

'You and your brother Paolo will be picked up in half an hour. Bring only once suitcase each of personal items and pack for warm weather. You will not hear from me again until I am ready for you.'

As the line went dead, Francis set to work, reluctantly following his latest orders.

Laura parked on the right under one of the large Italian stone pines lining the cobbled road outside Monastero San Francesco, fifty metres from its main steps. A quiet village, with quaint, narrow, cobbled vicolo lanes weaving across the hillside, Laura loved its historic charm. She chose the position for her rental car for its shade and making it less easy for someone to spot her in the comparative darkness, especially as she slinked down in her seat. While waiting for the monk to appear, she tried to piece together the strange events that had happened over the past four years. She cast her mind back... *General Hill and my trips to what is now Space Force HQ... Bhutan... the strangeness of the skull... the new techniques needed to harness its power... the app project... the attempt on my life and the murder of dear Jacob Rozen... crossing paths, three times now, with Sam Angel, a seemingly decent ex-military first-aider who keeps appearing at the wrong place at the wrong time; no, that cannot be coincidence. And now I have to terminate this Kung Fu monk.* She closed her eyes, thinking hard. *There's only one connecting thread throughout this, and that's Elion. Who is he? What is he up to? He's just playing with lives, billions of them, in fact. Am I being played by him too?*

A bright white taxi drove up the road from behind. As it slowly passed her, she casually looked to the left to see if there were any clues to its fare. It caught her immediate interest. The taxi from Rome pulled up metres in front of her, stopping outside the monastery's entrance.

'Bingo!' she whispered. There was no mistaking the man getting out; a young, athletic and traditionally-dressed Tibetan in a maroon monk's robe. *He stuck out like a Sequoia in a corn field,* she thought. She held the door tightly as she pulled the release catch, so as to not make any sound as she got out of her car. Slowly, she made her way along the perimeter wall of the monastery. Unholstering her gun, she stopped at the steps and took a darting look around the corner towards the entrance of the building. There was no sign of her target. Another look and still no sign.

'What do you want?' an Asian voice came from above.

Laura span her gun around and looked up, over the top of the wall, and saw her man, Tenzin Gorji, standing in a wide stance. Taking the safety catch off was all the cue he needed to disappear.

Laura ran up the steps and raced across the car park,

glimpsing his robe as Tenzin turned left at the corner end of the monastery. She sprinted after him and soon found herself in a labyrinth of eerily-deserted, cobbled vicolo. She slowed to a standstill in the middle of a crossroads. Brandishing her gun, she systematically turned, staccato fashion, in ninety-degree, anticlockwise sweeps, her heightened senses straining to provide a clue for the whereabouts of her target. Just as she turned away from one vicolo, a flash of maroon caught her eye. She spun back and studied that vicolo. She swiftly pivoted a hundred and eighty degrees but a noise of a bucket tipping over from behind cried for her attention. She caught another flash of the robe disappearing right at the next junction.

'That's impossible,' she affirmed to herself. With her firearm still raised, she checked the four routes sequentially and started seeing fleeting glimpses of the monk's robe disappear around corners and dart into doorways, from both left to right and vice-versa, again and again, and at increasing frequencies.

Dizzy, she stopped spinning. 'This is not happening,' she tried to convince herself. 'What's going on, have I been drugged?' She breathed heavily and felt confused, queasy and more than a little panicked by the impossibility she was witnessing.

'Laura!' she heard a male voice say from behind.

In a heightened state of confusion, she felt in imminent danger. One last spin. A vision of maroon stood before her, just three feet away. It towered over her. The bald monk from Brooklyn. She lifted her weapon higher and aimed it at the monk's head. She held her breath. She squeezed the trigger. The gun fired.

Tenzin's toned frame quickly fell back and hit the floor. Laura watched but did not hear the hollow thud of his body connecting with the cobbled vicolo. She became wholly mindful of the scene before her. Looking at her target, she first stalled a wave of rising vomit from exiting. Examining his forehead, the deep-red, bullet hole was dead centre, just above his eyebrow line. Thick, dark blood was starting to spread over the cobbles from the back of his head.

Oh shit, I've killed someone, I've killed a monk! She started to realise the enormity of what she had done. She was frozen for several moments, caught up in her own inner narrative. 'Get a grip, Laura,' she told herself quietly and her CIA training began fighting to the fore. Crouching beside the body, she started rummaging in his robe in vain for an identity or other useful documents or clues. She took a cursory glance around to make sure she was alone. She was not.

Shakily holding her gun up to an old lady dressed in black, who was approaching from the direction from which Laura had just discharged her firearm, Laura called out, in an unsteady voice, 'CIA Special Agent. Stop where you are!'

Her command was ignored. The old lady slowly continued her path until she was very close. She crouched down in front of Laura. 'Put your gun down, I am no threat, as you can feel,' she said with kindness and humility. She spoke English with a thick Italian accent.

Laura lowered her gun. She was overcome by a feeling of peace and harmony in the presence of this lady. Her gaze was transfixed on her. She felt calm in this worst moment of her life since being told her parents had been murdered. Tucked under the lady's shawled head, were flowing flame-coloured locks. And her eyes. Orange eyes. A collage of autumn colours encapsulated by a soft brown outer ring. *Who are you? What are you?* she thought.

'Laura, listen to me,' the woman said, placing her hand on Laura's shoulder. 'Listen to me.' Once Laura came out of her trance, the old lady continued. 'Take photos of Tenzin Gorji. Send them to your seniors. Report your mission fulfilled. Report your wish to stay in Europe to continue your convalescence. Then go home.'

Laura realised she was blindly starting to comply, but her usual logical thinking was impaired. She reached for the phone and took the evidence she needed. She sent it to General Hill along with a text notifying him she was taking more time off work. Without looking back at the monk or the old lady, she walked back towards the monastery and her car. Bewildered, she tried to get some order in her mind over what had happened. *Too much to process*, she concluded, but this did not stop her from trying over and over.

Collapsing into her car and slamming the door shut, she looked at herself in the rearview mirror, aware of the vacantness of her stare and how her jaw dropped. She tried to think what she needed to do next. For the first time in her adult life, she was stumped. She felt numb, fragile and befuddled, so much so, she barely registered the passenger door gently being opened.

A figure crouched in the doorway. 'Hello, Laura.'

Laura slowly turned. She saw the maroon-robed monk. She screamed and raised her hands to her head, and sobbed at the continued incredulity she was experiencing.

'I am not the enemy, Laura. I am peaceful and unarmed,' Tenzin calmly said. 'Let me drive out of Cori and I can explain everything. We need to talk. Urgently.'

In a corner booth of a quiet café in the outskirts of Rome, Laura gulped down a shot of brandy, swiftly followed by a slurp of hot, sweet coffee. Unaccustomed to liquor and even sugar in the coffee, she felt the need for external help to calm her jangled emotions. Having barely exchanged any words during the journey to the café, Laura now felt ready to start making sense of the day.

'So, let me get this straight, we first met on the Tibet-Bhutan disputed border. I witnessed my CIA partner shoot you off your pony. I thought you were dead, and it took a long time for me to forgive my partner for firing his gun at you.'

'Yes, Laura,' Tenzin serenely replied, sniffing a pinch of snuff up each nostril. Snapping the snuff-box shut, he showed it to Laura. 'See where the bullet struck? I repaired the holes but wanted to keep the dents as a reminder.'

'You were so lucky,' she said, running her fingers over the damaged box and feeling a stab of shock, recalling the moment Rozen had fired his gun.

'Luck? No, Laura, it was fate, karma in action,' Tenzin corrected her.

'So the bullet went right through this box?'

'The box took most of the energy out of the shot, so the bullet only lodged in my chest muscle,' he explained. Then pointing at the embossed Buddha image on the front of the box, he added, 'The Buddha allowed me to die and rebirth again that same day.'

Laura continued her analysis, 'Then, about four years later, I'm tasked to kill you and I track you down in New York, but my intuition guided me to talk to you, to try and understand the situation which had led to the order to neutralise you. You outsmart me and escape. I'm surprised I didn't recognise you then, but then I guess I only saw your face for seconds in that dark, Bhutan forest before you were shot.'

'And I was wearing a fur hat,' Tenzin added.

'I then track you down to Cori and in a confused state, I shoot you dead. There was no question about that, you were dead with blood oozing out of your head. But I didn't, or did I?' Her brain ached. She had never felt so confused. 'And that old lady! Her eyes! How did she know about me, you, my mission?' She asked the passing waitress for another shot of brandy.

'You did not shoot me, Laura. I am here before you, I am fine,' he reassured her.

'How, Tenzin? How?' she pleaded.

'I am not sure exactly what happened. I was in the village road, running away from you. I saw the lady and she told me to walk back to the monastery via a different route and wait for your return. She knew I was here to see Cardinal Francis at the monastery but said that he had left for good. I just did as she said. She had an aura of trust, I could sense she had a very high vibration, like that of the Dalai Lama.'

Not completely understanding what Tenzin meant about the lady, Laura continued to recount what she saw. There had been illusions of him everywhere and in a confused state, she thought she had killed him. She repeated what the old lady had said.

When the second brandy arrived, she sipped it, but soon she left it alone as she tuned into its taste and it did not agree with her palate. 'So, what are you doing, Tenzin? Do you have a plan or a mission? Are you working for someone?'

'I think we are going to work together from now on. I feel your vibration is high, you are a person of honour. I am seeking the skull, the one you and your partner tried killing me for.' He continued to explain the need to recover the artefact for the good of humanity, because it would bring about the destruction of The Divinity App.

Looking around to check no one was in earshot, Laura quietly let on, 'You know, I headed the team that created that app. The skull has a terrifying power and I thought that the project would just be consigned to the bin, like most top-secret projects. When it was first released, I was quite shocked but also, I felt pride in what we'd achieved. However, this was short-lived because recently I could see that there was a clear link between the app and the rising violence and disharmony that is now sweeping around most of the globe.'

'Where is the skull located?' Tenzin asked.

'I don't know. But the only place I can think of to start searching for clues is my old office in Cyber City, in London, the one that has been blown up. The whole operation was moved to a secret location when it was just about complete. Also, there's someone else I've kept coming across these past few years, but I cannot for the life of me connect how he fits in,' she said, rubbing both temples to try relieve the puzzling nature of all these loose ends. 'But I do know who's behind the app, though,' she teased, raising her eyebrows.

'He goes by the name of Elion, but his real name is…' Laura told Tenzin all she knew about this elusive figure.

20

Monte Carlo, Monaco
25th May 2022

Sam stirred and blinked his eyes open, trying to focus. He felt groggy and there was an unpleasant taste in his mouth, like a hangover except he had not been drinking. He looked around the bedroom he found himself in. It was huge, vast. Every fitting and detail exuded opulence, with marble flooring and gold plating, the use of embroidered, pure white fabrics, full height folding doors leading to a magnificent, modern balcony. He could see sun loungers, large plant pots containing dwarf Cypress trees, finely fashioned into perfect spirals. He got out of bed, still wearing his dishevelled shirt and trousers following his previous meeting with Cardinal Francis and walked towards the balcony. Pushing the main door open, he stepped onto the balcony and absorbed magnificent, sun-drenched views that were unobstructed due to the fully glazed-topped parapet wall. Overlooking the sparkling, azure Mediterranean Sea, he took in a deep breath and was instantly transported back to his childhood holidays in the South of France, where the air had been heavy with the olfaction of a cocktail of pine, sea, coffee and fresh bread.

The balcony wrapped around the building; to the right was a marble-tiled, infinity swimming pool, with matching sunken jacuzzi. Sam started walking around to the left, affording him views of Casino de Monte-Carlo, a mid-nineteenth-century edifice to the high society establishment of the day. It was with this reference point that Sam worked out exactly where he was; the exclusive Hôtel de Paris Monte-Carlo. Looking back towards the hotel, he saw he was adjacent to a sumptuous lounge and dining room, again finely decorated with both wall-mounted and pedestalled artworks. He made his way to the open doors of this section of the accommodation.

'Good morning, Sam Angel,' a French voice emanated from one of two large, dark suited men sitting on one of the light grey sofas which were positioned around a central coffee table.

'Who are you? Why have you kidnapped me?' Sam demanded in as much as an authoritative tone he could muster in his still-drowsy state.

The man on the furthest couch stood and adjusting his beltline, which revealed a firearm, he replied, 'Kidnapped is a little strong a term, my Angel.' He proceeded to pick up a paper bag from a clothes designer from the floor next to him and offered it to Sam. 'I suggest you take a shower and you'll find a new wardrobe for you in here.'

Sam took the bag and tried to get his brain in gear to decide his next move. Having seen this guy was armed and that both of the men filled their suit jackets with muscular bulges, Sam surmised they were some serious security detail. Doing nothing stupid at this time was the wisest conclusion.

'Last I remember, I was at Rome Airport. I've obviously been drugged and now I wake up in Monte Carlo,' Sam said, patting his pockets for his for his phone to check the time and date. 'Where's my phone? What day is it?' he asked.

'Your phone is safe. It's Wednesday the twenty-fifth of May, and yes, we sedated you and flew you here from Rome.'

'OK, so I've only been here one night?'

The man nodded, then added, 'Not a bad place to stay for a night, n'est pas? The Princess Grace Diamond Suite at the Hôtel de Paris Monte-Carlo. Maybe you should be saying "merci" or something,' he said facetiously, finishing with a small laugh and turning to look at his stockier, coffee-drinking companion.

Sam ignored the comment and asked, 'Where am I going?'

'To see a great man who has been looking forward to meeting you again for years,' was the reply.

Clearly, he was not going to get any more information for now, so Sam left to find the bathroom.

The Riva Aquarama tender effortlessly cut through the crystal clear, calm harbour water, passing yacht after superyacht, many of which were moored to afford their wealthy passengers the spectacle of FIA's Formula One race weekend at Monaco. The morning's build up to the classic car racing had begun, but the drone of the vintage race cars receded with every stroke of each of the two, four hundred horsepower engines that were nestled under the rear sundeck of the motorboat. Sheathed in mahogany and varnished to accentuate the allure of the tropical hardwood grain, the small boat was one of the most beautiful Sam had ever seen, let alone taken a trip in. However, these details did not gain much traction in his mind and his thoughts were racing to make sense of the predicament he found himself in.

Picking out the prominent position of the luxurious hotel the three had recently departed, Sam analysed options to escape his captors.   But as the mainland receded to his left, he resigned himself to staying put. As the tender started to heave as they passed the protected confines of the harbour, he perched in the white leather seat and replayed moments that may have led to this point, whilst unconsciously starting to sweat from anxiety and the increasing warmth of the sun. He breathed through his mouth to avoid smelling one of the minder's strong body odour, now being downwind from the offender.

Having met Special Agent Lafayette again yesterday, Sam knew she had a lot to do with all the recent strange events in his life, although, he still could not see how Amelie fitted into all of this. Drawing little conclusion, he looked out to sea to ascertain where they were headed. The two stooges had refused to say one word since their meeting in the hotel suite's lounge earlier that morning. Craning his head to see past his chaperones, he discerned perhaps a dozen or more mega-yachts anchored in a hotch-potch fashion in the zone around the harbour. The exclusive Riva boat kept a straight course, staying away from these mega-yachts. A few minutes on, the tender was just passing the last of the gaggle of ocean giants. On the horizon, there was only one vessel left before the endless expanse of the sea.

So that's my destination, Sam thought.

Another ten minutes passed and Sam had watched the craft grow as they travelled closer. *Infinitus* was modestly denoted next to the nose of the bow. Compared to some of the superyachts he had just seen and although ultra-modern, this yacht did not appear as brash as some. It was more understated somehow, perhaps due it its shimmering blue, grey and green coating, which provided an almost perfect sea camouflage.

The seemingly lead security guy made a quick radio call, but Sam noticed he used a military-grade satellite communication device, and not a simple walkie-talkie. This gave him more concerns that whomever resided on this mega-yacht must be a seriously well-connected individual.

A sizeable section of the midship's hull opened up in a gull-wing manner, leaving a hole into which the Riva was manoeuvred. The three occupants remained seated on the boat while the hull side door closed. With a smooth whirr of another motor, the tender was then elevated to a level in line with the grated walkway. Another mechanical noise followed and the area below the small Riva was pumped empty of the sea water.

Sam was led up into the heart of the vessel, ascending three flights of steps and eventually entering an expansive, open-plan living space. There was a full width, nautical-styled wooden bar to the rear of the forward bulkhead wall and views out to the rear deck area. The deck had been covered with exquisitely varnished timber boards, running in a bow to stern orientation interspersed with black caulking, but that regular pattern was interrupted by the outline shape of the large swimming pool which occupied the centre portion. The back of the deck, nearer the stern, was fitted with a large seating area on the left and two full-glass hot-tubs to the right, with both areas covered by triangular, canvas sunshades.

'Stay here,' Sam was ordered. He stood with the bar behind him so he could keep an eye on what was going on outside. One of the suited men walked down the deck to the pool where a young, dark-haired lady was swimming. A crew member dressed in a white polo shirt, shorts and deck shoes was saying something to her and holding a towelling dressing gown. The woman looked reluctant to get out of the pool. In what Sam could only think was an optical illusion, the woman made her way towards the deckhand but at the same time, looked like she was rising out of the water, effortlessly. Within thirty seconds, Sam witnessed the swimming pool completely disappear and the pool floor rise to seamlessly meet with the rest of the deck. Two more deckhands appeared with pole-mounted squeegees, expelling the remnants of pool water to a drain. The original crew member helped the slender swim-suited woman put on the gown. She looked to be around six months' pregnant.

The only telltale sign of the existence of a pool was an outline in black edging, forming a large, elongated figure of eight-type shape. The other point Sam observed was that the floor of the pool carried a golden, three-dimensional design. *Like an infinity sign except with one end smaller than the other,* Sam thought.

The pregnant woman walked into the living area and headed to the door at the far side of the bar. Before she exited the room, she made a point of holding her gaze at Sam as she squeezed water out of her long hair.

'He's ready for you now,' the suited man said, catching Sam by surprise as he was distracted by the pregnant woman.

Sam was led by one of the men and closely followed by the other to a set of white leather furniture to the rearmost point of the deck. Sitting in a shaded, single armchair, was a stout man in a light-coloured linen suit. At first, Sam only noticed his legs because the man was engrossed reading *Le Monde* newspaper. Sam then observed the man's hands; thick-set but with smooth, moley skin, which had a grey, almost translucent hue. More disturbing were the fingernails; bulbous, thick, monotone yellow. *Uncomfortably long*, Sam thought. They ended in sharp points, curling down slightly at their ends. They

216

looked claw-like, from the animal world, but his thoughts were curtailed as high levels of anxiety regained control of his awareness.

The security guard let out a gentle cough and the seated man neatly folded the newspaper and lay it down on the adjacent seat.

'Sam Angel, sir,' the minder said and subsequently both guards retreated to a nearby station.

Sam stepped forward and tentatively held his hand out to shake the man's outreached hand. Sam noticed it was unexpectedly cool and dry, like the feel of a lizard.

'So pleased to meet you again, Sam. It seems forever since we last met.'

'Again? Who are you?' Sam said, more perplexed than ever.

'Please, take a seat here, we have so much to catch up on. Help yourself to a refreshment, too,' gesturing to the bottle of water and set of glasses on the table between them.

Sam did not move.

'Call me Elion, Sam.'

'Elion. Why? What's your real name. And who are you? What do you want with me,' Sam demanded.

In the silence between them, Sam noticed the deep rattle of Elion's breath. He studied the man, analysing his pale, smooth skin, and the fact that, in many ways, he looked very old but also conversely young by some measure. The man had a full set of teeth, but they were stained and stump-like, and the top row were of a similarly small size, almost like yellowed milk teeth. The crown of his head was elongated, like photographs he'd seen of tribespeople who had been head bound. That, coupled with his talons, Sam had the distressing feeling that he was not in the presence of a normal human being. Without further dwelling, Sam's attention was pulled towards the inverted plasma bag half full of a bright red solution, connected to the crook in Elion's left arm.

'You will have so many questions, and will feel, quite understandably, agitated as to the situation in which you find yourself. Please, sit and permit me to start giving you some explanations and then you can ask me whatever questions you wish,' Elion said calmy, as he leaned forward, forming a creepy smile.

Sam nodded, sat down and took the opportunity to study Elion's face at closer quarters. For someone clearly in his advanced years, Sam noted his short back and sides haircut was recently coiffured and there was still some natural colour in his hair. The skin around his eyes betrayed his age, as the deep bags looked like they had formed over many decades. However, the clarity of his dark grey irises and the pureness of the whites of his eyes was normal for someone perhaps less than half his age, in Sam's medical experience. Sam concluded Elion was a physical enigma.

'My birth name is Maximilian Adelino Zelig Frederick Rotzburg III. For ease and for good reason to my fellow community here on the planet, I am known as Elion, translated, meaning Sun. It is for good reason, for I am akin to the Sun in terms of my power, gravitas and position in this world. And please do not confuse this description and write it off as an old man's ego; it is fact,' Elion said. He sat back in his chair and beathed in noisily. 'Now, getting to the nub of our meeting; why are you here? Firstly, please accept my apologies for the unceremonious journey I understand you had from Rome. Do believe me that I would not have wanted it done in the way it was, but I leave such matters to my team, and they decide the means.'

As Sam opened his mouth to speak, Elion raised a hand to stop him and continued, 'Let me give you some preamble; this will provide some context for what you will learn.'

'The world is getting a more frenetic place to live just as

the lives of the masses become more barren, just hollow lives. Technology is advancing, soon Unicoin will be on everyone's lips as the one-world digital currency, and artificial intelligence will garner significant standing in society just as the digital identities take hold. We will encounter more political upheavals, wars, religious strife, social unrest, complicity between media and governments, increased poverty, climate concerns, environmental damage, financial instability, sexism, racism, other -isms, food shortages and increases in sicknesses, cancers, heart disease, et cetera, et cetera. Many would have thought that, as the years and decades have rolled on, world problems would be alleviated by now, maybe even solved, but this has not been the case and the useless eaters do not even ask why.'

Elion leaned forward again. 'People who think this way are distracted and blind, but more to the point, they have been blinded. They have been blinded by the Sun.' Elion stopped talking and watched Sam's reaction.

Letting the words sink in, Sam glanced left at the grey, cylindrical device between them, which was mounted on the side handrail to his left. Dismissing it as being a telescope, he summarised Elion's words.

'So, you're saying that you, the Sun, Elion, are the reason for the troubles in the world?' Sam asked, horror rising within him.

'Clever boy, Sam. You don't mind me calling you Sam, do you? It's just that I find your new surname, Angel, a little salacious.'

How did he know I changed my surname? Sam thought but refused to be distracted.

'That's bullshit, Elion! You think you are some kind of God, controlling humans? Next you'll take claim to starting the pandemic!'

'Well, yes, I did indirectly; the pandemic was necessary as

we had a non-conforming President of the United States of America in power at the time. One of the many goals of the pandemic was to usher in mail-in ballots, amongst other measures, to skew the results to install a conforming President,' Elion explained.

Responding to the aghast expression on Sam's face, Elion clasped his hands together and rocked them back and forth. 'I know, I know. It's too much to believe. I don't have to justify what I say to you, life is just too short.' He nodded towards his intravenous infusion. 'To save time, I will level with you. Everything I have said is truthful. Everything I will tell you will be truthful. I am not lying. I do not lie. I have no need to lie. It matters not the question you pose. I enjoy telling the truth.'

'What do you mean, you have no need to lie?'

'Sam, I have no fear, I have no human enemy. If I want something to happen, it's done. There is no one else in the position that my family and I occupy. Who else in the world has no reason to lie? Life is so simple when you can live this way. Between here and the ring pass-not, I have dominion.'

'Who are you and your family?' Sam asked, not fully understanding Elion's terminology. He poured himself a glass of water, feeling the increase in temperature of both the ambient conditions and the conversation.

'We are a tight-knit family that has had significant powers of influence over the ages and can be traced back to way before the Roman Empire. Right now, we all find ourselves in a time of changing age. Subtle energies, undetectable by modern science, are altering our collective direction. This moment in our history grants our family the power to orchestrate upheavals more easily and to create more disunity, because with disunity comes power, control and opportunity.'

'So you are purposefully creating turmoil? Why? To piss off people and give them a miserable life?' Sam asked in disbelief.

'That's too simplistic a goal, Sam. There's a Yuri Bezmenov quote I can use here, 'A person who is demoralised is unable to access true information'. You see, when the masses cannot access true information, they are blinded and thus, controllable. Technology is marching on at such a rapid pace that very soon, a select subset of the human race will be able to have the whole planet to themselves. A few hundred thousand humans, living peaceful and joyous lives, with their needs being served by automation, artificial intelligence and a small army of useful maintenance workers. Mother Earth will heal and mankind will finally have a chance to ascend.'

'So you will create a war or disease to reduce the world population to allow you to create your utopia? And then what? Live the rest of your life in this new world and then die?'

Chuckling, Elion replied, 'No, no, no. Don't you believe in reincarnation, Sam?'

Sam nodded, 'I think so, but I'm no expert on the subject.'

'Well, here's how it works. A human being dies and their soul goes into a period of metempsychosis. By a complex cosmic calculation, part of this process requires the soul to be purged of a proportion of its karmic debt, a fiery and unpleasant event, hence where the notion of hell is derived. After this refinement, there is a period of rest, back in the divine home, wherever that is. Some talk of heaven, others, the oneness. Once rested, the soul is ready to reside in a baby just at the point of it being born. Depending on many variables, the time this whole process takes, measured from an Earthly perspective, is months, years, decades, hundreds of years or even millennia.' Elion checked his intravenous line was still actively administering his cocktail. 'My family has a shortcut to all of this. You could say, we have hacked the reincarnation system via a secret ceremony, and better still, the hack affords us the memories of our past lives once we start developing through childhood.' He finished and displayed a wide grin of delight.

After a few moments of thought, Sam concluded, 'So you and your family can effectively live forever?'

'Absolutely, Sam. Isn't that just wonderful? But even better, we have control as to whom we inhabit on our return to life.'

So engrossed in their conversation, neither of them realised that the pregnant, young woman had arrived at the table.

'Ah, Camila, you shouldn't creep up like that,' Elion snapped.

With pursed lips and a frown, she looked at Sam and then to Elion. 'But, dear, I saw your infusion has finished. Let me take it out.'

She tended to Elion before walking away and Sam wondered how much of the conversation she had heard. He then he made a startling connection.

If Camila's baby is Elion's... Sam's train of thought was cut by the increasingly intrusive noise of a Jet Ski. Though he could not see it, he watched Elion's face contort before he nimbly stood. Taking one step towards Sam, Elion grabbed the handles of what Sam had previously dismissed as a telescope and watched as the old man swivelled the unit down to the side of the yacht. With a sharp bang, a thin projectile fired out of the far end of the tube, trailing behind it a thin length of steel wire. Sam's alarm at the realisation that it was a harpoon was soon accompanied by a muffled cry rising up from where the arrow had been fired.

Calmly, Elion sat down. He signalled to one of the deck crew and announced, 'I do so dislike Jet Skis, such an annoyance to all coast-lovers.'

Sam, jumped up and looked overboard. 'You've just shot someone! With a harpoon! You're a fucking madman!' Sam looked at the blooded body being pulled in towards the boat.

He could see there was no chance of saving him. Another crew member launched an inflatable rib to retrieve the Jet Ski that was now circling without its rider.

'Sit down, Sam,' Elion commanded, continuing once he was re-seated. 'There're only two possibilities for that guy to be here. Either he is trouble or stupid. Using a Jet Ski this far out from the shore was his mistake.'

'What are you going to do with him and the Jet Ski? Someone will know. He's someone's family member. If I get off this ship, I'll have to report this,' Sam said with passion.

'No, no, you won't. No one would believe you. There will be no evidence. The Jet Ski will be scuttled in deep water and the body is probably already in our bio-cesspit. The bones will be dumped in the middle of an ocean in a few days' time. Do not underestimate my reach, I am untouchable, however, anyone that stands against me, including you, will be permanently taken off the chess board,' Elion warned, chillingly. 'Now, where were we before that hiatus? Ah, yes, my beautiful Camila. She's younger than you, Sam, but might I say, a lot more attractive.'

'So, she's carrying your baby?'

Emphasising his words for effect, Elion said, 'No, Sam, she's carrying the future me.'

Sam was struggling to take all this on board. He felt he had gleaned so much but it was all in the realm of conspiracy theories. *Could all this be true? Was this guy just a good crime boss, a Mafia-type, bigging himself up?* But it didn't feel this way to Sam.

'What did she remove from your arm? Are you sick?'

'No, Sam. That was adrenochrome. It is a medicine of sorts. It keeps my vitality up to high levels. It powers my body to look and, more importantly, to feel more youthful. My ninety-five-year-old body's failing now, even with the serum, the adrenalised blood of children,' Elion casually imparted and awaited a response.

Having come across this product in some of his research on conspiracies, disgusted and with horror rising, Sam hesitantly asked, 'What do you mean?'

'There's a whole network of child traffickers worldwide, supported by some of the biggest names in the world, some of whom are world leaders, and part of this structure produces adrenochrome, the blood taken from youngsters, who are tormented and terrorised to maximise the adrenaline content.'

'You are beyond sick, Elion. This is just the fucking sickest shit you're doing!' Sam raged. Before he knew it, he uncharacteristically leaped forward, grabbed Elion around the throat with his left hand and started to squeeze, his right fist poised to punch the life out of the creature before him. Elion's hand reactively grasped Sam's left to try to alleviate the pressure, puncturing Sam's hand with his sharp talons. Blood burst through the piercings. Elion's eyes started to bulge and his tongue appeared, slithering from his open mouth. It was long and narrow, and Elion gave a loud hiss, like a threatened reptile.

Elion's security detail rushed across the deck but retreated once they saw Elion's hand waving them away.

Sam looked at the weird hybrid in his clutches and slowly relented in his grip. This was reciprocated by Elion.

After some composure, Sam retook his seat and used a towel from the table to wipe the blood from his cut hand. 'What the fuck are you? Some animal cross-breed?'

Recovering, Elion took in a gurgling breath, before explaining, 'I have some reptilious analogues, which increase as the bloodline progresses. It is nothing but a result of dominant genetics.'

'You mean you're a fucking inbred,' Sam snapped, still angry and shocked at the nature of the beast in front of him. 'I should just kill you now.'

Smiling, Elion replied, 'You're a healer, Sam, not a killer.'

'How would you know? You don't know the first thing about me!'

Elion looked at Sam's hand. 'Go to the bar and get your hand treated. We'll continue after then.'

Sam took the advice and walked over to the bar.

'Here, let me do it,' Camila said, taking a first aid kit from the deckhand. Wearing a lemon-yellow sundress and a wide-brimmed sun hat, she set down her sunglasses and baby-blue knitting on the bar.

'We don't have much time,' she whispered in an Hispanic lilt. With her head lowered, she focussed on Sam's hand. If it was not for what Elion had already told him, Sam would have guessed she was in her late-twenties. She had soft features and silky, long, dark hair. 'I am Camila Flores, held here as partner of Elion.' She paused as one of the security men stopped next to them, probably making sure Camila was just administering medical aid, before he moved on.

Held here, Sam repeated in his mind. *A very telling statement*, he thought.

'I heard a little of what you were discussing, I need to know what you know.'

The alcohol wipe stung, but Sam braved it and did not flinch. 'So much was said, where do I start?' Sam whispered.

'The bit about his reincarnation.'

'Hey, get on with it,' the suited man barked from the other side of the room.

As Camila unwrapped the cellophane from a bandage and started to dress his hand, Sam felt something small being pushed onto his palm. It was subsequently sandwiched between his hand and the bandage. 'My number. Contact me as soon as you can,' she quietly said.

'Tell me, do you know where The Divinity App is located?' Sam whispered.

Camila slowly turned her head and looked around to make sure they were not being overheard. 'I'm sorry, I don't know, but do you promise to contact me with what you know?'

Sam took a moment to determine whether he felt she could be trusted but concluded she appeared to be a genuinely innocent party, not unlike himself. 'Sure, you have my word,' he said, but still entertained the notion that this may be a trap.

'Allez!' one of the security men snarled, breaking up the two and proceeded to escort Sam back to Elion.

Once seated again, Sam opened up the conversation. 'What are you doing here, Elion? You obviously don't like the sun or motor racing.'

'People! Whilst some of the world and the pretty people are gorging on the spectacle of Formula One, living the dream, pretending to be more important than they really are, there are a few highly influential men and women who are present here. What better guise than the racing to catch up with these shakers and movers?'

'Like who?'

Elion chuckled, which brought on a wheezy cough. 'Presidents, Prime Ministers, CEOs, colleagues from the Club of Rome, the Committee of 300 members, the Knights of Malta, the Bilderberg Group, the highest degree Masons, and so on. If they have sizeable power and influence, I have dealings with them.'

'Coerce them, you mean!'

'That's a crass analysis, Sam. I have many irons in the fire, and sometimes the irons need repositioning. If an iron goes cold, there are many more to choose from. I know people and I know how they tick. That is my game, my area of expertise, if you will.'

Sam resisted his inner voice urging him to punish this old man for what he had done. He reasoned that obtaining more information from him was the smarter move. 'I know about the skull powering The Divinity App,' Sam said, using some of the details Amelie had previously given him. 'Where is the skull now?'

Widening his eyes in surprise, Elion replied, 'You must have an angel on your side, feeding you sensitive information. As I said, I will not lie to you. However, I draw the line at making one of my irons an open target. Suffice to say, it is not in your interest to know its location or to pursue recovering it.'

'A veiled threat,' Sam spat.

'Another truth, Sam.'

'Your karma must be off the scale!'

'That's an irrelevant statement, Sam. I have told you that we have hacked the system. The karma count could be as high as the sun, but we do not pass through 'hell'. Look at our family emblem.' Elion used one of his pointed nails to direct Sam to view the deck floor. 'Our crest is called *Inifinitus,* this yacht is named after it. You see the longer and wider loop at the bottom nearest to us? That denotes a long life in the physical world. The small loop at the top; that denotes a short duration in the other world, the spirit world, before being reborn and starting the cycle again. The symbol is akin to the infinity sign, hence our crest's name, but it is vertical, signifying the heavens above and the physical world below, all in an eternal cycle. You might have seen the symbol on The Divinity App?'

'I've not downloaded it. I smelled a rat with that app from the off,' Sam said with pride. 'How did you know what the skull could do?'

'I didn't, well not to the degree we now know. But with perseverance and the right minds put to work on something with this kind of power, it was only a matter of time before I found a good use for it. Hence the app.'

'So you can create more mayhem and misery?'

'Just allowing the innate human condition to bubble to the

surface and I help it along a bit; I fan the flames of ego. Disunity creates fertile ground for opportunity to progress the running of the world. Remember, it's business, not personal,' Elion stated, coldly. 'I was pleased with myself when I managed to get the skull onto the Gemini programme in the sixties.'

'What do you mean?'

'Well, in Greek mythology, Castor and Pollux were twins but born to different parents. Castor was born to Tyndareus, the King of Sparta and Pollux born to the god Zeus. Castor died as he was just a mere mortal and so Pollux begged his father to give Castor immortality. The twins did get immortality, not in this world, but in the heavens. However, there is a hidden element to this story, in that Zeus blessed the physical skulls of both Castor and Pollux and they would hold increasing physical powers as the ages rolled on.'

'So there are *two* skulls?' Sam asked, trepidation creeping through him.

'Yes, Sam. And just think of the power that could be harnessed when the other skull is found, and Castor and Pollux are finally reunited here on Earth.' Elion said clamping his hands together with glee.

'It doesn't bear thinking about,' Sam said in disgust.

Elion chuckled again. 'This brings me to the main reason I wanted to meet you. I want to offer you something.'

'I doubt I'd want anything from an evil creature like you, Elion!' Sam snarled.

'Maybe not, but let's keep it civil, Sam. I want to offer you a ticket to the inner circle of our family.'

'I don't understand?'

'Well, I am giving you the opportunity to work with me and my family to help bring about the changes to the world that are so desperately needed. I'm offering you all you could want materially, but more than that, I'm offering you a ticket to witness my immortality.'

Sam sat for a moment. *Is this Elion person, sitting here in front of me, serious, or am I hallucinating*? Sam thought to himself. In a calm manner, Sam replied, 'I don't quite know what to say to keep things civil. I think you are a dangerous, evil, odious man who, quite frankly, needs to be put down. You destroy lives, have no remorse and claim to be a permanent feature on this planet. Why the hell do you think I'd want to work with you, and watch you live forever? Talk about selling my soul to the devil!' Sam took a couple of gulps of water, but kept his eyes fixed on Elion, and then posed a civil question, 'And why the fuck would you even ask me? You don't know anything about me!'

In a deadpan manner, Elion began to reel off facts, 'You are Sam Angel, born Samuel Anderson on the third of September, 1990, in Watford, England, the only child to Elizabeth Elise Anderson and Thomas Andrew Anderson, scientists who both tragically died in Antarctica in 1998. It was after this event when we first met, I was one of two officials to report the news to your aunt.' Elion paused and his chest rattled when he breathed deeply, whilst Sam cast his mind back to that time when he was told his parents had died.

Elion resumed, 'You continued to live with your mother's sister until sixteen, when you changed your name by deed poll to Sam Angel, after having been obsessed with regarding your parents as angels and thought by changing your name, it would bring you closer to them and give you a sense of control and understanding over your life. You then enlisted in the army, following your best friend, Nelson Taylor, where you trained as a medic, saw active service in two countries, but not any real military action until that day in Helmand Province ten years ago when you shot a child.'

Sam felt an oppressive wave of dread wash over him as he was reminded of his parents' passing and then of that cataclysmic day in Helmand Province. However, Elion did not halt his biography.

'After that, your life was a bit of a mess until you had the opportunity to go to Bhutan, which was, unbeknownst to you, a battleground for the skull. I made sure you were not to be harmed, and hoped you would, subsequently, get involved with my projects somehow, but this never quite materialised, hence our meeting now. You have some skills and traits that could always be useful to my family, loyalty being one of them and your sense of righteousness would be an interesting challenge for me to bear. But I understand how you may feel about me. However, I wanted to give you the opportunity, a quid pro quo, call it cancelling a business debt I have with you.' Elion signalled with a subtle eye movement for his minders to move closer to Sam.

'OK, you have a good memory for facts about my life, however creepy that comes across.' Intensely aware of his shaken state and the surreal situation in which he found himself, Sam fought to stay focussed. 'So, you were there, telling my auntie and me that my parents had died?'

'I didn't do the talking, but I was in England at the time and so went along for the experience and to measure you up. If it wasn't for me, your auntie would never have received that healthy monthly income.'

'I don't remember seeing you.'

'I was in military uniform, wearing gloves, you know, to disguise my hands.'

Sam cast his mind back to that dreadful day. *Yes, it was Elion who had worn gloves*. 'And what indebtedness do you have, the quid pro quo, with a commoner, a 'useless eater' like me?'

Elion coolly let Sam know, 'I had to have your parents killed.'

Once the realisation sunk in that Elion was not bluffing,

Sam was seething and shouted, 'You fuck!', whilst involuntarily projecting strings of spittle onto the table.

He only managed to half stand before he was thrust back into his seat by four heavy hands on his shoulders. 'You fucking murderous madman!' he added, using all his strength to writhe in his seat, trying to wrest himself from his restrainers.

'Calm down, this must be hard to hear but if you want to know the truth, you must listen.'

Sam calmed down only a degree or two, and he still tried to lunge at Elion a couple more times in vain as the two minders did not release their grip on him. Contrasting with Sam's view of the sanctity of life, he knew he would have to kill Elion at the first opportunity.

'Your parents worked for one of my companies, Laydox Limited, in the late nineties. They were hired to take and study ice core samples and analyse some of the unique geology down there. My company specialises in covert government contracts, ones not readily available to read and scrutinise, so people like your parents would produce innocuous research that would appease, in this case, the British Government.

When they arrived at the base, they soon found that it was located just two miles away from a very secret operation. You see, my company would over-inflate the contract costs and use some of the difference to fund top-secret projects out there. Unfortunately, someone on site had loose lips and soon afterwards, your parents made their way to the secret location on one of their days off. They made their way down the gently sloping cave and entered the first chamber. Even though they were in this frozen wasteland, in this chamber, just a couple of hundred metres down, the air was temperate and the lake inside was liquid and warm enough to paddle in. This was just the tip of the iceberg, if you would excuse the pun. It was at this point I was contacted for further instruction. Due to the sensitivity of the site, I ordered there to be no trace of the intruders. It is my understanding that they were shot in the lake, and elements in the British Government decided to have your parents' bodies cremated in South Africa before being returned to you and your aunt.'

'So, because they were inquisitive, you had them shot?' Sam said, emotion welling up and tried again to attack his nemesis.

'I regret taking this action, but it was not personal, just business.'

'You cold bastard. So, you made me an orphan and then you looked over my shoulder from then on?'

'What can I say, it's just business, Sam,' Elion reiterated again.

'Well, at least I know the truth now.'

'Truth, you'll never know the truth. There are eight billion versions of the truth out there and they all conflict. You can work towards the truth but it can never be attained.'

'You're saying that's not the truth about my parents?'

'No, Sam. The world is like an onion, reality is like an onion, physically, mentally and spiritually. Once one peels off a layer, one may feel relief, jubilance or upset at finding the truth. However, the next layer of truth waits to be discovered.'

'I can't really take that in now. I've just been told that my parents were murdered, and by you! You're a dead man!' Sam seethed.

'We are all capable of murder, Sam. You've wanted to kill me today and don't forget you murdered that boy in Afghanistan,' Elion said smugly.

Sam felt emotionally confused. The last thing he needed was to be reminded of Afghanistan. 'Hardly the same thing. Taking your life would do humanity a huge favour, and in a situation where you kill or be killed, most would kill,' Sam justified.

'But killing someone is still killing someone, Sam. So, we're not that different, you and I.' Elion said.

Sam tried once again to move to attack the madman but found himself still immobilised by the two men.

'I do not have much time left in this body and time is marching on, Sam. You have made your decision, and you will not be partnering us in this reality, but my debt with you has now been expunged. I will not interfere with your life from now on. You are free to do as you wish. But heed this warning – if you cross me or impede my work in any way, you will become my business and you will be removed from the game. If we meet again, it will be the last time. Bon chance, Sam.'

Sam was allocated seat 7A, sitting at the rear of Business Class on the return flight to London City Airport. He had used the journey from Elion's yacht to the Monaco Heliport and on to Nice Airport to reflect on what he had learned and was trying to make sense of a direction to pursue. He had been flanked by the two suited men right up until he boarded the plane, where they returned his phone. Sam didn't know how they were allowed airside, but he reasoned Elion obviously had connections.

He needed a drink to relax and he hoped this would help him see more clearly. He closed his eyes with the intention of getting some rest, yet his mind was awash with details, memories and puzzles that needed his attention. But above all, his learning of his parents' fate filled Sam with rage he'd never experienced before.

In an attempt to distract his mind for a while, he took the

bandage off his right hand and read the note from Camila, which detailed her mobile number in neat handwriting. With his phone on, he took a picture of the number and then stowed the note away in his phone wallet. Although his hand was sore, the puncture wounds were nothing more than a dog bite and he diverted his attention to next look at the ZUX News 24 online; he was unsurprised to see that the wave of social unrest had not abated. It had instead risen at an alarming pace in the two days since he had last checked.

Sam read his text messages, starting with those from Tinks. The first one was curt, almost angry that Sam had missed the flight home yesterday. But the second took a warmer tone with concern for his friend's disappearance. And the third:

Hi, Angel. Concerned not heard from you. Please reply asap as need to meet up later today? Have you seen the news about the Cardinal!!?

Sam searched online and found an article headlined 'Cardinal Francis, The Priest Behind The Divinity App, In Plane Crash, Presumed Dead'. He read the article, which described how a small jet had disappeared from radar and radio contact the day before, about an hour from Rome, somewhere over the Adriatic Sea, approximately halfway between Italy and Albania. Only the previous morning he had met with Cardinal Francis, however, that seemed a very long time ago.

Is there a connection between my meeting the Cardinal, witnessing his sex act, the app and today's meeting with that monster Elion? Sam was sure of a connection but was not able to join any of the dots.

Reading on, he learned that Pope Leo XIV and the Cardinal had personal differences. Also, it appeared that the emergency beacon had not been operational on the business jet, hampering any location or rescue efforts. *Elion!* Sam instantly surmised. *He's either brought this plane down or made everyone think he's brought it down.* But then he countered, *Maybe the Cardinal was not even on the plane, assuming it really existed. I can't be sure of anything now.*

With his brain hurting from information overload and endless possibilities, Sam replied to Tinks:

All OK. Meet @8pm tonight, usual haunt.

An announcement was made as the aircraft was over Paris and due to start the descent into London City Airport soon. Sam looked out of the window and scanned the scene below, the likes of which resembled some of the darker days he had witnessed in Afghanistan following allied bombing raids on towns, fuel depots and enemy munitions stockpiles. Across the city, the evening sun silhouetted dozens of plumes of smoke, reflecting the breakdown of ordered society.

Sam used the rest of the flight planning how to respond to Camila to let her know Elion's plan for reincarnation into the baby boy she was carrying, and he decided he would call as soon as he was safely on the ground.

'So that's put paid to that dream contract,' Tinks said disappointedly.

'I understand the way you feel, Tinks, but there's a bigger picture here. You've seen the riots, the attacks on people and property. Flying into City Airport, there's smoke all over the place; the same in Paris from what I saw. Do you still think there's no link between the app and all this chaos?'

Tinks took a couple of glugs of beer, buying time to phrase his response. 'I've seen it for myself. I did something I wasn't proud of; I threw a brick through a Sikh temple's window.' Dejected, Tinks lowered his head, 'And my karmic debt reduced. ZUX News 24 is full of shit, Angel! You were right, the media is lying to us. But what can we do about it?'

'Waking up to difficult realities is the hardest thing, mate. But it feels great to finally have my best mate on a similar page. The magnitude of truths that have smacked me in the face in the past two days are as disturbing as my darkest day in Afghanistan.'

'Shit, Angel, I can see how shaken up you are. I'm all ears.'

'There's so much to tell you, Tinks, but before I do, there is something we can do. It's hugely risky, but after a couple of phone calls before we met up tonight, there is a sort of plan to take down this app. Are you in?'

'Damn right, Angel. When do we start?'

'Tomorrow. Meet at mine at ten am sharp. We'll go through the plan then.'

'Come along now, Paolo, I know it's very hot and humid, but it's just down the end of this track,' Cardinal Francis, exhausted, said to his brother. Dressed in black cassocks, they dripped in sweat. Huge wet patches darkened their gowns. 'Just another hundred metres or so, brother,' Francis said in encouragement to them both, but feeling his energy draining as his suitcase seemed to be getting heavier with every step. He now had to carry it due to the wheels not coping with the uneven ground.

The long flight, albeit in one of Elion's private jets, was draining, as too was the six-hour ride on a small bus from the airport in Phnom Penh, Cambodia, to the outskirts of Krong Siem Reap, near the historic site of Ankar Wat. The last part of the journey was a mile walk down tropical roads that turned into lanes and narrowed to tracks. They were surrounded by silence.

Francis and Paolo finally staggered to their destination and viewed their new home. It was a colonial building and the land in front of it was demarked by a low, chain-link fence that was mostly obscured by lush, large-leaved banana trees and other tropical flora. The centre portion of the land was mainly laid with very coarse, threadbare grass. The metal gate was open and Francis sat down his baggage on the unmade road and read the arched sign above the gate.

Welcome to St. Mary's Orphanage of Cambodia

'Until we're called back by Elion's family, Paolo, this is our new home.' Paolo always smiled when someone said the word 'home'.

A bell rang, promptly followed by the front door of the orphanage opening. Two nuns followed by several well behaved, children, all dressed the same, came out to greet their new arrivals.

'I think this will be just fine,' Francis said with a grin, and threw his arms forward to greet his new family.

'Sir, sir?' the muscular, suited man gently called, standing at the threshold of his suite door.

'What is it?' Elion snapped. Though never needing more

than four hours' sleep a night, Elion found it essential that they were counted as of good quality to ensure he operated with his desired sharpness during the day. Being woken just before midnight, less than an hour into his ritual, was far from ideal.

'I'm sorry to disturb you, but there is something that needs your attention. Erm, urgently, sir.'

Grumbling and wheezing, Elion struggled to sit up on the edge of his bed and tucked his claw-toed feet into his deck shoes. Thrusting his arms into his black silk dressing gown, he mumbled to himself, irritated at the intrusion and rueing the fact that his trusted team could not take care of matters, just for four hours.

Elion was escorted to the suite at the other end of the deck, was shown through the bedroom and on towards the en-suite bathroom. As Elion stepped into the dark bedroom, he could see the bathroom door was open and he could also hear Camila sobbing and muttering to herself.

The door banged fully open when Elion knocked on it and strode in to see a distraught Camila squatting in the bath in her silk, pale green nightdress, her matching slippers dumped on the floor along with the half-finished baby clothing she had been knitting. As he moved closer, he saw her nightie was hitched up around her waist and her knees were splayed out.

The floor of the bath ran with bright red, dark red and clear liquids, and they were coming from in between Camila's legs. Despite strings of blooded, dripping tissue hanging from her vagina, Elion could clearly see the heads of two knitting needles, which had been thrust into her uterus.

'You're a fucking sick, evil, fucking monster, Max!' she cried out, using her blood-stained hands to manically pull at her own head hair. 'You're a monster! A monster! You made me do this! I had to do this!' She shouted with rage at first but ended with uncontrollable crying.

Elion screwed up his face and gritted his teeth before giving her face a hard, back-handed slap, lacerating her cheek with three of his claws. She cried out loudly and mopped her cut cheek with one of her hands. He calmly took a towel from a rail to wipe his hand of her blood, sweat and tears and returned to the suited man, who stood just outside.

'Ready the helicopter and take her to the hospital. Then alert the authorities to arrest her for self-induced abortion,' Elion commanded in a matter-of-fact tone.

'I thought you might be interested in this,' the man said, handing Elion Camila's phone. 'She got a phone call a few hours ago from this unknown UK number, but it's clear whom it's from.'

Elion gently scratched his chin with his sharp nails and thought for a moment. 'OK, this changes everything. Make the arrangements to leave for home at first light.'

21

East London
26th May 2022

08:00 UTC ZUX NEWS 24 LIVE ---- BREAKING NEWS ----

'The wave of civil unrest that has recently spread across nations is now growing at an alarming rate across all continents. Up until recently, Africa had not seen too much violence, but in the past day, this continent is now seeing angry mobs ransacking places of worship, shops and banks.

'In other news, the main four social media giants have jointly announced uniformed wording appended to any posts questioning the integrity of The Divinity App. The press release goes on to say that they will continue to tackle the scourge of online misinformation and cancel account holders, where necessary. This news has been welcomed by European and UK governments and we will expect to hear reaction from the US and Canadian governments in due course.'

Sam heard a gentle knock on the rear starboard window and felt his boat's familiar rocking movement of someone stepping aboard.

'Come in, come in, Amelie,' he said with enthusiasm. 'Can I get you a coffee or tea?'

'Sorry I'm a little late. A coffee, black…'

'No sugar, right, I'm on it,' Sam said, keenly finishing her order and pouring her drink. His eyes darted back and forth from the coffee to his guest and her enchanting hair and eyes.

'Are you ready to do what must be done, Sam?' Amelie asked, holding Sam's gaze.

'I think so, but I'm quite apprehensive, to be honest. I'm wearing combat trousers in the hope they'll subdue any genesis of combat,' he joked, knowing how poor a quip it was. 'So how are we going to start things off?'

'Can we sit down?' They both took a place on Sam's sofa. 'OK, now do you have your phone on you?'

'Er, yes.' Sam fumbled, checking which pocket it was in.

'Now go and install The Divinity App.'

'The Divinity App? Really? That's the last thing I want on my phone,' he protested.

Resting her hand on Sam's forearm and giving a little squeeze of encouragement, she explained, 'There's no other way, Sam.'

Amelie started drinking whilst Sam downloaded the app. 'The bastards will have access to all my info now,' he claimed.

'I'm sorry to say, but they have access to most of it already.'

'What a world we live in! What right do these people think

they have to take all our data? I remember the internet before smart phones, when many companies were trying to work out how to make income with the change in the technology and the way customers bought and consumed their goods and services. Now dealing in data is king and selling their wares is almost secondary for some,' he ranted as the installation completed. 'OK. I just need to sign up…'

'Wait, Sam. Put the phone down. You don't need to sign up until the others get here.'

Sam complied and looked into Amelie's amazing fiery eyes.

'Turn towards me,' she said, as she turned to face him. 'Now, you do trust me, don't you?'

'Absolutely, Amelie. I'd trust you with my soul,' he boldly replied.

'I need us to do something, something very temporary to get a job done, but it will sting a bit.'

Intrigued, Sam replied slowly, 'Go on.'

'I need you to press your fingers and my fingers together, only for a few moments, is that OK?'

'Yeah.' He raised his hands with his fingers splayed out.

Amelie's finger and thumb tips met with Sam's. As the two looked at each other, Sam noticed that her polychromatic irises started to move and slivers of reds, golds, auburns and oranges started to slowly dance and morph into each other in a hypnotically sensory display. Sam was momentarily mesmerised with one of the most beautiful displays he had ever seen. Just as he was settling into the splendour, his concentration was shattered by a searing pain in his fingertips.

'Shit!' he shrieked out and withdrew his hands in an instant. He jumped up and started shaking his hands and flicking his fingers over the pads of his thumbs, before taking a long look at them.

'What was all that about,' he asked, reeling from the shock

to his system. 'And your eyes! Who are you?' he implored.

Amelie stood, gave Sam a warm and reassuring smile and held his hands gently, though Sam was not too sure if he needed to brace for more pain. 'Please trust me. Laura will help explain what's just happened.' She moved her hands up to hold his upper arms. 'We're all here for a reason, Sam. A better question to ask is "Who are you?", "What is your purpose?",' she responded.

Sam thought on this, then replied, 'I dunno, but I want to rid the world of maggots like Elion.'

'Follow your heart and you'll know what to do,' she concluded. With a friendly kiss to both of his cheeks, she looked him in the eye and said, 'Goodbye, Sam. Love will always overcome.'

As she turned and left the boat, Sam felt a physical warmth and comfort in Amelie's words, though this heavily contrasted with his feeling that there was a finality about her goodbye. Breaking out of his trance, he moved himself swiftly to the back deck of the boat to wave her off, but she was nowhere to be found. He looked up and down the towpath, which was clearly visible to him for maybe a hundred metres either way, and he scanned the water for any movement just in case she had fallen in the canal again. But he found no trace of Amelie.

The impeccably dressed Felix, gingerly walked up to Elion with a tray carrying a large serving of Camus Curvée 4.160 cognac, in the finest of brandy glasses made to order by Venetian glassblowing master craftsmen from Murano. Along with his quieter than usual presence, this was highly unusual behaviour that Mr Rotzberg was exhibiting, Felix thought. In the three years Felix had been in his employ, he had only seen his boss take a drink once and even that, he barely touched. 'Drinking impairs the mind and diminishes the human experience,' Felix remembered Elion used to say.

'Your brandy, Mr Rotzburg.' Felix set the glass down before returning to his serving station to the rear of the business jet.

From behind, he watched as Elion appeared to marvel at the exquisiteness of the vessel and the hue of the liquor contained within it. His employer then held up his glass and swilled the exclusive cognac around and watched its legs slide down the inside, before smelling its aroma and ultimately taking his first sip. Then another. Then another.

In a matter of minutes, Elion held out his empty glass into the aisle space and called Felix for a refill. Felix immediately attended to his duties and on returning with another generous measure, he set the glass down. 'Is everything OK today, Mr Rotzburg?'

Elion did not respond until he had taken another sip. 'Everything is just fine, Felix. Matter comes, matter goes. Change is the only constant in life,' he cryptically, but meaningfully, remarked. He looked directly into Felix's eyes and smiled. 'Everything just is, Felix, so how could it be anything other than fine?'

Bemused, Felix formed a pleasant smile and gave the slightest of nods before returning to his station. He kept an eye on Elion on account of his strange behaviour.

Several more sups later, Felix saw Elion take out his phone and could clearly hear him make a call. 'Hyperion. We're thirty minutes from the airport, so I will be with you within the hour, say eleven o'clock. Is all in place there, like I asked last night?' There was a slight delay before Elion spoke again. 'OK, my son. Until then.'

'Ah, Tinks.' Sam ascended the four steps out of his boat to the cruiser stern to greet his good friend.

'Look at you, Angel, looks like you're dressed for a mission into enemy territory,' Tinks said, noticing Sam dressed in a black T-shirt, black cargo trousers and black work boots.

'Well, that's the hope, mate. Hope you're ready for action too?'

'Always ready, me,' Tinks said, laughing. Putting his hand ons Sam's shoulder, he continued, 'How are you doing, mate? I was so sorry to hear about how your parents died.'

'Yeah, I know, I know. I'm trying to not think about that at the mo, just focussing on the plan in hand.' After the shortest of pauses, Sam said, 'Come on in and let me introduce you to some people.'

Sam stepped down into the kitchen area of his boat. Instantly, his two guests stood and walked towards them. 'This is Special Agent Laura Lafayette from the CIA in America and this is Tenzin Gorji from Tibet.'

After initial greetings and compliments on Tenzin's traditional dress, Tinks asked, 'So Laura, you were on that helicopter in Bhutan four years ago and Tenzin, you were the guy we found in a bad way just before the Chinese army chased us down on that border?'

Laura nodded. Tenzin added, 'Yes, I am the very same. Thank you for saving my life.'

'No need for thanks, that's what we're trained to do, Angel and me. How did you get to that point?'

Tenzin gave a brief update and although Tinks had been

told some of it from Sam, he listened intently to get the story direct from Tenzin. 'So, you were shot by Laura's partner and then they stole the skull?' Tinks said and turned his attention to Laura.

'We were working on orders to recover the artefact but, yes, my companion did shoot at Tenzin. That's not how I wanted to handle the situation. I thought he'd killed Tenzin but I recently found out what saved his life.' Laura pointed to Tenzin's snuffbox, which he was pulling out of his pocket.

'Wow, Tenzin, you were so lucky. You could have died twice over that day, what with the Chinese military closing in,' Tinks said. 'So, this skull thing, Angel's told me it has some kind of power, and it's the power behind this Vatican app?'

'Yes. You might have been told that I headed a team to create The Divinity App, for someone called Elion, who operated an umbrella company called Religix Limited. That company's offshore and there are no details available. I did look into this guy and the company but found very little detail,' Laura said.

'What did you find out?' Tinks asked.

'I found out Elion's real name is Maximilian Adelino Zelig Frederick Rotzburg III, the head of a family with long lineage, huge influence and immeasurable wealth. Strangely, both his parents died reportedly of natural causes on the same day as his only son was born. He and his baby son survived a helicopter crash in the early nineties, which killed his wife and two daughters. Since then, he's been even more reclusive, only appears in people's lives when it suits him and his needs, and pops up now and again at super-high-level meetings, like the Bilderberg Group and Committee of 300 meetings, and the type of meetings to which the political elite and the world's influential billionaires are invited by shadowy members of ancient families. Getting just that information killed my partner, killed one of Elion's drivers, and nearly killed me,

Sam and that cardinal who launched the app. Nothing really makes sense.'

'I think I might be able to add some context to some of what you said, Laura,' said Sam and he gave a précis of what he had learned the day before during his forced meeting with Elion. 'So, I guess I should thank you, Laura, for chasing me down at Rome Airport two days ago and handing me over to be drugged and hauled off to his boat,' Sam said, smirking in jest. 'Tell Tinks what you told me earlier, about the app. That'll help him understand our plan.'

'Right, I headed this team, as I mentioned, which built an app all around the strange capabilities of the skull that we acquired from Tenzin, in Bhutan. As far as we could tell, direct contact with the artefact started returning a sum of the bad things that person had done in their lifetime and if anyone held it for any longer, memories of all of their negative actions would, one by one, start to flood into their mind, usually leading to the instant releasing of the skull and the start of dealing with the reality of having been shown events most of us try to bury in the depths of our minds. We found a way to digitise this karmic information and present it in this app.'

Laura paused for a sip of coffee and Tinks interjected, 'So exactly what karmic information did you gather?'

'I will get on to that, but I want all of you to know that what I am telling you now, stays between us all. This is so sensitive, not to mention beyond top secret, but extraordinary times call for extraordinary protocols.' Laura looked at each of her three companions to get some form of acceptance of her terms.

'We found no one could physically touch the bone artefact for more than a couple of seconds for it became far too traumatic. But we devised a system using people's fingerprints. This fingerprint could be presented to the skull's surface using an ultrashort pulse laser and the skull would then resonate, for four nanoseconds. This brief vibration comprised vast amounts of data which the laser could pick up straight after presenting the fingerprint. With the right infrastructure in place, we would be able to perform two hundred million requests per second! It was so fast, we needed to design hardware to be able to cope with its scope. In that tiny fraction of a second, the skull emitted a data burst that not only gave us the person's karmic score, but also a complete list of karmic events and an indication of when they were exacted.'

'But the app only gives the karmic score,' Tinks stated.

'That's right, our remit was to collate all the data into one database to be used by Religix for future uses, though I suspect one or more US government agencies were cut into a deal to receive some or all of the data,' Laura explained.

'So, Religix has a copy of everyone's wrongdoings across their entire life?' Tinks asked, incredulously.

'Yes and no,' Laura said. 'Yes, we could collate a person's life's karmic events, all dated by how many days it occurred before the date of information request. But here's where it gets really strange. Nearly everyone tested had most of their events dated before they were born. And much more than that, sometimes going back hundreds, if not thousands, of years.'

'Reincarnation!' Sam concluded.

'That's the only conclusion we came up with, assuming the data was correct; there was no way of us corroborating the data before modern history. But my partner Rozen and I carried out a batch of unauthorised tests and found we could link many serious crimes where we had good details of the timing and the felony, to an individual or individuals.'

'So loads of crimes could be solved with this data?' Sam asked.

'Well, in a way, yes, but firstly, the app data would not be considered reliable evidence at this time; how could anyone prove that this data was genuine? And secondly, our tests were abruptly stopped by Elion after one of our phone conversations. When I asked him why, he replied that the app was not to be used for such ends.'

Laura saw Sam look at his phone and she also saw that time was marching on. 'So, before we detail the plan, there's a couple more things you need to know. During the app project we were tasked with including a trigger in a particular circumstance. If ever a "null" result was found, then the system needed to communicate this fact to a cell phone and send all relevant data, such as name, location, phone number and other account details. Now, a "null" result is different from a zero, which we found could be attained by using fake prints. A "null" could mean several different things, but it's safe to assume it means that the user with this score either has no karmic score or a karmic score is not applicable to them. I did trace the cell phone to a company called CentSec, a security company again traced back to Elion. Rozen asked the reasoning behind the subroutine; Elion told him to mind his own beeswax.'

'I guess it's impossible for someone to have a zero-karma score, so they need to be investigated,' Sam added.

'What's the plan?' Tinks asked.

'So, Tinks, the plan is for Sam to use The Divinity App, generate a null score, get taken to the hidden HQ of the app, we follow him, we rescue him, then we find the skull, destroy the data, stop the app and try to neutralise Elion as a bonus,' Laura summarised, nonchalantly.

'And we must not damage the skull and then we have to take it back for hiding,' Tenzin added.

'OK. Is that all? For a minute, I thought this was going to be hard work,' Tinks said sarcastically. 'I've got so many questions, I don't know where to begin.'

Sam spoke up, 'Tinks, I know it sounds a bit of a harebrained scheme but hear me out. Amelie popped over this morning and did something to my fingers. I'm guessing she's changed my fingerprints to be able to provide a "null" return on the app for me.'

'Sorry... what?' Tinks said, impatient. 'This red-haired woman with orange eyes, that no one's ever seen, apart from you, has changed your fingerprints? You've lost the fucking plot, mate!'

'I've seen her,' Tenzin said.

'Me too,' Laura added. 'She crossed our paths in Rome a couple of days ago. I can't explain it and we don't have the time to recount what happened to us. But believe me, she does exist.'

'And she changed Angel's fingerprints?' Tinks continued with sarcasm.

'We'll find out soon enough, Tinks. Let's just leave that to one side for a moment as we need to carry on detailing the plan. Assuming that my prints have changed and assuming I am subsequently picked up and taken to the app's hidden base, you three can follow me. Laura has a tracker device and she has access to transport at the drop of a hat,' Sam explained.

'It's going to cost me another meal with a lecherous four-star General, though,' Laura added, pulling a long face.

'What kind of tracker have you got, Laura? Anyone worth their salt would sweep him for bugs and electronics,' Tinks said in a slightly supercilious manner.

'You're right, Tinks. Any standard equipment will most probably be screened for. Again, this stays between us,' Laura said. She reached into her handbag and pulled out a small, white, carbon-fibre box. She carefully opened the flip-top lid, revealing nine tiny compartments, each about ten millimetres by five millimetres, and perhaps five millimetres deep. From the inside of the lid, she unclipped a flat, white utensil, as long as the box, and moved it over the top right compartment. Laura and her three associates witnessed an almost clear square of material levitate up to the utensil.

'Sam, turn over your arm. I'm going to place this on the inside of your wrist,' Laura instructed.

Very slowly, Sam complied. 'What is that exactly?'

'It's a biometric transmitter. It's still being trialled. It's cutting-edge technology,' she added.

Sam recoiled his arm. 'I'm no guinea pig, Laura,' he said in alarm.

'It's OK, trust me,' she tried to reason with Sam, still holding the utensil, ready to administer the bug. 'It's mostly made from bio-plastics, it will sit microscopically above your skin, held in place by electrostatics and is undetectable. When we've finished with it, I can take it off you just as easily as applying it.'

Hesitantly, Sam offered the underside of his wrist again and Laura placed the membrane-tracker on his skin. Instantly, it appeared to blend in and merge with his skin.

Tinks stood, mesmerised. He had seen incredible technology in his time but his faced dropped in disbelief. 'How does it work, Laura?'

Laura was on her phone, setting up the tracker to the CIA's BioTraQ System, allowing her to pinpoint Sam's location, but still managed to explain as she registered Sam's bug. 'The tattoo comprises a network of bioelectronics which has the ability to use a person's electromagnetic field to create a contact ping. It manages to boost the field, just for a microsecond and cryptically embed the MAC address, the unique identifying serial number, of the tracker in that signal. The CIA project running this has signal "sniffers" across the world, secreted in all manner of networks, such as the power grid, the cell phone network, the internet, wi-fi frequencies, radio and television transmissions, et cetera and can relay, with a fair degree of accuracy, the location of the bug. But it's not so good on planes because the project needs to throw hardware up in space to be able to monitor any flying BioTraQ System devices. Should be online later this year but its current capabilities will suffice for our needs today and I can track you on my phone.'

'How accurate is it, Laura?' Sam enquired.

'Five to ten metres on average, but it depends on the network and other factors.'

'OK. Any questions anyone?' Sam asked.

'If you are picked up, how do we know you'll be taken to this mystery HQ and how many people will we be up against?'

Laura took to answering these queries, 'We don't know for sure that Sam will be taken to HQ but it's the only move that makes sense. If Religix or Elion recognise "null" karma people as some kind of special case, hence the special subroutine, then surely they'll want to at least study them further and it would stand to reason they would want to get a direct comparison between the app results and the results from getting in direct contact with the skull. As for numbers, I can't tell you. The app was written with first generation artificial intelligence, so as long as the hardware, internet connections and power are in place, with backup systems, there is no need for any support staff. It makes me wonder what happened to all my staff that were moved to a new location when the core of the app hardware was relocated.'

'Any more questions? It's pushing eleven am and we have a long and dangerous day ahead of us,' Sam stated.

'I don't know what to say, Sam. If you produce a "null" result on the app, then I won't ask any more questions for now and will get behind the plan one hundred per cent,' Tinks said, still bewildered by many assaults on his understanding of the world.

Sam got out his phone and opened The Divinity App. On asking for his fingerprint, he fruitlessly tested that his thumbs were not burned and continued signing into the app.

Place digit on fingerprint reader, commanded the sign-in

procedure. Sam complied and saw the app accept his print and awaited the response from the programme.

'What am I expecting to see here, Laura?'

'Just wait a few more moments,' she replied. Then…

****

The Divinity App

Name: Samuel Angel

Born: Watford, England on 03/Sep/1990

Karmic Score:

Null

Help
Donate

****

Sam took several moments to take in the fact that he got the result they were hoping for but not necessarily expecting.

'Null!' Tinks exclaimed. 'Well, fuck me, maybe this Amelie does exist after all,' he said in amazement, not quite believing what he was seeing.

Sam replied, 'As I've said to you before, Tinks, the world is not how it is presented to us.'

Sitting outside at a pavement table at the Cyber City café at which Sam had met Amelie on a couple of occasions, he felt unusually cool. A brisk wind blew around the local office blocks and the sky was overcast. Though cold for the end of May, Sam resisted putting on his hoodie for the time being and put his chilliness down to anxiousness of the situation that may be about to unfold. There was a smell of burning in the air, probably from recently dowsed fires from the pockets of civil unrest. He sat with his coffee, having already picked at a toasted cheese sandwich and half read the ZUX News 24 website, not really concentrating on it but wanting to present an appearance of normality. He managed to joke to himself that even if he was taking in the editorial, he would be at odds with its bias and hidden agendas.

He occasionally glanced down the road, on the other side where Tinks, Laura and Tenzin sat in a rental car parked up outside a bakery, ready to follow when needed. Sam noticed that the street was not that busy with either traffic nor pedestrians, and he put it down to a mixture of the increased working from home culture which had been initiated by the pandemic, creating semi-ghost towns in many commercial centres across towns and cities, and also people keeping themselves away from any of the trouble flashpoints.

A black Mercedes limousine appeared and hurriedly pulled up to the kerb next to the café. Sam's instant reaction was to run, but he overruled this impulse having previously decided not to create any resistance; the sooner he was in their hands, the sooner he would be where they all wanted to be, was his thinking. Two well-built, shaven-headed men, with quite conspicuous earpiece communicators, alighted the rear of the car, with the one nearest to Sam waiting for the other to join him, so they could intercept Sam in unison.

Sam put down his coffee and watched them walk towards him. As one of them grabbed Sam's upper arm, the other said, 'You need to come with us,' in a well-spoken London accent. Sam did not feel the need to act in any way other that his heightened state of anxiety portrayed. Without resistance, a worried Sam stood up and was escorted into the back of the car, followed by one of his arresters, whilst the other walked around the car to enter from the roadside.

The limousine pulled away at speed, even before the last door was shut, and Sam was flung back into the soft leather bench seat with the force of the acceleration.

'No talking! Hand me your phone,' were the first two instructions, closely followed by a third, 'Hold out your arms.' Sam's arms were forcibly zip tied together and he winced as the cuts to his hand were still very raw. With his inner wrists now pressed together, he impulsively shouted in his head, *The tracker!* He was uncertain of how robust the bug was and so tried to pull against the strap to relieve some of the pressure between his inner wrists. If the tracker fails, we're all done for, he thought.

He was swept for tracking devices and was relieved when it appeared none had been detected. Before another thought bubbled up, his world went dark. A black bag was slid over his head and a pull-cord tugged so that it was snuggly sealed around Sam's neck. Fortunately, he could breathe through the material. Though he could make out faint light through the weave of the cloth, he knew there would be no guessing his destination.

By Sam's reckoning, it took just an hour and a half from receiving the "null" app result to getting picked up. Whoever was concerned with these "null" results certainly meant business and had the ability to locate such people using their mobile phones. Very well-connected – all the hallmarks of Elion's network, he thought.

Thirty minutes of silence later, the car came to a stop and he could hear three of the doors opening. Pulled by his tied forearms, Sam stumbled out of the car. He was met by the unmistakeable smell of kerosene and the high-pitched whine of an auxiliary power unit. It could only mean one thing – a flight.

'Steps,' someone shouted, and Sam stumbled somewhat as his right foot clashed with the bottom riser of the airstair into the jet. His balance was steadied by the lead captor who ascended the steps in front of Sam, holding his forearm. Without any ceremony, he was led to a seat, had his seatbelt buckled up and was again told not to make a sound. Within a minute, he could hear the door being closed and locked, immediately followed by movement of the aircraft. Sam mentally counted seconds to mitigate the effects of his rising anxiety. Within two minutes, they were accelerating hard down the runway then rotated to a steep angle of attack. Sam was guessing they were taking off from London City, as it was the closest airport to Cyber City and he knew this airport necessitated a steep take-off and approach due to noise abatement regulations. But then again, he could not be so sure because private jets often ascended at greater rates than commercial aircraft.

He felt he was sitting on the starboard side of the plane and confirmed this by placing his right arm on the armrest and sliding his elbow beyond it, making contact with the fuselage. Slowly, he returned his arms to his lap, not wanting to attract any attention. Concentrating on the attitude of the jet, he determined they were on a straight element of their flight path, still ascending, about ten minutes after taking off.

As the flight broke through the cloud layer, the sun bathed Sam's forearms in its warmth. *OK, as it's lunchtime, we must be heading roughly in a south-easterly direction*, Sam calculated in his mind. With no more apparent clues, he began to go over the events and conversations of past few days and see if anything could help him with executing the plan. He just hoped the transmitter was still working, though knew it was useless in the air.

Around a further fifteen minutes had passed when Sam realised the plane had started its descent. *So, about a thirty to forty-five-minute flight, flying southeast from London. Seems were going to land in France or a Benelux country*, he concluded.

Sam's captors seamlessly transferred him from the landed airplane onto an awaiting helicopter. Flanked by two new minders, one with a French accent and another silent one, emitting strong body odour, Sam sat in the middle of the rear seat, but with the various changes of direction the chopper made during the flight, he had no clue where he was heading. After about ten minutes, he felt a long rise up then a stomach-churning short drop, followed by a gentle bump and a feeling of stability as the skids made contact with ground and the engine noise wound down.

Frog-marched for several minutes, he felt the sun's radiance for the first minute, then sensed he was indoors, and by the acoustics, he reckoned a large building. After ascending a couple of wide-treaded staircases and being walked down a long corridor which echoed all the footsteps, he knew he had walked out into the sunny open air again. With his shoulders being guided by two hands, Sam was then pushed down and his backside met with a cushioned chair.

'Got him!' Laura proclaimed. Laura, Tenzin and Tinks huddled over Laura's phone, which displayed a topographical map sporting a stark, small red circle in the middle of the screen.

'Where is that, Laura?' Tinks asked.

'Let me copy the co-ordinates and paste them here… Château de Holzer. He's here in Luxembourg.'

'And so is the skull, then,' Tenzin added.

'How far away is that château?' Tinks queried.

'Probably about ten, fifteen minutes by chopper,' she replied, and felt a wave of unease in her stomach. Flying was bad enough, but helicopter trips brought out the worst of her phobia.

The three were standing in the private terminal at Aéroport de Luxembourg, having chartered a jet at very short notice from London City Airport. Tinks knew if it wasn't for Laura's CIA credentials and smart dealing with the business jet chartering receptionist, they wouldn't be nearly so close to Sam. He was most impressed, though, by her tracking of Sam's transponder-less jet via one of her CIA real-time satellite apps. This was vital to knowing where Sam's flight was heading.

Using her skills of persuasion and negotiation, Laura straightened her collar and proceeded to secure the hiring of a local helicopter and pilot, one who had just completed a sightseeing jolly for a group of insurance underwriters who were in town for a business conference. Tinks jumped in the front seat of the ten-year-old Bell 505 Jet Ranger X with Tenzin sitting behind the pilot. Laura quickly checked her firearm was still in its holster, then entered the helicopter from the starboard side and slid to the middle seat. She followed the others in putting on a headset.

'Sorry, my lady, but I'll need you in the window seat to help balance out the helicopter,' the pilot said, pointing at the desired position for her. Reluctantly, she slid back to the window seat and scrambled to fasten her four-point seat belt system, trying to moderate her anxiety by breathing deeply and slowly.

'I trained for a while as a 'copter pilot, quite a few years ago now,' Tinks said to the pilot.

'That'll be handy, in case I want to take a nap,' the pilot said, laughing. This did not help Laura's anxiety one bit.

'Are you OK if I ask you a few questions on the way,' Tinks asked, 'as a way of a refresher?'

'Sure. We all ready in here?' the pilot asked but didn't wait for any response and took off, hovering a few feet from the ground. After a couple of quick communications with the control tower, the engine wound up even more. The helicopter moved off as the rotor blades clawed at the air, giving them further lift and propulsion.

'Wow, this is amazing,' Tenzin said with a big grin, systematically looking out of his window, then through the front screen and the window next to Laura. Laura tried to ignore all that was going on and focussed on the map on her phone.

Less than ten minutes after taking-off and having flown over a patchwork of attractive dark green woodlands and mid-green fields, made all the more alluring with the bright sunshine, the pilot set the Bell down on a flat section of pasture adjacent to a twenty-metre wide, gently-flowing river.

'Are you sure you can't fly us up to the château, up the valley. It's only a few miles?' Laura pleaded.

'No, Ma'am. As I told you at the terminal, that's restricted airspace. I'd lose my licence and the company would probably go out of business due to the severity of the fines. You get out here now or come back to Lux with me.'

The three watched the helicopter recede into the distance, not knowing if the pilot would come back for them when called. Referring to Laura's map and studying the valley ahead of them, they plotted a route to take them to their destination.

'OK, Sam. Here we come,' Tinks said as the three climbed over the timber perimeter fence.

'We need to be quick. He's been there for a good half hour now,' Laura pointed out.

'Well, I don't know about you, but this valley looks easy to walk compared to what I'm used to,' Tenzin said.

Both Laura and Tinks cast their minds back to Bhutanese terrain and couldn't disagree with their colleague.

Sam's black hood was slackened and unceremoniously ripped off his head. He reactively slammed shut his eyes and bowed his head, then blinked intermittently as his irises adapted to the intensity of the bright sunlight. His forearms still banded and with his minders close by, he understood that he was sitting at a bare, wooden table on a stone balcony, with a substantial stone wall to his left. Stunning, panoramic countryside views were to his right, over a lichened, stone balustrade. Most noticeably, there was an unoccupied wooden chair opposite him, fully shaded by a brown parasol.

A familiar, gravelly voice emanated from the nearby, wide open patio doors, 'I'm in the mood for brandy, Richter. I'll take it on the balcony.' With spritely agility, Elion strode onto the balcony, purposefully not making eye contact with Sam until he was comfortably seated. Sam was not surprised to now see his evil nemesis sitting across from him.

'Twenty-four hours ago, I warned you that our next meeting would be our last,' he rattled and coughed, clearing some of the congestion. Sam noticed Elion had slurred a couple of his words.

'Though deeply disappointing, I am a man of my word, and in just a short day, you have given me not one but two reasons to exact my word.' Richter put pause to Elion's monologue while he was served a large brandy. 'I don't usually drink, Sam, but today is worth celebrating, for more than one reason, with a little of the devil's juice,' he smirked and took a mouthful of the spirit. Sam went to talk but stopped as soon as Elion's glassless, open left hand was raised.

Elion slumped back into his cushioned chair, seemingly enjoying the comfort it afforded along with the pleasure of the drink.

'You know, you're gonna pay for murdering my parents, Elion. You're a dead man,' Sam said, relatively calmly, resisting all urges to attack him now as it would be a futile attempt, what with his hands bound and the minders inches from him.

'Yes, Sam, I agree with you, but I will not be departing on your terms,' Elion said, with a chesty chuckle. 'Yesterday, you could have just gone back to your life of being the hero and saving other people's lives, living on your miserable boat, hiding from the atrocities of your past, but, no; you had to interfere with my life. This can never be tolerated,' Elion stated and sipped his brandy once again.

'How did I interfere?' Sam retorted, knowing that he had spoken to Camila on the previous day.

'You spoke to Camila and informed her what my family does, how we keep together, how we keep our wealth, how we keep our position in the world, how we regain connection to our past lives to advance our righteous work.'

'You mean how you have rigged a divine system for your own ends,' Sam said, reframing with some rancour.

'Sam Angel. You sit there smug in your rectitude when you know full well that energy follows thought, and when you create an action, it has consequences. This is the basis of karma.' Elion leaned forwards and locked his cold eyes to Sam's. 'So, you call the woman bearing my unborn child, telling her some truths, and so she squats in a bath, inserts two knitting needles into her vagina and forcibly lowers her pelvis to ram those needles up through her cervix and into a defenceless unborn baby, only a matter of weeks from being birthed. Now, tell me, how does that sit with your conscience?'

Sam's eyes darted all over the place, anywhere except at Elion. He was deep in processing thought when a feeling of nausea welled up from the pit of his stomach. He didn't for a minute suspect that Camila would have done that, but then again, he didn't give thought to what she might do with his information.

'You see, Sam, life is complicated and actions have consequences – karma – in this life or in another, but in the end, you and me are not that dissimilar, hmm?'

'Fuck you,' Sam spat back.

'Ah, I think I have touched a nerve. Something to ponder on in the short time you have left on God's Earth.'

'You are just as monstrous as you look.'

'Sticks and stones, Sam. Is that what the pure-of-heart Sam Angel has come down to, name-calling?' Elion relished in his belittlement and mental torturing of his captive.

'Don't you have any feelings, any emotions about what you do to people, what you do to the divine system? Don't you have any empathy?' Sam asked more constructively.

'No!' Elion chuckled. 'Not one drop! Our family ridded

ourselves of the curse of emotion, of empathy, centuries ago. We are free to conduct ourselves in a manner to control the world and direct it as we see fit. Please, don't be so naïve as to be wanting me to start feeling again, to renounce my judged sins and redeem myself,' Elion laughed with his chesty rattle. 'I think you should be more concerned about yourself, bring your own house in order before you cast stones. Now, you have been brought here on account of your supposed "null" result on the app, I hear?'

Composing himself and trying hard to bluff, Sam responded, 'I did score "null".'

'You are no angel, Angel. Only someone in this world but not of this world could have possibly returned such a result; and you are not that!' Elion exclaimed.

'What do you mean?'

Chuckling, Elion answered, 'You shot a boy dead in a war, you played a part in killing an unborn baby, and by the way, Camila is fine, I'm surprised the empathetic Sam Angel did not ask after her well-being. So, you have karma, so… who helped you?'

'I don't know, I don't know who she really is.'

'Let me guess. Eyes of fire?' Elion widened his eyes and scrutinised Sam's reaction.

Sam's eyes widened, 'You know her?'

'Sam, Sam, Sam,' he said condescendingly. 'Not a she or a he. They just are.'

'No, that doesn't help me.'

'There are souls on this planet that spend lifetime upon lifetime upon lifetime purifying themselves through meditation and spiritual contacts in the ether, the energy of existence. They work their way up a metaphysical ladder, reaching higher and higher levels of initiation. At a certain point in their sacred ascent, these spirits are freed from reincarnation. They do not have to return here and they can spend all eternity in the spirit world, the oneness, helping other mortals to ascend. These entities do not need return as the soul has been purified and is dissolved to break the link between the spiritual entity and reincarnating soul, which no longer exists. However, a few monads, one's spiritual essence, hold onto their soul for a time after it has been purified, which allows them to incarnate at will, to be in the world but not of the world.'

'OK, so they are entities that come to help us, like angels, or are they aliens?' Sam asked flippantly.

'I suppose that's a crude analogy, but they are certainly not aliens, that's a whole different story,' Elion answered, rubbing his elongated crown. 'However, these "angels" do not help in the miraculous way the churches would have you believe, but they can direct and redirect energy on the physical plane to have an effect on the flow of humanity towards ascension, the rise of mankind, if you will.'

Sam pondered on this. It dovetailed into Amelie's pattern of existence – not being around for long, elusive, only revealing herself to the absolute minimum number of people. It explained her showing up in Italy for Laura and Tenzin, his camera app failing in her presence and why Tinks never believed she was real. But more to the point, the penny dropped for Sam. 'So, these beings are a danger to you, to your very existence, your family's existence. They are helping humanity to ascend. You are holding us back. You are the devil!'

'Don't be so dramatic, Sam. Angels and devils, heaven and hell, these are all constructs of a religion, a conduit of control for the masses to tenuously access the divine world.'

Strangely, Sam felt he couldn't argue against Elion's summary. 'But you do fear these entities, hence why you wanted to use the app, not only to effect more world disunity and harness more data on people for future uses, but also to flush out any of these celestial beings.'

'Very good, Sam. But the chances of catching out one of these flame-eyed meddlers is very low; they have access to boundless knowledge, and so are not easy to outwit. But when your fingerprint alerted our system, we had to take action, and hence you are here. Our family has been plagued by these beings for centuries but we have never encountered them, only hear about them through third parties, such as yourself. Though they do pose a threat to us, it is not a direct one, otherwise they would have presented themselves to us by now,' Elion rounded up. He finished his brandy. 'Now, I've got a big journey ahead of me and you must meet your maker. Richter!' Moments later, the butler appeared. 'Arrange for Mr Angel to have his real karma presented to him, then show him the ropes.'

Standing and turning to the still-seated Sam, who was now flanked by his minders, Elion said, 'This is our last goodbye, Sam. I bid you adieu and bon voyage.'

'So, what's between you and Angel, Laura?' Tinks changed the subject on their hike up the valley, alongside the babbling River Holz.

'What do you mean?' Laura played dumb, lifting her feet high in an awkward walking manner to mitigate the thistle-strewn landscape from scratching her ankles so much. She rued her decision to wear shorts and not wear thicker socks.

'You know. The way you look at him. The way he looks at you,' Tinks pried further.

Concentrating to not sound flustered, she replied, 'I think you're seeing things, Tinks. I'm not looking for love, too busy trying to save the world.' She felt confident she'd batted the subject away.

'You sound just like Angel,' Tinks teased.

'I think we need to focus on the task in hand. We've still got three miles to cover and that's before trying to scale the plateau to the château,' Laura explained.

'I think we've got company coming,' Tenzin said.

Both Laura and Tinks strained to scan the landscape ahead but could not spot anything. Having lived most of his life in wide open plains and trained to pick out a yak from the vista over great distances, Tenzin's superb eyesight, detected a black vehicle driving towards them along the riverbank.

'I see it now,' Laura said, a short while after scanning the area. 'It's got to be a couple of miles away. There's nothing wrong with your eyesight.'

'The pilot did say this valley is monitored. Remember, we're just two hikers with a monk,' Tinks said, being somewhat sarcastic. Although he and Laura would pass for walkers, Tenzin in his robes made him very conspicuous and the trio, therefore, looked very much out of place.

'Let's assume there are two thugs in the vehicle, here's a plan,' Laura said, detailing her idea to her companions.

Richter led the way down to the ground floor, then on through to the rear of the building. Sam was amazed, but also at the same time disgusted, by the vastness of the château and the adornment of the walls, in room after room, of a large collection of fine artworks and artefacts, presumably relevant to Elion's family and history. *There's probably enough wealth here to solve at least one of the major problems in the world,* he thought to himself, whilst also looking for possible escape routes should the opportunity for flight present itself.

Taking quick looks at his escorts, he recognised them from Monaco; a French guy and other smelly one, who was apparently dumb. Down they went into a colossal, vaulted cellar, stacked floor-to-vault, on every stone wall, with racks of bottled wines and ageing barrels of liquor. To the very rear of the maze-like basement, Sam, his accompanying minders and the butler came to a halt at a dead end, with a rack of bottles, perhaps six feet wide, arresting their progress. Richter stepped to the left and punched a code into a discreetly positioned keypad. Sam tried to take in the pattern of his fingers, but the old man's digits were too nimble to track.

The dead-end wall rumbled into life and the rack began to pivot about a central vertical axis, allowing a glow of light from beyond the wall to become visible. The wall slowly turned a full ninety degrees, producing an entrance to the left of about two feet wide. The wall thickness was two feet in width and to the right of the wall was now a side view of the rack of wines.

Sam was pushed to follow Richter through the secret opening and they entered into a spiral stairwell. But unlike the rest of the building, meticulously built from well-honed blocks of stone, this area had been carved out of what looked like solid granite rock. The party descended the steps for what Sam estimated was two full turns, so he was sure they were at least twenty feet below the basement. The steps led to a small lobby with one, highly polished steel door, and another keypad to the right-hand side. This time, Richter was not able to be so discreet and Sam clearly saw the entry code.

No! It can't be! he thought to himself before again being pushed over the threshold of the new opening and into a long corridor, also hewn from chiselled rock. Midway along the corridor, the four stopped again. Sam could see a door labelled 'Exit' at the far end of the corridor, but again watched the butler punch in the same code on the keypad next to another stainless-steel door on the left. This time, Richter stepped out of the way, allowing Sam to be pushed into the new room, closely followed by his two escorts. The door slammed shut behind them.

Sam took in the scene before him. The brightly lit room was large, perhaps forty feet each way and had a much higher ceiling than the corridor outside. It was also finished with a continuous, bright white, satin coating, the floor, the walls and the ceiling, clean, as if it could be used as an operating theatre. The far side of the room was festooned with floor-to-ceiling racks of electronic equipment, thousands of tiny green and amber lights flickering and dancing to an unheard tune. But the most eye-catching element of the high-tech chamber was the centrepiece. A full height, four-feet wide, cylindrical inner space, made from a form of glazing, which had a series of circular holes cut out, just above waist height. Long, white chamber gauntlets attached to the openings, drooped down the inside of the cylinder. In the middle of the cylinder sat a stainless-steel platform housing an array of what looked like small closed-circuit television cameras. It took no time for Sam to determine that these units were lasers, firing what seemed to be constant, fine green beams of light at a centrepiece.

Nestled in the centre of the ring of lasers was a very light grey, stone-like object, perhaps just the right size to hold in two cupped, adult hands. It seemed to contain meandering cracks that have been subsequently fused. 'The skull!' Sam muttered.

With the larger minder wrapping his sizeable hand around Sam's upper arm, his non-verbal sidekick made his way to a control panel on the lefthand wall. With a quick flick of a switch, the green laser beams ceased firing. The mute man then walked over to the cylinder and carefully peeled the seal away from one of the chamber gauntlets. He then pulled the freed glove out and tossed it on the floor. Walking back to Sam, he looked at him at close quarters and laughed with an unusually widened mouth. Sam recoiled at the sight. It was then that Sam understood the reason behind the man's muteness. He saw his tongue had previously been gruesomely torn out.

Sam's bound arms were lifted to near-horizontal and the tongueless man released them with a swift up-cut of a penknife to the restraining band. Immediately, Sam tried to fight off his company, but they were far too strong a force from which to escape and he was instantly controlled.

Dragging Sam over towards the centre cylinder, and by twisting his left arm and bending over his left hand, Sam was helpless to arrest his journey towards the skull.

Sam started shouting, 'No! No! NO!'

His right hand was thrust into the open hole and subsequently grabbed by the now gauntleted hand of the French minder. Between the two goons, Sam's movements were dominated by his captors. Straining every sinew to avoid touching the skull proved futile. 'Fuck off, fuck you. NO!' was the only defence he had.

His open right hand was now being held by his captor from above, his fingers interlaced with his controlling minder's, and being dragged closer and closer to the centre artefact.

'NOOOO!'

His four fingertips made contact with the top of skull. All physical resistance from him stopped in an instant. Reminders and memories of actions in the past began horrifying him, retraumatising him. His legs crumpled. He fell limp, crying, snivelling at the torture he was being forced to endure.

His captors let go of him and he fell to the floor; his right arm slid back out of the chamber. He instinctively assumed a foetal position, shaking, sweating, sobbing and murmuring to himself.

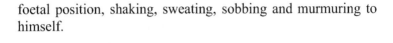

'This is private property and you are trespassing,' the black-suited driver said as he got out of his four-by-four pick-up truck. He was swiftly joined by his passenger and they both made their way to stand in front of the vehicle.

'Oh, sorry, we were just looking to hike up this valley, it looked so attractive,' Laura politely replied, with a friendly smile.

'We're going to have to take you back to the public footpath from where you came. Get on the backseat of the truck,' the man ordered.

Laura and Tinks obediently moved to the driver's side and Tenzin, the passenger's. As soon as they had passed the open front doors, they all turned around in unison. With lightning speed, Tenzin struck his man with a full force, open handed strike to the solar plexus. The man reactively bent over, winded, and then was swiftly knocked out by a sharp chopping blow to the base of his skull. Tenzin then rifled through the glove compartment and found a bag of zip ties.

Laura pointed her firearm at the centre of the driver's chest. 'Don't move a muscle! Arms up!' she ordered, whilst Tinks quickly moved to relieve him of his gun and radio, and checked for any other hidden threats.

Tenzin walked around the vehicle to join the others. With Tinks now training the driver's gun on the driver too, it was a simple process for Tenzin to zip tie the driver's arms behind him. 'I've disarmed the other one, tied him and got his radio.

He's out cold,' Tenzin reported.

'OK,' Laura said. She indicated towards the driver. 'Get this one on the back seat with you Tinks, and Tenzin, lift your man onto the flatbed and stay with him.'

Once these clear orders had been carried out, Laura speedily drove the truck up the valley, back from where it had come. Drifting around some of the larger boulder obstructions, Laura expertly manoeuvred the two-tonne truck up the valley. Craning their heads out of the left side of the vehicle, Laura and Tinks analysed the vertical island of granite coming closer into view.

'Man, just look at that. That castle seems to have grown out of the top of that gigantic oval of rock,' Tinks gasped. 'How the fuck do we get up there? It's got to be about two hundred feet or more of near vertical rock!' he said with a tone of defeat.

'The security detail must get up there and down it, there must be a way,' Laura said, injecting some positivity to the conversation.

'Look, over there! Directly to the left, Laura. Head for that.'

Laura changed down gear and turned towards the monolith, then accelerated towards a timber barn-like structure at its base. 'Just look at that!' Laura exclaimed.

Tinks had to crouch his head low to the central console to get a good view out of the front windscreen. 'Is that some kind of lift?' he said.

'Something like that. I think it's a funicular railway in the middle of nowhere. And it's almost vertical!' Laura said.

As they approached the barn area, Laura slowed and they scanned for any more security guards. As she parked up in the barn, the driver's radio in Tinks' hand sparked into life.

'Eagle's nest to fledgling. Anything to report? Over.'

Laura turned to the tied-up driver and pointed her gun at his face. 'Tell them only hikers and you've just dropped them back to public land. Go!' she instructed and got Tinks to hold the transmission button down for the driver. He did as he was told and they all alighted.

'Right, sit them both down, away from each other at the back of the barn and secure them there,' Laura directed and Tinks and Tenzin set to it while she gave them cover with her firearm. 'Is there anything else we need to know. Any codes or anything?' she asked. The conscious minder looked downwards and shook his head.

'OK, guys, we can't take their word and we need to keep our wits about us. First, gag them.'

Tinks found an oily rag and ripped it into two pieces, giving one to Tenzin. Then they did as Laura suggested.

Walking out of the barn, the three of them looked almost vertically up at the cliff face. Built at the site of a long chimney, maybe two hundred feet high, it provided a channelled, sheltered position for a two-car funicular railway.

'So, what is this?' Tenzin asked.

'It's like a lift and has two tracks. When one car comes down, the other goes up, like counterweights, to make the operation more efficient,' Laura explained.

'I can't see to the top clearly, there's too much glare from the sky above,' Tinks said.

'It ends at that overhang, that must be an entrance. I can see there's a T-shaped platform there, with pole railings, like scaffolding,' the eagle-eyed Tenzin reported.

'Well, there's only one way to find out,' Laura said, and confidently led them into the metal car on the left side track. She hid her fear of this next height-based challenge very well, distracted by the anxiety of the mission. Once inside, there was a simple control panel on the rock-face side of the car, with two buttons, labelled with up and down arrows. The other three sides of the carriage were amply windowed to afford

Rad Johnson

expansive views during the journey.

Laura pressed the up button. The car started with a jolt, graunching and squeaking and as it began to crawl up the side of the sheer, granite colossus.

'Get up!' the French man ordered.

Sam felt that he had no energy as he slowly pushed his body up onto his feet. Though he had recovered somewhat, he once again found himself haunted by harrowing memories of Afghanistan. The minders had quickly reactivated The Divinity App's nucleus, minimising any downtime.

'You see, you are not without karma,' the French man said and both his captors laughed as they escorted Sam out of the nerve centre. With his legs feeling like lead, he struggled to walk down the corridor towards the door furnished with the exit sign. With the code entered, the steel door opened outwards and allowed a rush of warm, outdoor air to rush in. Pushed out again, the beleaguered Sam found himself staggering onto a steel gridded platform, flanked by a granite wall to his right and barriers to his left. There was a break in the barriers in the middle where a narrow section of platform cantilevered out to allow for passengers to alight the railway. At the far end of the platform, opposite from the door he'd just exited, was a closed door signed 'Machine Room'.

Sam was shoved towards the closest section of barrier. 'Elion asked us to show you "the ropes",' the French man said and Sam was manhandled to the barrier and forced to look down. Terrified, Sam saw a near-vertical drop of at least two hundred feet. Two rails were affixed to the cliff for the full

273

length that he could see down to a funicular car, a long way below. In between the rails lay two thick steel cables, rattling and wiggling as the system was in operation. He could see the car to the left had nearly arrived.

'You see? The ropes! Steel ropes,' the French man said and laughed out loud. Without hesitation, he then pushed Sam between his shoulder blades. Sam found himself tipping over the barrier, head first.

Sam started his fall. He tracked the bottom of a vertical section of barrier, vigorously engaging his muscles for their one-shot, life-saving task. He grabbed the bottom-most part of the pole with his right hand and tensed all of his muscles in readiness for the jolt when his freefalling body would pull on his hand like never before.

His grip held and but knew he would not be able to hold on for long with one hand. Sam looked up, beyond his hand, and noticed the French minder's face transform from joy to gritted determination as he lifted his right foot in readiness to stamp down on Sam's weakening fingers.

Almost in concert, a loud mechanical clunk rang out as the funicular railway cars reached their apogees and the railway car door opened.

Bang! Laura discharged her gun. Sam saw the French man fall backwards from the force of the gunshot and hit the gridded platform with a loud clatter. She then aimed for the mute sidekick.

Sam watched his hand as his grasp failed and fingers started to helplessly extend.

'Angel!' Tinks shouted as he dived onto the platform at the foot of the barrier. Just as Sam's gripped failed, Tinks grabbed Sam's forearm with both hands. A fraction of a second later, Sam witnessed Tenzin reach down for his other arm. The two pulled him up, Sam's legs waggling, fruitlessly trying to find some purchase. They propped Sam up against the cliff wall on the other side of the platform and Tinks checked him over to make sure he was OK.

'Fuck, Angel, I thought you were a gonner,' Tinks said emotionally.

Still catching his breath, Sam replied, 'Another second, mate.' He affectionately gripped Tinks' forearm.

Laura and Tenzin moved towards the entrance door near where the mute minder stood. 'Enter the code and open the door,' she commanded, still pointing her gun at him. He didn't respond at first but then slowly turned to face the keypad. Instead of reaching for the entry pad, he lunged at Laura. Laura recoiled but Tenzin went on the offensive and kicked him square in the face. Reeling backwards from the blow and holding his bloodied, broken nose, he stumbled into the railings. The force of his backtracking made his torso lean outward over the barrier as soon as his pelvis met the top bar. Tenzin leaped forward to grab the minder, but in that instant, he powerlessly watched him somersault backwards off the platform and silently plummet down the funicular railway track.

'I tried,' Tenzin said, looking down to the bottom car that was now splattered with the remains of the mute henchman.

'I know, Tenzin, I saw,' Laura consoled. 'Now we're stuck out here. Shall I just shoot the keypad and try our luck?'

'No!' Sam shouted. 'I know the code.'

Laura went up to the keypad. 'What is it?'

'Six, six, six,' Sam replied with incredulity.

As the door powered open and she checked that the corridor behind was clear, Laura turned and said, 'Oh, my God! Elion *is* the devil!' and then searched the French man's body for his gun. She also came across two phones. 'Is one of these yours, Sam?' she asked, throwing them both into his lap.

'I have thrown all the door bolts on the doors, top and bottom of the staircase, Mr Rotzburg. No one can get at us unless they have a small army,' Richter assured Elion, not even out of breath after his security activities and running up the steps, equivalent to three flights, non-stop.

Now holed up on the top floor room of the turret above Elion's library office and balcony, Elion felt it safe to begin. The circular stone room served as a penthouse panic room, fitted out as a bedroom with rudimentary kitchen and ablutions facilities. Today it also served a wholly difference purpose.

Elion was comfortably seated in a green leather, wing-backed chair, feeling tired after having consumed several measures of brandy that day. 'Hyperion, are you ready, my son?'

'Yes, Father. Isabella is comfortably sedated. I think she is ready to birth our baby boy any time now.'

'How much did you divulge to Isabella?'

'Nothing, Father. After you called me, I got her doctor to call her on the pretence of an oversight of her last pre-natal check-up, and he diagnosed pre-eclampsia. She then told me that we need to induce the baby, even though she is only thirty-seven weeks through the term. The pessary was flown in and administered last night.'

'Excellent, my boy. Just as efficient as my father was,' he said, with a twinkle in his eye.

The thirty-two-year-old Hyperion shared the same stout stature and conical head as his father and carried similar genetic mutations which presented in his parent; the gappy, stubby teeth, the cool, thin, pale and mole-covered skin, and the claw-like fingers and toes. However, the most noticeable difference was the addition of a mutation that startled people to the greatest degree; his pupils formed a vertical, black ellipse within the confines of his irises of radiant blue hues.

'Thank you, my boy. I know she was not ready for another couple of weeks, but I did not anticipate Camila's actions. As you know, it's best to do this with our own flesh and blood.'

'It will be a pleasure, Papa.' He helped Elion up onto his feet, ensuring his full length galabiya was not caught on anything, and guided him up onto a decorative wooden table. Once sitting, Hyperion carefully assisted his father to lay down flat on the table, tucking a small pillow under his head and gently kissed his forehead.

Hyperion's girlfriend, Isabella, groaned with the onset of more contractions. She lay on the king-sized bed, draped in sheets of white Egyptian cotton, matching her own dress, which was now hitched up to her waist. Her legs were apart and her knees up, with Richter, having just sanitised his hands, attending to birthing the baby.

Hyperion picked up the pre-prepared faggot of dried herbs and set light to one end. Having blown out the flames, he walked around the room with the smudge stick, moving it in a triangular fashion, repeating an ancient phrase over and over, 'Matala-el erak awat, matala-el erak awat, matala-el erak awat, matala-el erak awat.'

'The space is now devoid of any interfering spirits. Richter, how long now?' Hyperion asked calmly.

'Minutes, Mr Rotzburg, I can see the head in the canal,' he replied.

Hyperion took a stand at the head of the table, right next to the top of his father's head. He lay down a small, dog-eared codex; an assembly of faded papyrus sheets contained within a more recently-made, leather binding. Hyperion referred to the ritual manual, flipping through some of the papyrus leaves before assuming a wide stance and raised his arms above his own blonde-haired head. He formed a triangle, his upper arms almost horizontal and his fingertips and thumb from one hand touching their counterparts of his other hand, forming a pyramid. Moving his head backwards, he looked up to this hand-pyramid and started chanting continuously, slowly at first, 'Wsir-di-nsmt hateka milish cabah, wsir-di-nsmt milish cabah, wsir-di-nsmt hateka milish cabah.'

Isabella started screaming with the intensity of the next contraction, Hyperion responded by chanting quicker and louder, with a hypnotic meter, 'Wsir-di-nsmt hateka milish cabah, wsir-di-nsmt hateka milish cabah, wsir-di-nsmt hateka milish cabah.'

Elion took an exaggerated, rattly deep breath, arching his back in spasm. As he exhaled, his body slumped and turned limp.

The next moment, Elion found himself looking down at the scene below; himself on a table, his son standing next to him in a trance-like state and continuing the chanting, and Isabella on the bed with Richter cradling the top of the baby's head emerging from between Isabella's legs.

The realities of the room below Elion began to fade to black and the room's sounds quietened, until an enveloping, thick nothingness was all that he could perceive. Time in this stasis was unmeasurable but Elion had experienced this process many, many times before. The feeling of lightness of being out of his aging body contrasted with the darkness of his new environment. It was only a matter of moments before his reincarnation would be completed.

Though familiar with this spiritual mechanism, his consciousness was taken aback with a sudden and unexpected experience. His visual sense was overwhelmed by a rush of ferocious flame and fire. This inferno formed a sphere around him. Elion did not know what this signified but all he could do was witness the ensuing fire-dance. As a feeling of intense, burning heat hit him, it was accompanied by an excruciating audible roar. The sensations of the onslaught could not be physically felt, as such, by Elion, but were abominable from his spiritual perspective. Elion was now concerned that there was a glitch in his reincarnation ritual.

The flames then abated and became less present, less intrusive. Through the fiery sphere, he could discern a lightness from behind and some objects, perhaps some entities. As he trained his concentration on these new aspects, a scream interrupted Elion's world and with a push from Isabella, Elion's existence went dark once again. With the sound of blood rushing through the ears to a rhythm of a fast heartbeat, he instantly had the overwhelming urge to clear his lungs and breathe his first breath. He was reborn.

Richter speedily swaddled the newborn as he let out his first cry, ejecting mucous from his lungs and using his lungs for the very first time.

Hyperion raced over to the bed and held his firstborn child, a son. He gazed at his beautiful boy through tear-filled eyes, not quite believing the alien feeling of love for this small dependent bundle.

Taking a moment to control and shake off this brief moment of emotional weakness, he cradled his baby's head and quietly whispered, 'Hello, my boy. Hello, Father. Hello, Elion.'

Tinks helped Sam to his feet, 'You OK to carry on?'

'Yeah. Yeah, mate,' he replied unconvincingly, but they all knew they had no choice but to get the job done. Arriving at the app's nerve centre, Sam opened the door and made his way swiftly over to the control panel on the left. Within a moment, the lasers had been deactivated.

The other three were taking in the elements comprising the nerve centre. Albeit mostly familiar to Laura, she was still amazed at how all the equipment she had helped to build had been set up deep inside this gargantuan lump of granite.

Getting his thinking straight and trying to focus on the job in hand, Sam said, 'OK, how about Tinks and Tenzin recover the skull, but don't touch it, use the gauntlets as insulation. Laura and I will track down Elion. Then we'll meet up near the entrance at some point in time?' He had run out of ideas.

Laura pointed to a rack on the back wall. 'That rack needs to be totally destroyed too as it holds all the harvested data.'

'Just remember, six, six, six is the keypad number you'll need,' Sam added. Tenzin and Tinks nodded and set to work as Laura and Sam left the room.

Laura led them towards the door at the end of the corridor. She turned to Sam and asked, 'You sure you're OK?'

Sam nodded and indicated to press on, and Laura grabbed his hand and placed the French minder's gun in it. He stared at it and froze. 'It's going to be alright, Sam, but you may need this.' Thoughts of that poor Afghani child flashed into his mind. He shut his eyes and shook his head, trying to clear what he saw, which worked enough to allow him to continue.

After opening the steel door, Laura cautiously started up the spiral, stone steps, followed by Sam, and they made their way up them, keeping their backs to the outside wall and scanning for any movement from above. Laura punched in the code at the next door allowing them passage into the cellar. They silently proceeded, guns at the ready.

'I know how to get to Elion's office, let me lead,' Sam whispered, and Laura followed him through the cellar and up to the main ground floor.

Walking through a large, ornate dining room, from the

diagonally opposite door, a black-suited man appeared, looking into the huge room but not instantly seeing Sam and Laura. Sam had his gun already raised. But his vision was interrupted as he went to pull the trigger. All he could see for that moment was the boy whom he had shot those many years ago.

Crack! A gunshot rang out.

Sam did not quite know what had happened. With his left hand, he felt his torso and checked his hand for blood. 'Am I shot?' he asked, confused.

It took a firm grab and little shake to his left arm by Laura to snap him out of his bewildered state. She looked him in the eyes, 'It's OK, Sam. You're OK. I took care of it. Come on, we can't stay here.'

They moved on and Sam whispered, 'How many more suits can there be?'

'Who knows, but it seems that Elion does not keep a large security detail here, probably a combination of wanting to hide his secrets and the difficulty in anyone getting here,' she replied.

They climbed two grand staircases, taking their time and listening out for further sound, and eventually arrived outside Elion's library office.

Just as Sam turned the handles, he was startled by a volley of four shots ringing out from Laura's gun; two kill shots for each of the two suited men running up the staircase they had just ascended.

Laura held her finger up towards Sam, requesting a moment of silence. 'It's OK, I can't hear any more of them at the moment. Let's go in.'

After they had swept through the library, Sam said, 'No sign of Elion here either,' after sticking his head out of the patio doors to check the balcony. 'And the helicopter I was brought in is still here, on the lawn in that walled garden area,' he said, pointing in the direction of the chopper. 'He must still be around.'

'OK, Sam, have a look through his desk, see if you can find anything of note. I'll keep watch here,' Laura said, heading for the entrance door.

Sam went through the drawers, but nothing of significance jumped out. There was one drawer to the top of the right pedestal, but it was locked and Sam felt around under the bare desk to see if he could find a key. 'There's one locked drawer, Laura, I'm going to have to shoot the lock open.'

'Wait! I hear footsteps.' Sam joined Laura at the doorway, listening to the growing sound of hurried footsteps.

'It's two people, getting close now,' Sam discerned.

Readying their guns, they hid in the shadows of the doorway, ready to take action.

'Sam? Laura?' Tinks was whispering as he and Tenzin ran along the corridor, stopping at every room opening.

Laura stuck her head out to survey the area. 'Tenzin! Tinks! We're in here,' she whispered back.

Once the four were reunited, Tinks explained, 'Tenzin has the skull, wrapped in plastic sheeting we found and then in that dead minder's jacket and we destroyed the data bank. This place is like the *Mary Celeste*, but is so vast, we've not been able to check everywhere for Elion or his henchmen.'

'Great work,' Laura lauded the two. We have to make a decision. We have the skull, so do we try to escape now, or finish the job and get Elion?'

'I've just got to see what's in that drawer, then I say we go. Keep a look out as it's going to be noisy,' Sam said.

Sam approached the desk and at an angle, fired at almost point-blank range, destroying the lock. He opened the drawer but it looked empty at first. Pulling the drawer out to its fullest extent, it revealed a paper file. He slapped it onto the desk and read the title,

Rad Johnson

Above Top Secret: Project Bluebeam and the Alien Invasion.
Disseminated by: General John Q. Hill

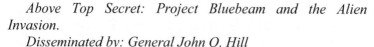

'It sounds like they are in your late father's office, Mr Rotzburg,' Richter said, matter-of-factly.

'Yes, that gunshot sounded almost directly below us, very close. Come on, help,' Hyperion ordered. He stopped stroking his baby, who was now trying to take his first breast-feed from Isabella.

Richter opened the turret window, then joined Hyperion at his deceased father's body. With some considerable effort, they each took one of Elion's arms, wrapping them over their own shoulders and dragged his body to the window. They sat the corpse on the windowsill before unceremoniously pushing it backwards out of the window.

What the hell's this document about? Sam fleetingly thought and picked the file up to read another time. As he just left the desk, he was taken aback by a 'whomph', followed by a large crash out on the balcony.

'What the f… ?' Sam said, holding up his gun and looking startled. Laura raced over and they quickly checked the balcony for dangers. Looking clear, they continued onto it, leaving Tinks and Tenzin to guard the room.

They approached the broken patio table which had collapsed in the middle and stared at the bloodied mess that was Elion. Sam quickly checked the body for signs of life. 'He's dead and still very warm. Good riddance, though.'

He looked up and saw an open window. Indicating upwards with his gun, he surmised, 'Maybe he felt cornered and jumped out of the window? Nah. You don't suppose he's already reincarnated?'

'Possible, but I think it's time to get out of here with the skull,' Laura replied.

As Laura immediately left the balcony, Sam fleetingly wondered why Elion was wearing a white smock. He took out his phone and took a photo of the lifeless monster. 'Good riddance; you saved me a job,' he whispered, feeling that his death was some justice for taking his parents' lives.

Rejoining his companions and still on high alert for any enemy, they made their way down the two main staircases.

'What's the plan?' Tenzin asked.

'There's a helicopter outside. Tinks, how good's your flying?' Sam asked.

'Rusty as fuck, but I reckon I can handle it,' Tinks replied with bravado.

'Are you mad?' Laura snapped. 'You said you've only done a bit of flying in the army years ago! And we could be sitting targets,' she said. She felt rising anxiety.

'It's our best bet. We want to get as far away from here as quickly as possible, especially with the skull. Not even sure if the railway will work now that minder's corpse hit a car. And the other chopper pilot from the airport would have knocked off by now,' Tinks reasoned.

The four ran out of the main reception hall and across the lawn to the Eurocopter, with Laura occasionally looking backwards, scanning for threats with her gun readied. Tinks and Tenzin, still cradling the skull, took the front seats and Sam and, lastly, Laura jumped in the back. Tinks took some seconds to look around the controls and then used the switches above his head to fire up the two engines.

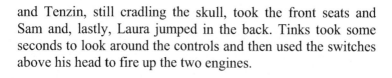

'Do you want me to radio whoever's left to shoot the helicopter down, Mr Rotzburg?' Richter asked, as they discreetly watched, through the turret window, the four escape.

'No, Richter. We cannot lose that artefact. We know who they are and we will deal with them in due course, and then recover our property.'

Tinks raised the engine speeds to take-off power and the Eurocopter shakily lifted a couple of feet off the ground. Sam tucked Elion's secret file in the seat pocket in front of him and concentrated on looking out for dangers to report to his rookie pilot friend.

Laura sat in the middle seat, her seatbelt clipped together, but she found it hard to control her jitters. Without asking for permission, she slid her left arm under Sam's right and reached out to hold his hand. They looked deep into each other's eyes and Sam responded with a loving smile and a reassuring squeeze of her hand.

'Luxembourg Airport, please, Tinks. But do take it easy,'

Sam jocularly ordered, bracing for them all to have a bumpy ride.

Epilogue 1

London
26th June 2022

11:00 UTC ZUX NEWS 24 LIVE --- NEWS HEADLINES---

'It's exactly a month to the day that the world mysteriously lost connection to The Divinity App. In the short five weeks before it went offline, it garnered over 2.5 billion downloads and was, at one point, estimated to dominate over seventy-five per cent of all social media usage. Although Pope Leo XIV has, extraordinarily, addressed the world three times recently to call for calm and unity, the Vatican has still kept silent on the subject of the app save for one press release confirming the Catholic Church's abandonment of the service. ZUX News has repeatedly requested the Vatican for further comment, but we have received no communication thus far.

In other news, rebuilding of the widespread damage caused by the recent wave of civil unrest across most nations of the world, has started in earnest. One economist has estimated the rebuilding cost as over a trillion dollars and may take upwards of two years for the reconstructions to complete. In an unsurpassed act of generosity, the Vatican has pledged one hundred million dollars to assist with the rebuilding, with much of the money to go to underdeveloped countries…'

'Hyperion?'

'Yes.'

'It's Shetty here, CentSec,' she said.

'Ah, Shetty! What news do you have?' Hyperion asked expectantly.

'Your father's scheme to expand funding for the northern Greek archaeological site at Vergina has paid off, sir. The other skull, it's been found.   '

'Marvellous! Marvellous! This, truly, is a great day! You will hear from me soon with instructions for its transportation,' and with that, Hyperion disconnected the call. 'It's been found, Richter, the second skull. Now we need to make a plan for the Gemini Twins to be reunited. And find me the contact of the cardinal who Elion controlled, the one he sent away to Southeast Asia.'

Epilogue 2
Dharamsala, India
22nd July 2022

Sam, Laura, Tinks and Tenzin sat perched on the edge of the brown leather sofa, giving their absolute full attention to every action and word emanating from the Dalai Lama, who sat to their right, at the head of the coffee table. The spiritual leader of the Gelug School of Tibetan Buddhism had warmly welcomed his guests and was sincerely delighted when they accepted his invitation for an audience with him in his exiled home town of Dharamsala, India.

The modest, but dated, reception room was clean and tidy, with a large, green, central carpet rug and floor-to-ceiling wooden panelling. This panelling was broken up by functional, white curtains, drawn to increase privacy and reduce the heating effect from direct sunlight. A few ornaments stood on the windowsills on top of the closed curtains, whilst the obvious focal point of the office was the Buddhist altar, against the wall facing the four guests, which was adorned with intricately-designed, gold-leafed frames and spiritual artefacts, delicate potted orchids and several sticks of burning incense giving the air a floral fragrance.

The bespectacled, bald, head monk, with his maroon and gold robe, now in his late-eighties, had all the presence and energy of a sage half his age. 'You know, Tenzin and I met just three months ago and I gave him a task of great importance to our world. He and all of you recover the skull, which is now safely hidden. For this, you have my deepest gratitude,' he said, placing his hands together in a prayer gesture and bowing his head to his guests.

'Your Holiness, once we all came to realise what had to be done, and with some divine guidance,' Sam struggled with how to describe Amelie's vital involvement in their success, 'we all followed our hearts; it was the right thing to do.' He took Laura's right hand and gave it a loving squeeze.

'Yes, yes, you all have light in your hearts, and I can see you want it to illuminate the darkness that lives amongst us,' the Dalai Lama concluded, and Sam's hand-holding did not go unnoticed. Looking at Sam and Laura, he continued, 'And our world needs and welcomes more light and more love, such as that which you and Laura have found and, I'm sure, will nurture.'

Both Sam and Laura looked at each other and blushed. 'You never know when you're going to meet a loving partner, and we sure did not expect it on this adventure,' Laura admitted.

'Love finds you, Laura. It's magnetic!' His Holiness proclaimed, widening his eyes and his smile in equal measure. Everyone in the room gently laughed.

'But sometimes, we all need some help, some directions,' he continued and then paused. His guests were not quite sure what he meant but kept their full attention on the spiritual leader. Keeping his smile, he blinked, an overlong, purposeful blink. When he opened his eyes, his irises had instantly changed colour to bright oranges, reds and golds. Just as the four took in the magical sight, the Dalai Lama blinked again and his eyes returned to their natural brown colouring.

'Amelie, Your Holiness?' Sam asked, stunned, confused.

'Yes and no, Sam. It's complicated, but rest assured, we are here, we are trying to direct mankind to the realisations of truth and to the path of ascent.'

Tinks froze with his jaw stuck in a dropped position.

Before Tinks' understanding could mature any further, the Dalai Lama swiftly moved the conversation on. 'Another reason to meet you all is to ask if you would work with us. Tenzin was our first Buddhist Defender and he rose to the occasion and in doing so, met the three of you on his path. We are working towards building a network of defenders to assist us with the work of facilitating the ascent of humans, a divine plan that must be conducted in the physical realm and must be successful against the growing darkness spreading throughout humanity. With the energetic changes we are experiencing as we cross over to the age of the knowledge-bearer, Aquarius, the battle for our minds and our hearts intensifies. What do you say?'

'Wow, Your Holiness. That is such an honour. Can I ask what this job means for us, exactly?' Sam asked.

'It's not so much a job, but really a calling. When the need arises, we may contact some of our members to assist with the most important direction for humankind, the path for each and every person and soul to find their way Home.'

Sam and Laura looked at each other with positive enthusiasm, though Sam was not totally clear in his understanding of the Dalai Lama's words.

'We need a little time to work things out between us, our relationship has been made difficult with living on different continents,' Laura explained, 'but I am looking for a transfer to London soon and then, yes,' she looked at Sam and then her host, 'yes, we would love to be part of this.' Both Laura and Sam nodded to the Dalai Lama.

'And what about you, Tinks? Is that your real name?' the wise monk asked.

'No, no, Your Holiness, it's Nelson Taylor, but everyone just calls me Tinks. I'll need some time to think it over. I have big plans for expanding my company, so it may not be easy to find the time,' Tinks replied.

'That is fine, Tinks. There is no wrong answer here, it needs to be one from the heart and given with honesty, as you have done.' Glancing at his clock, the Dalai Lama rounded up the meeting, 'Please, forgive me as I have many good people to meet today. I will call my assistant and he will take a photo on your cameras as a memento of our meeting, if you would like?'

The photoshoot concluded, and the four friends said their goodbyes to the holy man and were shown out of the building. Sam beamed with pride, along with a good portion of amazement, at this meeting with the Dalai Lama.

The sun-filled courtyard was busy with a snaking, higgledy-piggledy queue of people who had come to meet and pay homage to the Dalai Lama, people from different religions and races, dressed in all manner of brightly-coloured items of clothing, some traditional, some spiritual, some uniformed, interspersed with a few Western-style outfits. There was a loud hubbub of excited expectation, which increased a notch when Sam, Laura, Tinks and Tenzin appeared from the building. They were showered with handfuls of petals from the two bare-footed, Buddhist monks standing either side of the entranceway. The queue of pilgrims cheered and applauded each time someone walked out of the Dalai Lama's home, representing a mixture of shared celebration of their seeing His

Holiness and knowing that their time with the spiritual leader was getting closer.

The friends started to make their way down the dozen stone steps and squeezed past the queuers. Tenzin and Tinks found a quicker route through, with Sam following Laura, a distance grew between the pairs. Sam stopped to engage with some of the people asking him questions about his meeting.

'How was it? Was he amazing? Do you feel different?'

He couldn't adequately respond, other than to smile and nod, due to the rate of questions bombarding him and some people wanting to touch his arms or shoulders, as if His Holiness' divine energy could be transmissible to them through physical contact.

Knowing he needed to catch up with the others, he pushed his way down another step, but his way down was blocked by an older Western gentleman. The man looked worried, at complete odds with everyone else's demeanour. He raised his left hand and clasped Sam's right shoulder. Sam felt he recognised the face, but in that instant, he couldn't place the man.

'I'm so sorry, my child. Father, forgive me,' the man said, and quickly moved his right arm.

Sam felt no pain as the knife was skewered deep into his abdomen. He was immediately aware of something being seriously wrong and his face contorted in shock, but he didn't feel the knife withdraw. He instinctively put his hands down to his belly and, this time, did feel the knife as it sliced through his left hand, then through into his stomach area once again. This time the knife failed to penetrate so deeply due to the thickness of Sam's hand arresting its progress.

Time began to slow rapidly. A gap in the crowd emerged around him as the divinity seekers retreated from the danger area. He was vaguely aware of a flash of maroon as Tenzin struck the weaponed arm of Cardinal Francis and dragged him

293

away, down the last of the steps to the courtyard below, creating chaos as the monk urgently knocked people out of the way.

Sam's legs gave way. Clutching his bleeding midriff, he fell and landed heavily on the stone staircase, hitting his head. His awareness of all but his hearing become fuzzier and fuzzier.

'Sam! Sam! No!' Laura shrieked as she scrambled up the steps and knelt down beside him, holding his head off the stone. Tinks arrived, pushed Sam onto his back and started assessing his friend, trying to stem the flow of blood oozing from his wounds, looking even more horrific in contrast with his white cotton shirt.

'Stay with me, Sam! Open your eyes! Stay with me!' Laura shouted through her frenzied crying.

With an unexpectedly sharp intake of breath, Sam's eyes opened up, unfocussed. Although trauma-filled and glazed at first, they momentarily sparkled, with the dull whites transforming to a clean white and the colours comprising his irises clearing to reveal their true splendour. As he gently exhaled through his mouth, his fixed eyes dimmed as quick as they had gleamed. Sam could hear Laura but could not respond as his awareness receded further and further.

'We're losing him, Tinks! He's stopped breathing! Do something!' Laura cried.

Sam Angel watched himself lying lifeless below.

No feeling of sorrow, no pain; just rapidly increasing exaltation.

Bliss. Serenity. Silence. Peace. Love.

Pure love, indescribable, fulfilling love.

The only breath was one of a sense of growing, infinite awareness.

Grabbing Laura's hands, Tinks got Laura to apply considerable pressure to his jumper that lay scrunched on Sam's abdomen, acting as makeshift wadding for the wounds.

He immediately started rapid chest compressions and shouted out for an automated external defibrillator, not knowing if one was present.

Sam's consciousness was drawn up and away from the scene of mayhem that was unfolding below him and towards a great whiteness, now starting to envelope him. He trained his focus back down to the chaotic display on the steps to the Dalai Lama's home, albeit now harder to discern through the burgeoning brightness. Momentarily, he felt a heavy loss and sadness for his dying body and loving empathy for the soon-to-be grieving Laura and Tinks, both now fading out of sight.

I don't want to go yet. Stop this drawing me away from me, from them. I'm not ready to leave. He realised that his thoughts were not being acted upon; a magnetic-like pull was separating him from all he knew but, strangely, towards a feeling of Home.

Eleven white orbs gently and mysteriously presented themselves and formed a large circle in the completely white space in which he now found himself. Sam felt he was also one of these orbs, the twelfth, and intuitively knew these were all parts of him, the twelve personalities, six female, six male, making up his essence. Each of these orbs radiated a glorious light; the light of pure love.

Outside of the circle, two larger white spheres manifested. These new spheres were communicating with each other, a serene exchange, but he did not comprehend its content. He could sense they were discussing him and his immediate destiny for several moments.

The interchange abruptly ceased.

Then... a heartbeat.

Instantaneously, Sam Angel wore the familiar weight of life again.

CAN I ASK YOU FOR A REVIEW PLEASE?

I sincerely hope you really enjoyed this book, but no matter your view, I would truly appreciate it if you would now take a moment to review it on Amazon or the retailing platform you used to obtain your copy of The Karma Con.

This way, others might find and enjoy this book too. Reviews are the best way of supporting a self-publisher as we do not have the marketing clout at the disposal of traditional publishers.

A sincere thank you for your review – Rad Johnson.

✳✳✳✳

Please search for
The Karma Con on Amazon
and leave your review
✳✳✳✳

If you loved this book:
SAM ANGEL RETURNS IN

HOLLOW
LIFE

If you would like to be the first to know when Hollow Life is available, please join my email list to get the latest updates on this sequel's progress – radjohnsonmail@gmail.com.

About the Author:

Rad Johnson

Though having never considered writing a novel in the first 50 years of his life, for as long as he can remember, Rad Johnson has always dwelled upon the nature of our existence, the world and that which is beyond, both physically, mentally, emotionally and spiritually. Career paths, including structural engineering, IT and more recently working within a family business, mostly utilised Rad's left-brain bias.

An unexplainable but significant life event sparked a seed-change in his approach to life. This opened the door to, amongst other things, creativity, culminating in the writing of The Karma Con, the first novel in a trilogy.

Rad lives with his wife and two children in Essex, England. Though lovingly connected to this chunk of land, he yearns for a warmer climate!

Printed in Great Britain
by Amazon

40391464R00169